FLAKE IT
`til you make it

CHRISTMAS
Falls
SEASON 2

BETH BOLDEN

1. Sugar Plum Park
2. Dancing Sugar Plums
3. Santa's Workshop
4. Nutcrackers
5. Ginger's Breads
6. Tidings & Joy
7. Santa's Helpers Animal Shelter
8. Frosty's
9. Gingerbread Cottage
10. Jolly Java
11. Holiday Hope Foundation
12. Jingle Bites
13. Town Hall
14. The White Elephant
15. The Snowflake Shack
16. Mistletoe Movies
17. Christmas Falls Festivals Inc
18. Festival Museum
19. Rudolph's
20. Season's Readings

Chapter 1

"I can't believe this," Rocco said incredulously, partly to Rebecca, the employee he'd inherited from Holly and Joelle, who'd owned Jolly Java before he'd bought it from them, and partly to himself.

Rebecca shot him a frank look. "It's been this empty in the afternoons for a week," she said. The one thing he could say about Rebecca was she could make a mean latte and she was unflinchingly honest. Okay, that was *two* things. Two whole things! Rocco gave a weak cheer, and she sent him another one of those questioning looks as she cleaned the tables scattered through the little coffee shop. It was quaint. It was old-fashioned.

When Rocco had taken it over maybe it had been a little *too* quaint, maybe a little too old-fashioned. He'd spruced up the interior. Painted the walls a modern coffee-with-a-hint-of-cream brown, with darker espresso trim. New tables and chairs.

He'd modernized the equipment. The logo. He'd changed out the beans the owners had been buying for years for a higher quality Italian brand. Stopped buying baked goods from Joel at Ginger's Breads Bakery, putting out a full gourmet spread of pastries that he baked in the back kitchen. He'd put *his* stamp on it, the Rocco Moretti stamp. And since Morettis were scattered across the whole US now, spreading their culinary magic, he'd thought that would be a welcome stamp.

His first realization that maybe he'd made a misstep was when four customers complained the day he debuted his special fall drink. Not the pumpkin spice latte, like the original Jolly Java had been famous for, but a new creation he'd come up with, a marzipan latte that apparently nobody wanted. Pumpkin spice! Like Rocco would ever be that freaking basic.

It was disappointing and frustrating, but Rocco had still been sure these were just growing pains.

Everyone said the tourist season, when Christmas Falls hosted its huge holiday themed festival, was crazy, and he'd be packed.

And he did have customers. A steady enough stream of tourists in the mornings, but most locals had abandoned him and Jolly Java. After ten AM, the place was deader than a doornail. He'd never even gotten a chance to implement his new lunch menu.

Instead of a cozy cafe full of regulars whom Rocco knew by name and by order, he had a lot of tourists he saw maybe once or twice, and a few Christmas Falls residents who didn't visit with the regularity Holly and Joelle had described.

It was not the community-forward, familial atmosphere he'd hoped for when he'd taken every penny he'd earned from fourteen to twenty-eight and bought this place.

Rocco slumped down to the front counter.

He'd been so sure he'd win over the town with good Italian cappuccino and his delicious pastries.

But instead, the majority of them had started going to Ginger's Breads, even being willing to trade his high-quality espresso for the free self-service coffee Joel served with his baked goods.

Rocco had been in the line in the grocery store just the other day and had gotten to listen to one woman complaining to the other about the changes—and how she'd started saving a bundle by not getting her oat milk latte every morning.

"I told you," Rebecca said as she approached the counter, where Rocco was gently banging his head against the reclaimed wood. *That* he hadn't needed to replace, because the coffee bar itself, stretching across one side of Jolly Java, was gorgeous.

"I took the turmeric and goat cheese scone off the menu! I added pumpkin spice back on," Rocco argued. The scone *had* been a stretch, and he'd known it, but he'd also envisioned a future where the townspeople of Christmas Falls had been willing to have Rocco expand their palates.

"Yeah, you gotta win them back somehow," Rebecca said, sympathetically.

Her empathy, while kind, felt like poison in his gut.

What if he failed . . .*no*, that was not even an option. Morettis didn't fail. Especially not in any kind of food-related business.

His grandmother, whom everyone called Nonna, had started a famous chain of Italian restaurants in the Napa Valley, restaurants that his cousin Luca now ran with an expert hand, along with his six other siblings. Luca also owned a gourmet bistro in the tiny town of Indigo Bay, South Carolina, with his husband, Oliver, and tourists came to town just to eat there. Dante and Beatrice, his parents, ran their own little jewel of an Italian restaurant in the hills of San Francisco, and it regularly made lists of "Best Italian in the City" and "Best Neighborhood Spot." Some of his parents' clients had celebrated twenty anniversaries at the same goddamn table.

And here was Rocco.

Three months here and already a has-been.

"I've tried to spread the word that pumpkin spice is back *and* god help us, gingerbread, too," Rocco said, motioning to the artistic chalkboard sign sitting just outside the door.

Rebecca leaned against the counter. Lifting Rocco's head so he'd stop *thwacking* it against the counter.

"Stop that. You're gonna give yourself a concussion, and then what are you going to do? Listen, these people are creatures of habit. Most of them were born here and grew up here and never left. Jolly Java is a part of that tradition. Give them that tradition back."

It was hard to give something back to someone when he'd been so eager to change it it felt like he'd barely given the original a second glance. Sure, he had Rebecca as a resource, but every time he suggested making a change back to what they'd had before, she'd given him one of those looks that said, *but that isn't going to fix it.*

Well, he *had* to fix it.

"I'm *trying*," Rocco said. "I gave them goddamn pumpkin spice back, didn't I?" He shuddered.

"It's not about flavors, though that certainly isn't going to hurt you." Rebecca's mouth quirked into a little smile. "You know that."

"I spent the last two weeks trying to get the festival committee to consider letting me supply the cookies for the tree lighting, thinking maybe I could convince the town to try me again." When Rebecca shot him another one of those looks, he kept going. "I was even going to serve goddamn *normal* things, I swear. Chocolate chip and sugar and snickerdoodle and peanut butter. I showed up more than once with baskets of cookies. Fresh baked! And you know what they said?"

Rebecca sighed. "I can only imagine."

"Joel's handling it. Joel knows what he's doing. Like I don't know what I'm doing!"

"You did take pumpkin spice off the menu." She was smiling again, and yes, it sounded very stupid when she said it now.

His head had just been building castles in the sky.

"Holly and Joelle supplied cookies *every year* to the tree lighting before last year. Joel does it one year and he 'knows what he's doing'!" Rocco made a frustrated noise and re-started banging his head, before Rebecca stopped him again, grabbing him by a handful of dark curls.

"You'll figure something out," Rebecca promised. "You're a smart guy. You're good at this, when you get out of your own way."

"Thanks," Rocco said dryly. "But we Morettis aren't just 'good at this'! We're spectacular! We're fabulous! We're fucking *synonymous with flavor and experience*."

"No? Are y'all as dramatic as that, too?"

Rocco laughed, because otherwise he was going to cry. "Believe it or not, I'm from the undramatic branch of the family."

Rebecca joined him, downright cackling with delight at this impossibility. "Would one of your cousins be on his knees by now, rending his garments and banging his fists on the floor?"

It was easier to keep laughing, and even easier still when Rocco considered this. "Absolutely," he said. "Gabe, yes. He'd be beside himself. He's so fucking emotional. And Lorenzo? Yeah. He'd be right alongside there with him, unless it messed up his perfect hair. Luca? He'd have issued an edict ordering everyone to return, or else."

"Or else?"

"There'd be a town coup if Luca was in charge. Governmental change number one would be a law requiring everyone to visit Jolly Java once a day."

"Well, there's always that," Rebecca said lightly.

"There's always that," Rocco retorted morosely.

"Well, one positive about being slow today is that we can close early, for the tree lighting," Rebecca said. "You gonna head over?"

"So I can eat perfect Joel's perfect cookies? No fucking thank you," Rocco said.

"Rocco," Rebecca chided.

He sighed. "No," he murmured. "I'm not in the mood. Maybe I'll take up that whole tray of pastries and gorge myself on the couch, watching the worst TV I can find."

"I think *Real Housewives* has a Duluth edition, these days," Rebecca teased.

"Ugh, that might actually be better than thinking about how I've messed this up," Rocco said.

Rebecca whacked him on the shoulder before turning and heading to the front door, flicking off the *open* sign, grabbing the chalkboard sign, and tucking it behind a row of barstools that stood on the new tall bar that ran alongside the big picture window.

Rocco had imagined people sitting there, working on their laptops and enjoying the beautifully decorated streets of downtown Christmas Falls.

That had not happened.

"Come on," she said, "you're gonna come with me to the tree lighting. It's your first one here, you can't miss it because you're throwing yourself a big pity party."

"I'm not exactly in a festive mood," Rocco argued.

"Doesn't matter." Rebecca shot him another look, but this one was softer, affectionate. "In Christmas Falls, everyone's welcome. Even grinches."

"I'm not a grinch." In fact, Rocco had actually kind of looked forward to living in a town with this much affection for and attention to the holidays. It felt like when he'd been a kid, he'd never gotten much of that kind of season-long revelry. Other than the celebration on Christmas Day itself, when the restaurant was closed, in December it always had been packed with revelers and holiday parties and office celebrations. His parents certainly hadn't *ignored* him, but that was one of their busiest times of year. In fact, starting at a young age, Rocco had often been drafted to help.

He'd been excited about being part of this community expression of pure holiday joy.

That was before he'd lost all sense of community *and* joy.

"I'd hope not." Rebecca reached over and brushed one of his curls back from his forehead. "Seriously, you can't just sit at home on the couch and feel sorry for yourself. It's not healthy."

"In this mood, sulking feels *great*," Rocco said.

"Yep, you're definitely tapping into that overdramatic Moretti side," Rebecca said, chuckling. "I'll let you sulk for approximately two point five hours, but then you're gonna come with me to the tree lighting."

"Fine," Rocco said. "I'll do it. *Then* I can sulk in peace?"

Rebecca laughed. "All you want to, Moretti."

"Sounds like a plan."

He'd just made it upstairs to his little apartment over the coffee shop when he got a text.

Hey, call me when you have a sec, it read, from his cousin Luca's husband, Oliver.

Rocco had spent the last year in Indigo Bay, soaking up every little thing Oliver, a master baker who owned a charming and popular bakery and cafe in town, had to teach him.

He'd originally gone out to the east coast to save up additional money for his nest egg, but the bonus had been that Oliver had been willing to show him just about anything he asked about, and more. During the ten months he'd spent in Indigo Bay, he'd learned more about how to be a business owner and a baker than he had in the last few years before that.

It was one of the reasons why when the opportunity to purchase Jolly Java had come up, he'd jumped at it. He'd felt *ready*.

Now, he just felt like a failure.

His first foray into ownership and he hadn't just not brought in *new* customers, he'd alienated the ones he'd inherited.

Rocco debated just not answering him, but Oliver had given him *so* much, it felt wrong to return that with silence.

Besides, he was family, now, and Rocco had learned from an early age that you didn't just ignore family.

He dialed Oliver's number and set it to speaker as he flopped down onto the couch.

The owners of Jolly Java had just put in the second floor when they'd decided—when their daughter moved with their granddaughter to Florida—to sell. They told Rocco they'd intended to rent it out to tourists during the holiday season and to use it for storage the rest of the year. Along with some of his other changes to the main space, he'd expanded the bathroom and even put in a little kitchenette, but for the rest of his cooking, he went downstairs and used the big kitchen.

"Hey, I thought you'd be busy," Oliver said.

Rocco made a face. If he didn't want Oliver to know the truth, he should've waited to call him.

"Slow one today. It's the big tree lighting tonight," Rocco said. Like the tree lighting would have normally kept anyone away from Jolly Java. In fact Holly and Joelle had specifically told him that festival afternoons were always some of their busiest.

Ha.

Not today.

"Oh, that sounds so fun," Oliver said. "You gonna go? You made any friends yet?"

"You sound like my mother," Rocco complained. "Actually—a cross between my mother and your husband."

Oliver chuckled. "That's a terrifying thought."

"Yeah. Seriously." He paused. "So, what's up?"

"That marzipan syrup you did for that new latte on your menu? I wondered if you'd send me the recipe."

Rocco winced. "You really want that?"

"Sure, I do. It sounds delicious. I think the customers would love it," Oliver said and the confusion in his voice made it clear he had no idea why Rocco wasn't eager to give it to him.

"Well, at least someone might," Rocco said under his breath. Then louder, "I'll email it to you."

"Great. Thanks." Oliver paused, and Rocco could practically hear the wheels turning in his head. *Don't ask, don't ask, just don't ask.* "Everything alright?"

Dang it. He'd asked.

"Fine," Rocco said, but he could hear the high, false note in his own voice.

"Rocco, you know running a business is hard. But then I don't have to tell you that. You want to talk about it? Everyone has a bad day, every once in awhile."

"How about a bad month?"

There was only silence on the other end. Rocco wished he hadn't said it. Wished he'd kept his failure a secret.

"Is it going that badly?" Oliver sounded cautious. Careful.

"I fucked it up." Rocco rubbed a hand over his face. Knew the moment the words were out of his mouth this time that it actually felt good to tell Oliver and stop trying to grind it out alone.

He had Rebecca, sure, but he *hadn't* made any other friends in town. In fact, it felt like the exact goddamn opposite.

He'd been lucky they hadn't run him out of town already for refusing to make a pumpkin spice latte.

"What?" Oliver sounded shocked. "How could you? Rocco, you're *great* at this. The place looked awesome. Just perfect for you."

"That's the worst of it," Rocco said glumly. "It *was* perfect."

"Well, what happened? Tell me about it," Oliver coaxed.

"Ugh, so you know the marzipan latte? That's the problem. That's the whole problem."

"Huh."

"I changed too many things, too fast," Rocco admitted. "And I took a bunch of stuff people loved off the menu." He made a groan. "Including fucking pumpkin spice."

Oliver chuckled. "You didn't."

"I know." Rocco groaned again. "I *know*. It's back on the menu, but the thing is it pissed off some people, most of the regulars, and now they won't come back. I get some tourist business, but it's not the same. It's not Sweetie Pie's."

Oliver sighed when Rocco brought up his bakery. "Sweetie Pie's didn't start like you saw it, you know that."

"Yeah, but it still got there," Rocco said despondently. "I'm not sure Jolly Java is gonna get there."

Just saying it out loud made Rocco want to cry. He'd poured so much into this business. Every penny he'd saved starting back when he'd been only a gangly teenager, every time he'd put in a twelve or fourteen or sixteen hour day, doing what he loved, but that was *still* fucking hard work. He'd done it because of *this* day. But now *this day* had come, and it wasn't anything like he'd expected—and honestly, some of that was his own damn fault, and that made it even worse.

"You're gonna fix it," Oliver soothed. "You put pumpkin spice back on the menu, right?"

"Yes," Rocco said, laughing because it was better than crying. "And gingerbread, too."

"Good," Oliver said. "I've read about Christmas Falls. The community there is so fantastic. You can win them back. I *know* you can, Rocco. You won me over, didn't you?"

"You were easy," Rocco scoffed. "You were predisposed to like me. I'm a Moretti, and you're *married* to a Moretti."

Oliver laughed. "True. But you're still a good-natured, charming guy. Maybe you're not Ren, but you're no slouch."

"Nobody is Ren except for Ren," Rocco retorted, referring to his cousin Lorenzo, who had cut a swath through the eligible bachelors of Los Angeles with breathtaking ease.

"What I'm *saying* is deploy some of that infamous Moretti charm," Oliver said. "People *like* you. If they like you, they'll figure out they made a mistake."

"Does that mean I can't hide in my apartment, drowning my sorrows with Cherry Garcia?" Rocco asked. Even though he already knew that Rebecca wouldn't let him tonight, anyway.

"Absolutely not. Doesn't that festival thing start soon?" Oliver asked.

"Yep. Tonight, actually."

"There you go," Oliver said. "Go. Participate. Be part of the community. I know small towns. You're a stranger. Once you're not a stranger, you'll be part of them, and they won't hold the pumpkin spice thing against you."

"I don't know," Rocco said with faux gravity, "people take their pumpkin spice pretty goddamn seriously."

"Exactly. And now you know that. You've learned your lesson, and you won't make that mistake again." Oliver paused, and Rocco knew him well enough to know he was smiling. "Listen, being a business owner? Honestly, it's just making one mistake after another. The difference between successful businesses and the ones who don't make it? The owner's ability to learn from their mistakes and not make them again. And you're smart and you're flexible. You'll get there."

For the first time since things had started to go badly, Rocco felt like this situation could actually be salvaged. Like he might really turn this whole thing around.

"Really?" he asked.

"Yeah. Absolutely. I wouldn't lie to you," Oliver said seriously. "And, if all else fails, I'll send Luca out there to fix you up."

"No!" Rocco yelped. He did *not* want Luca Moretti, the now de facto head of the Morettis, Oliver's husband, and the culinary business genius of the family to come fix him. He wouldn't live through it—they *both* wouldn't live through it, probably.

Oliver cackled in delight at his vehemence. "Don't worry, I wouldn't."

"Can you . . ." Rocco hesitated. He didn't want to tell Oliver to keep a secret from his husband, but also . . .he wasn't ready to tell Luca he'd screwed things up here. Maybe when they were already on their way to being fixed, he'd be willing to tell his ridiculously competent cousin about it.

"Don't worry, I won't breathe a word to him. This stays between us," Oliver said. "You'll tell him when you're ready."

"Thank you," Rocco said.

"But don't be a stranger, either. You need help, you call me, okay?" Oliver's voice was kind, empathetic even, but there was the ring of steel beneath it.

"I will," Rocco promised.

"Good," Oliver said. "Now go out and mingle, okay? Charm the pants off some hot guy."

"Oliver!" Rocco squeaked, but Oliver just laughed.

"You young kids didn't invent sex, you know."

"I'm not *young*, and you're not *old*," Rocco said.

Oliver chuckled. "No, not even close. But still. Have fun, okay?"

"Okay," Rocco said and flopped back on the couch after he'd hung up. He should get up, take a shower. Fix his hair, even though all he'd end up doing was shoving a hat on top of it, in deference to the cold Illinois weather.

But he would, in a minute. First though, he was gonna enjoy this warm feeling—the feeling that told him that this wasn't over, not by a long shot.

Chapter 2

"Taylor! There you are," Mona Grayson, the mayor of Christmas Falls, exclaimed as he approached where she was standing back from the stage, set up in front of the still-dark tree.

"Right here, boss," Taylor said. "What's up?"

His old college friend, Joey, always joked that his deputy mayor job was little more than a glorified personal assistant, even though he knew better. When Taylor had listed out all the projects he'd spearheaded during his four years here, even Joey, who made a living not only being an in-demand business consultant, but a sarcastic smart ass, had been impressed.

He hadn't used the phrase, *you're a shoo-in* regarding the soon-to-be-empty city manager job, but Taylor had read between the lines and had let himself feel optimistic.

At least until the latest round of Mona's concerns.

"Oh good, you're here," she said. "I've got to have someone keep Heath Kelly from running away."

She gestured towards where Heath Kelly, former soap actor, Hallmark heartthrob, and when they'd finally gotten their conservative heads out of their even-more conservative asses, the male lead in their last three queer-themed holiday movies, stood.

And, even more pertinently, this year's Christmas Falls Festival grand marshal.

Next to the podium and the gigantic tree, was Heath, undeniably tall and undeniably handsome. Taylor could see Heath's gaze roaming over the growing crowd, his apprehension not particularly well-hidden. Even for a celebrity used to Hollywood's excesses, the festival was a lot.

A whole bunch of holiday joy.

Maybe a lesser man wouldn't admit it or enjoy it, but the truth was, Taylor fucking *loved* it.

Last year, Taylor had been convinced Jem Knight, the retired Charleston Condors defensive end and one of the town's most famous sons, would take a dive off the platform just to stop all the overly enthusiastic screams and catcalls.

"Go charm him," Mona said, giving Taylor a little shove. "Maybe he'll take one look at you, decide that he's been waiting for you for his whole life, and you can settle down together with three cats and a nice picket fence."

"Three cats?"

Mona chuckled. "Doesn't the other Taylor—"

"No. I don't need three. Just Meredith is fine," Taylor said resolutely. This was one of his favorite nights of the year. He was not going to tolerate comparisons to certain very famous female pop stars, not tonight, anyway.

"Taylor, you know this town. Maybe you didn't grow up here—"

"Mona," Taylor interrupted again.

"And *that's* another ding—and we both know it is, Taylor. This town doesn't particularly like change. And they don't like strangers. They don't like single, tall, dark, and handsome strangers, especially."

Taylor rolled his eyes, hoping that his outward disdain for the mayor's worry might protect that tiny flame of hope-tinged optimism deep inside him. "If that was actually true, they'd be way less excited to see Heath Kelly."

She laughed and patted him on the arm. "I do love you, Taylor. You're so funny."

"Don't say you'll miss me when you're gone."

"I'm not going anywhere," Mona said resolutely. That much Taylor could believe.

Mona had been the mayor for a long time, at least fifteen years, and she was as much a fixture of Christmas Falls as Christmas Falls was a fixture for *her*.

Someday, Taylor wanted to take her spot. But for now, he was going to be perfectly happy getting the city manager position he'd had his eye on for the last two years.

And old, curmudgeonly Mr. Granger, who'd probably worked for Christmas Falls longer than Taylor had been alive, had finally announced his retirement.

Taylor, who'd been learning the ropes from both him and Mona for the last four years, had seemed like the most natural fit. Mona had even cautiously said she'd give him a recommendation to take to the city council during the hiring process.

But he was young. He wasn't originally from Christmas Falls. And he didn't have a family.

Three strikes Mona couldn't stop reminding him about.

"Go keep that nice young man company. Flirt a little. If the town *and* the city council think you're interested in settling down . . ." Mona waggled her eyebrows, and Taylor knew he should laugh, but he could barely muster a smile. He wasn't interested in settling down. When he lay in bed, sleep elusive, and thought of the future, of what he wanted more than anything else, it was a job that helped him preserve what made Christmas Falls so special while adding just enough growth that the town didn't stagnate.

That might, eventually, when Mona had decided that she didn't want to be mayor anymore, empower him to run in her place.

"Right," Taylor said. He didn't remind Mona that Heath Kelly wasn't going to be interested in him, even if he was interested in Heath Kelly.

Which he wasn't.

Not even a little.

Yes, as Taylor wandered closer to him, he couldn't deny that Heath was very good looking. And famous. And rich.

Maybe Joey was right and his sex drive, ignored for too long, had finally shriveled and died.

But it was hard to be sad about that, especially when he was the only candidate for his dream job, and he was hoping it would stay that way. Then, her warnings about his three strikes wouldn't make much difference.

"Hey," Taylor said to Heath. "You thinking about making a run for it, yet?"

Heath gave him a semi-embarrassed smile. "I do this entertainment stuff for a living, so it shouldn't be so . . .so . . ."

"I get it," Taylor said, shoving his hands into his charcoal gray jacket.

"Well, you're the deputy mayor, so that means you signed up for this, right? You enjoy it."

Taylor did not remind Heath Kelly that he had *also* signed up for this. Albeit temporarily.

"Actually," Taylor said, "I love it."

Heath gave him a surprised look. And yes, okay, Taylor didn't look like a guy who was obsessed with Christmas.

He looked like who he was, on the outside, anyway. An urban guy in his early thirties, fit and decent looking, upwardly mobile with a job in marketing or IT or business, with a good wardrobe.

He *had* been that guy. He'd tried to be, anyway. It hadn't stuck.

If you peeled him open, underneath his thick, sober charcoal peacoat and navy cashmere sweater, he'd bleed red and green and glitter.

"Yeah? That's cool. I do this kind of thing, a lot. Comes with my job, too. All this holiday rah-rah cheer. But the funny thing is, I'm usually bundled up in the heat of August, sweating through my sweater and coat, wishing I could rip the scarf off and take a deep breath." Heath chuckled. "And the snow's always fake."

"Not so fake here."

Heath seemed like a decent enough guy. Maybe Taylor should be doing what Mona had suggested, but that easy charm that worked so well on the townspeople felt frozen when it came to a romantic possibility.

It hadn't always been that way.

"Nope," Heath said with a grin. "So I hear I'm getting a liaison, for, like, the festival events." He gave Taylor another quick once-over. "Please tell me that's gonna be you."

Taylor was flattered. Still frozen, but flattered.

"Actually, no," Taylor said apologetically. "That's going to be Murphy Clark. He carves the gnomes. I'm sure you've seen them around town."

Last year, the festival organizer, Griff, had convinced Murphy to do the liaison job, because by the time they headed into the five weeks before Christmas and the prime festival season, Murphy was always at a loose end. He'd already done all his work, throughout the year.

Plus, Murphy had an easy, quiet way about him. Supportive and friendly. When Griff had mentioned they should approach him again for the job, Marlene had argued that the only reason he'd agreed at all last year was because of the torch he'd been carrying for Jem Knight, last year's grand marshal.

But when they'd asked, to everyone's surprise, Murphy had agreed. He'd never be a people person, but after dating Jem for the whole year, Taylor could see that he'd begun to come out of his shell more.

"Oh yeah? The gnome guy? I think I met him at Rudolph's the other night. He's the one who's dating the really hot football player." Heath winced. "The one who replaced me last year, when I broke my leg."

"Yep, that's Murphy. Big guy. Gnome carver. Plaid-and-Jem-Knight aficionado."

"Cool. I liked him."

Taylor patted him on the shoulder. "You'll be in expert hands with him. The guy grew up here. He's practically Christmas Falls in a single person."

Heath shot him a flirtatious glance. "I thought that was you. Loving it so much here and all."

He should be flattered. He should not only be flattered, he should be listening to Mona's advice and taking Heath up on all these promising looks he kept sending Taylor's way.

When would he ever get to say he'd hooked up with a bona fide movie star?

If ego mattered, it would be full to bursting at even the possibility.

But Heath still left Taylor cold.

"I do love it," Taylor agreed. Patted him again. "Come on, Mona's getting ready to make her speech, and we're on smile and wave duty. You can say a few things if you'd like, but it's not a requirement."

"I can do that," Heath said, nodding.

"The mayor likes to flip the switch herself," Taylor explained under his breath as they walked towards the middle of the stage, slightly behind the podium. "Gives her a rush of power, or so she says."

"You ever interested in taking her job?" Heath asked, waving at where Mona stood.

"Being the mayor? Someday, maybe, but not now." He wasn't going to tell Heath that the real power in the town was working behind the scenes. That Mona was largely a figurehead.

"You'd be good at it," Heath said and thankfully left it at that, as Mona approached the podium to a raucous wave of cheers.

He started waving and felt better when Heath joined in, seeming to get the hang of it.

No, he wouldn't be making a run for it.

And no, Taylor wouldn't be inviting him to his bed, either.

The reason why?

The shining faces gazing up at Mona, and the unbridled joy in them as she flipped the switch. There was a power in that, but not the kind of power that Heath probably assumed it was.

It wasn't about the title. It was about understanding the true power of this town, the pulse of it that ran so steady and bright underneath every street and was the lifeblood of the festival.

The reason so many tourists came once and then returned every year, just the way that Taylor and his family had.

It was the power of happiness. Of nostalgia. Of hope and care and selflessness. And Taylor had learned, since he'd moved here four years ago, that he'd do anything in *his* power to protect that and to nurture it.

Taylor let Murphy and Jem collect Heath at the end of the lighting ceremony, and he wasn't sure where they'd be taking him, but it wasn't with him, and that was all he cared about.

Polite deflections were only going to get him so far.

Taylor was heading out of Sugar Plum Park, weaving through the knots of people carrying cups of steaming hot cocoa and cider, holding brightly decorated sugar cookies in their mitten-covered hands when Mona caught up to him.

He saw Mason over at his table, talking to a handful of people about the new foundation, and Elias in the crowd, handing out flyers for the pet pics event for the shelter.

"You heading out?" she asked.

For someone pushing seventy, she moved fast.

Taylor shouldn't be surprised by this, but he still was.

"Yep," he said. Though he already knew he was too keyed up to go home to his quiet little house, on its brightly decorated street. He'd stop by Rudolph's, grab a spot at the bar, and have a drink. The park was still full, and the after-party at The White Elephant would mean Rudolph's would be fairly chill tonight.

"You didn't go with Heath." Mona sounded disappointed.

"The guy's a movie star. What am I gonna do? Ask him to recommend me to the city council?" Taylor kept his voice light.

"You could have," she said sternly.

He shrugged. "He's nice. Handsome, too. But not my type."

"What *is* your type?" Mona asked, and Taylor knew he had to cut this right off, right now.

"Getting the city manager job. That's my type," Taylor said, layering in a joking undertone. "You'd better be careful, you're gonna give Nick Morgan a run for his matchmaking money."

"I just hate you're always so alone," Mona said, and there was truth in her eyes. Affection, too. She really cared about him. And the town too. She'd devoted fifteen years of her life to it. Well, maybe Taylor hadn't had fifteen years to give, yet, but he cared, too.

"And you hate that there's a handful of people on the city council who'll look at my application and wish I had a family," Taylor retorted lightly. "Wish I was older. Wish I was *settled*."

She smiled. "Yes, and that too."

"I'll figure it out," Taylor said. Even though he had no idea how he would do that. Maybe he could come up with a positive spin on *really fucking single and even more fucking alone.*

"Of course you will." Mona gave him a quick hug. "You're so smart, Taylor. And the best thing this town could have. I wouldn't be recommending you to take Martin Granger's place if I didn't think you'd be more than capable of doing the job."

"I won't let you down," Taylor promised.

She patted him on the cheek. "You wouldn't. Now go off and have fun, alright?"

Taylor didn't know if *quiet drink at Rudolph's* counted as fun, necessarily, but for him these days, that more than fulfilled the definition.

He walked over and had just settled down on a stool at the far end of the long wooden bar when a commotion behind him caught his attention.

Taylor turned and wished he hadn't.

Rocco Moretti, the new owner of Jolly Java, and the only man to come close to heating him up in the last few years, was approaching, muttering and gesturing, clearly upset about something.

Don't come sit next to me, don't come sit next to me, don't come sit next—

But Rocco looked up and down the bar, and even though there were several open barstools, took the one right next to Taylor.

Of course.

They'd met only once before, when in his official capacity, Taylor had dutifully gone to the coffee shop to welcome him to Christmas Falls as one of its new business owners.

It had been a completely routine sort of visit, one he'd done a dozen times before, except for the fact that Rocco's good looks and charm had left him stammering and awkward.

"Hey," Rocco said, leaning over right into Taylor's personal space. With anyone else he'd have shifted his barstool over a fraction, making it clear just how much he wasn't into having his bubble invaded by a stranger.

But Taylor didn't move.

He let himself stay for a minute and just enjoy all that fucking warmth.

"Hey," Taylor replied, adopting a very casual, very much, *I'll be nice, but I'd actually prefer to be left alone* tone.

Even in the middle of winter, Rocco's skin was a warm olive, like he'd just stepped off a plane from the sunny coast of Italy, his dark eyes bright and animated, full of fire. He tugged his hat off and dark curls spilled out, falling over his forehead.

Taylor forced himself to look away. It was annoying that Rocco Moretti was more interesting to him than Heath freaking Kelly, who was just here for a few weeks and would be a perfect way to break his long dry spell. Rocco Moretti, on the other hand, lived in town. Nothing with him would be simple, or cut-and-dried.

But apparently Rocco didn't get his memo about being left alone, because he leaned in even farther, and Taylor swore he could smell coffee on his skin, he was that freaking close.

He didn't like coffee, but he was afraid he liked Rocco.

"God, this town," Rocco said. "I want to love it, I do, but it's kind of driving me nuts."

"I think that means you *do* love it," Taylor said dryly.

He didn't need to ask what had Rocco so hot under his collar. He knew. Rocco's changes to Jolly Java had not all been welcome, and the town was a little pissy about that particular fact.

"Ugh, I think you must be right. We don't always like the people we love, right?"

Taylor wanted to ask what kind of experience he had with that, with *love*, but he didn't, because he wasn't stupid enough to flirt with Rocco Moretti.

"Yeah," Taylor agreed. He was predisposed to feel empathy for Rocco—they were both outsiders, and also undeniably because he *wanted* to—but Mona would probably caution him not to wade into this mess.

The town would eventually forgive Rocco, they always did, but right now they were giving him the cold shoulder. Punishing him for getting rid of their comfortable favorites and attempting to introduce them to goat cheese . . .or something.

Taylor had listened to several people complain one morning over his breakfast plate at The Snowflake Shack, and that seemed to be the conclusion they'd come to.

They didn't appreciate being deprived of pumpkin spice and they didn't want to like goat cheese.

Personally, Taylor didn't have skin in the game, as he didn't drink coffee and he was neutral on the concept of goat cheese, but he'd listened anyway. At the time, he'd told himself it was because he was the deputy mayor and it was his job and his responsibility to keep an ear out for relevant issues in the town, even if it was just gossip. But he knew, deep down, that wasn't *entirely* why he'd listened.

Someone had said, very loudly, the name *Rocco Moretti* and his whole body had perked up.

Kinda like how it was doing now.

"Did you know I delivered a dozen boxes of cookies to the festival committee? Hand baked. Hand packed. Freaking *hand delivered*. They wouldn't even listen to me." Rocco sounded disgusted. "And Joel isn't even who normally does it! Holly and Joelle did it *every single year* before he did last year's, because of an emergency. I should've gotten that job back."

Don't say it, don't say it, don't say—

"Maybe they thought you'd fill the cookies with goat cheese," Taylor said, saying it anyway.

Enjoying, way more than he should have, how Rocco's eyes lit up. In amusement. In passion. Probably in *everything*. Rocco was the kind of guy who never held back. Taylor didn't even realize how cold he'd gotten until he metaphorically stripped off his gloves and held his freezing hands up to that warmth.

Rocco laughed, long and loud, not worrying about any of the sets of eyes that swiveled in their direction. "They probably *do* think that. I'm gonna have to come up with a goat cheese cookie, just to piss them off."

"Maybe not," Taylor said hurriedly.

"Or maybe I'd be doing it to tempt *you* into Jolly Java," Rocco teased. "You haven't been back since that first time you visited."

Even if Taylor liked coffee, he'd have avoided Jolly Java on principle.

Self-preservation principle.

"I actually don't drink coffee," Taylor admitted. Stupidly, irrationally worried that his admission would mean Rocco would no longer be interested in talking to him.

That would be okay. You'd be okay with that.

"You haven't had *my* coffee," Rocco said, apparently not turned off, but in fact, intrigued by the challenge Taylor presented.

"My friend Joey's tried for years." Taylor rubbed his neck. Already feeling the prickle of inevitable disappointment. "Even in college, I wouldn't."

Rocco only looked more fascinated. "What did you drink instead? Don't tell me you don't drink caffeine? A hot, professional guy like you? I can't even deal with it if you don't."

Taylor's brain, mostly unaffected by Heath's obvious interest, stuttered to a complete fucking halt at Rocco's words.

"You think I'm hot?"

Rocco took his drink—unsurprisingly an espresso martini—from the bartender, and saluted Taylor with it. "Uh, yeah," he said. "That's not even a compliment. It's just a plain fact."

"Oh uh, thanks." Taylor tried to accept the compliment like it was nothing, like guys who looked like Rocco Moretti told him he was hot all the time.

Maybe they might, Mona's voice told him, *if you didn't freeze them out first.*

"Anyway, what *do* you drink? Please tell me you're not one of those clean-living types . . ." Rocco trailed off and gave him a look up and down, similar to the one Heath had given him earlier, but this one lit him right up. "Though you kinda *look* like one of those types."

"Uh, no," Taylor said, lifting his beer glass. "I'm drinking this beer, aren't I? I . . .uh . . .well, I've got a very secret, very terrible addiction to energy drinks, if you have to know."

"That stuff'll eat your liver," Rocco said.

"Believe me, that's what everyone says, and yet I keep drinking them." Taylor shook his head and chuckled under his breath. "Now you know the worst thing about me."

"I like it," Rocco said, surprising him.

"You do?"

"Yeah. Now I'm gonna have to tell you something. Um . . .well, you clearly already know about the pumpkin spice and the goat cheese . . ." Rocco glanced up at him, worry creasing his handsome features. "Don't tell me someone complained to the mayor's office?"

"No, no, nothing like that." He didn't tell Rocco about the overheard conversation at The Snowflake Shack.

"Okay, *phew*." Rocco looked relieved.

"They're gonna come around," Taylor said as reassuringly as he could. "I really liked the changes you've made to the place."

"Goat cheese and all?" Rocco asked.

"I've got nothing against goat cheese," Taylor said.

"That's *my* big secret, I guess. I love goat cheese and I want everyone else to love it, too."

Taylor chuckled. "Baby steps, Moretti."

"Yeah, yeah," he said. "I went too fast before. I get that now. I won't make that mistake again. But I just need to get people to come back—try the new-old stuff I've got. I thought maybe if I could get *you* in the door . . ."

"Ouch. Wanted only for my title," Taylor joked.

"You think you could get the mayor herself—"

Taylor winced. "Sorry to disappoint. She's a tea-only drinker. But I'll mention it to her."

"Ugh, this sucks," Rocco said, taking another long sip of his martini. "You've got it so lucky. Your new job's all lined up. You just gotta show up, right? And the city council will hire you."

"That is not . . . *not* necessarily true." Taylor hadn't meant to say so, but once he'd started he couldn't quite stop. "Mona's worried that I'm too young, too single, and then there's the fact that I'm not originally from Christmas Falls. It's probably not enough to kill my application, not since there aren't any other serious candidates. But if anyone else shows up? Ugh, I'm worried. I shouldn't be, but I am."

"She doesn't like that you're single?"

"Perpetually," Taylor said wryly. "She was trying to get me to hook up with Heath Kelly—thought maybe I could convince him to smile and wave next to me a few times, I think."

"And you didn't want to?" Rocco's jaw dropped. "*Heath Kelly*? Man, he is crazy hot."

"Maybe yeah, but not my type," Taylor said, embarrassed now. It was one thing to discuss his desert of a love life with Mona and another entirely to discuss it with Rocco Moretti.

"You could always ask . . .ugh, who's that matchmaker's name . . ."

"Nick Morgan," Taylor supplied. "But that's *really* not my thing, to be honest."

"I met him, too, and he was, *of course*, interested in hearing more about me, but I told him, I've got too much on my plate with this new business to think about a relationship but . . ." Rocco trailed off.

Taylor thought Rocco's reluctance to agree to Nick Morgan's schemes was more along the lines of never needing help getting a date than being too busy, but he let it go. At least until Rocco's eyes brightened, like he'd just had a brilliant idea.

"That's what we should do," Rocco said, snapping his fingers.

"What?" Taylor asked warily.

"Matchmake ourselves!"

Rocco might have been the first guy in what felt like ages to actually have a chance at melting his chilly exterior, but that didn't mean Taylor was ready to just *date*.

Not when the thought of Rocco made his palms sweat.

It would be like strapping yourself to a rocket, when you were only ready for a sparkler.

"It's not like you think," Rocco continued. "I don't mean *for real*, I mean . . .like help each other out."

Taylor's brain supplied all kinds of ways they could help each other out—in and out of clothes, specifically—but he shut down those thoughts hard and fast. He had a job to focus on getting. And Rocco had his business.

"I don't know what you mean," Taylor said.

"So my cousin did this, and it *seemed* crazy at the time, but it worked out, in the end. Worked like a charm, too. He fake-dated this guy to get his mom off his ass about settling down."

"And that *worked*?" Taylor sounded incredulous.

"Oh, it worked," Rocco said, shooting Taylor a very charming, unfortunately very convincing smile. "So, you need someone on your arm when you're going to festival events. And I need an in with the town. Some reason for people to start coming back to Jolly Java. You're the freaking deputy mayor—soon to be the city manager! What's more part of the town than *that*?"

It was an absolutely ludicrous idea.

Taylor wanted to tell Rocco flatly that he was not interested.

But he was.

Despite all the potential pitfalls and problems—not to mention the certified insanity.

"The final meeting of the council isn't until April. That's five months away. You really want to pretend to be my boyfriend for that long?"

Say yes. Say you absolutely do.

But Rocco just laughed. "Well, I can't say it would be a hardship," he said. "Plus, I'm gone for a month right in the middle of that time. I'm going to help out some family in Indigo Bay, for their Sweethearts Festival." He paused and suddenly looked worried. "That isn't going to be a problem, is it?"

"Let me get this straight. You're worried about being gone for a month between now and April, but *not* worried about faking a relationship for five months?"

"Oh, how hard can it be? A few smiles, some hand-holding, maybe even a romantic date or two, they'll all believe it, and then it's just a matter of keeping up the charade." Rocco leaned in. There was that smell of coffee again. But it was sweeter, too. Spicy, almost.

It was unexpectedly intoxicating.

Intoxication must have been the only reason Taylor said, "I'll think about it."

Rocco's nearness had totally gone to his head.

"Aw," Rocco said, having the nerve to both look and sound disappointed. "Come on. It could be fun. And useful. Emphasis on useful, if that's what you're into." He shot Taylor a particularly mischievous look. "I have a feeling you are, actually."

"Kind of comes with the job," Taylor said wryly. "The one I have, *and* the one I want."

"Are you really worried about not getting it? From what I hear, you're practically already hired."

Taylor shrugged and finished his beer, setting the glass on the coaster in front of him. "Yes and no. Yeah, I've got some strikes against me. But I'm the deputy mayor. The current mayor is endorsing me. And biggest help? There's no other serious candidates for the position. Not that people haven't applied, but I've got the most experience."

Rocco nodded earnestly. "So nothing to worry about then."

"Not according to Mona," Taylor said with a chuckle. But yes, he *was* worried. Whether it was legitimate or not. There were still a few weeks for possible candidates to submit the necessary paperwork to apply for the job. Someone else without his three strikes and with the same or better experience, and he might have to resort to something extreme.

Something like Rocco's semi-insane fake boyfriend scheme.

"But you *will* think about it, won't you?" Rocco asked persuasively. Like Taylor might have forgotten in the last two minutes. Newsflash: it was hard to forget when anyone offered to fake date you. Doubly so when it was a someone who looked like Rocco Moretti.

"I will," Taylor promised and slid off his barstool. "It was good seeing you, Rocco. And I'll tell Mona to stop by your place this week. See if that helps."

Rocco brightened. "Thanks!"

Taylor considered that after he'd paid his bill and walked out the front door. Would asking Mona to stop by be helpful? It would, if she would actually do it. On the other hand, Rocco was probably right and dating *him* would be a far better option.

The nosy town would be piling into Jolly Java for a chance to get a second look at the guy who'd finally hooked the deputy mayor.

Embarrassing, maybe, but true, nonetheless.

He lived in a little one-story bungalow down one of the side streets, within an easy walk of downtown and City Hall. Unlocking the door, Taylor hung up his coat and scarf and walked into the living room.

Meredith, his sleek gray cat, was sleeping on her favorite cushion, and as he walked in, opened one glowing amber eye. "Meow," she said, greeting him. Taylor went over and rubbed her head. Enjoying the way her soft fur comforted him. Maybe he was alone, but his life wasn't lonely. He had his work, which fulfilled him, and the entire town to worry about and to worry about him in return. And then he had Meredith to cuddle up to at night.

"Should've hooked up with the movie star," he murmured to her as his fingers sifted through her fur. "Would've been easier."

CHAPTER 3

THE NEXT DAY, AS Taylor walked into City Hall, waving to Abe, the security guy at the front desk, it was quiet.

Usually the day after the tree lighting it was, but it felt especially quiet as he walked through the halls towards his office. Most of the offices and desks he passed were unsurprisingly empty.

At least until he got to his own, and when he walked in, Mona was sitting in the chair opposite his desk, teacup in hand, concern written across her face.

"What's up?" Taylor asked, flopping into his chair and pulling a can out of the little fridge underneath his desk. Popping open the energy drink made him think, inevitably, about Rocco Moretti.

Not that since their conversation last night, he'd left Taylor's mind much.

In fact, it kind of felt like he'd taken up semi-permanent residence there.

Mona leaned forward. "I wanted you to be the first to know, Taylor. Someone new applied for the city manager job today."

Taylor's insides froze. "What? Who?"

"His name's Steve Mills. He grew up here, then left for college at eighteen. Finished, built a business, retired early, and came back here. He could be a serious candidate. *Serious*."

Taylor was trying not to panic. "So he's from here. Okay. But he hasn't lived here since he was eighteen. That's surely not ideal, either."

"He's forty-five, and I looked him up on social media—he's got a wife and three daughters." Mona made a face. "They've got all those family pictures up, you know, where they're all wearing matching outfits."

Taylor leaned back in his chair. He was panicking now. Undeniably. "Shit."

"I asked around. It seems like he sees this job as a way to boost his future political aspirations. To take my job eventually? Then to use it to run for state senator? Possibly."

"I . . .*no*." Taylor didn't know what to say. Would he have stepped aside if this Steve Mills guy was good for the town? Maybe he might have. Because even more than he wanted to be the one to help lead Christmas Falls into more decades of prosperity, he wanted it to happen, *period*. If Steve Mills was the person to make that happen, he'd have conceded.

But if he was only looking at the job as a way to move up the political food chain . . .well, Taylor *wasn't* going to let that happen.

He cared about his career prospects, sure, but he cared about this town even more than that.

He'd fight with every tool in his arsenal before Steve Mills used this town to get ahead.

"We're going to fight him, of course," Mona said tightly. "We both will."

"Yeah, we will," Taylor said. "But *how*? This isn't an elected position."

But Taylor already knew what *he* was thinking. What he hadn't freaking stopped thinking about, since Rocco Moretti had brought it up last night.

"This Mills guy is smart so he'll be around. At all the events. I guess he was at the lighting last night. You've got to match him. Remind everyone why you're the best candidate for the job, because you care so much about the future of this town. That maybe you weren't born here, but that it's in your blood now and in your heart. And if . . ." Mona trailed off, then shook her head. "No, I feel bad about trying to push Heath at you last night. You shouldn't need a family to look like you can successfully run a family oriented town. You do it now, and there's no real difference."

"But," Taylor hedged, "it *would* look better, right?"

She looked surprised. "It would, but Taylor, don't date someone just for this. Date someone because you genuinely like them. Because you don't want to bury yourself in work for the rest of your life." She shot him a reprimanding look.

Taylor couldn't say whether or not he genuinely liked Rocco. But he could say, at least, they'd be on the same page. And he did *not* bury himself in work, thank you very much.

"I've got a possibility in mind," Taylor said.

She looked shocked. "Heath, after all?"

"Not Heath." Though *God*, he would have been a hundred times easier and better at this, probably. Still. It wasn't like Rocco Moretti would be bad at this. He'd just be . . .complicated.

"Then who?"

"I've got this handled," Taylor said. If he told his boss the truth, that he and Rocco weren't going to be falling madly in love but only *pretending* to fall madly in love, he had a feeling what she'd say.

No, to everyone else it needed to look totally legit.

And what would be more legit than heading over, first thing in the morning, to Jolly Java?

It was decently busy for a Friday morning, especially after a big event.

The town—and its tourists—needed a shot of sugar and caffeine after a late night partying at the tree lighting.

Rocco split time between the register, playing at the friendly, charming new business owner in town, and the shiny rose gold espresso machine he'd had installed when he'd bought Jolly Java. It was a serious upgrade over what the prior owners had, but of course, not a single soul had mentioned how much better the coffee was.

No. They'd only mourned the loss of pumpkin freaking spice.

By ten, he and Rebecca had dealt with the crowd, then he turned to stocking the pastry case as Rebecca leaned against the counter and watched him.

"So," she asked, "what did you do after the lighting? Please tell me you didn't actually come back here and binge *The Real Housewives of Duluth*."

"I . . .uh . . .actually, I went to Rudolph's."

He did not mention that after his single espresso martini, he'd come home. Thinking the whole time, as he got ready for bed and lay there, sleep eluding him, of the insanity he'd suggested to Taylor Hall.

Taylor Hall, that tall, quiet hunk of a guy who had set his pulse racing the one time he'd stopped by Jolly Java, to welcome him to Christmas Falls.

Rocco had remembered the way his quick, brisk handshake had felt for ages after. For someone who pushed paper all day, he had nice hands. Big and not too soft. Just calloused enough.

Rocco shivered again, thinking about them.

What *had* he been thinking?

That they could solve both of their problems, possibly, and also the third one, which was Rocco's current dry spell.

"Oh yeah? Meet anyone interesting?" she asked casually.

Which told him that the bartender at Rudolph's, had probably noticed him talking to Taylor and had mentioned it to someone else, who'd probably spread it to the whole town.

Rocco rolled his eyes. "Who told you?"

"Mrs. Lil mentioned it to me when I walked to work this morning."

He'd assumed he understood the small town gossip mill from his time in Indigo Bay, but Christmas Falls had a whole other gear that he was still adjusting to.

"What else did she say?"

Rebecca grinned. "How cozy you two looked."

If Taylor had agreed to Rocco's plan, this would've been a great way to lay their groundwork. Spotted together once, and now the town was already ready to couple them up.

"We had one drink, and it wasn't even like we came in together. He was there and I just sat next to him."

"Lots of seats in Rudolph's," she pointed out.

And okay, yes that was true.

After they'd met for the first time, Rocco had done his research—easy in this town, where all you had to do to find out about anyone was ask—and discovered that Taylor Hall was gay and single and had not, in anyone's memory, dated anyone at all.

If he was dating or even hooking up with anyone, he was being so discreet even the town rumor mill hadn't learned of it, which meant that *his* dry spell was possibly quadruple Rocco's own.

Knowledge Rocco told himself he wasn't interested in and didn't need to do anything about.

But then he'd gone and made that suggestion last night. Half of the blame rested firmly with his own desperation to make this business work, and half was almost definitely generated from the kernel of that knowledge, buried deep inside, that he'd been unsuccessfully attempting to ignore.

"He *is* cute," Rocco allowed. There was nothing wrong with laying some groundwork just in case. Besides, it wasn't like he hadn't already told Taylor to his face that he thought he was hot.

"You should ask him out," Rebecca said. Still casually. But he could practically *feel* her eagerness.

"I don't think he's interested," Rocco said, but he didn't know if that was necessarily true. Taylor had that interesting polite-but-cold front, but for a second, Rocco had sworn he'd felt the same attraction he did.

He'd just hidden it better.

Well, that made sense, because Rocco didn't care about hiding it.

"You don't know that he's not," Rebecca said encouragingly. "You two would be so cute together."

"Not everyone wants to date," Rocco said, which *was* true.

He'd hoped to be far too busy for a boyfriend. Yet, he'd gone and sat next to Taylor anyway, at Rudolph's, and then had made that suggestion.

Really, he was lucky Taylor hadn't looked at him like he was nuts and gotten as far away from him as possible. Okay, he hadn't *agreed*, but he had said he'd consider it, in that quiet, considerate, restrained way of his.

That way that made Rocco want to know what Taylor Hall would be like when all that restraint melted away.

"You forget I saw you two the first time you met," Rebecca added slyly. "There was definitely some kind of heat there. He stammered more than once. Taylor doesn't *do* that."

"Maybe he was massively embarrassed that I was making a pumpkin spice-sized mistake," Rocco retorted.

"And you stared at his ass on his way out."

"Have you seen his ass? It'd be a crime to *not* look at it."

The front doorbell chimed, but before Rocco could straighten up and look at who'd come in, Rebecca said, "Keep telling yourself that, okay?"

"Why—"

But before Rocco could get the rest of the question out, he spotted why she'd said it in the first place, *and* why she'd said it all knowing and fond like that.

Because yep, there was Taylor himself, approaching the front counter.

"I'll be cleaning the tables," Rebecca said and then embarrassingly headed instead towards the back, making it crystal clear just what she was doing.

Leaving the two of them alone-ish, other than the pair of tourists by the window who were sharing a ham and gruyere croissant sandwich and a large pot of coffee.

"Hey," Taylor said.

"Come in to discover what you've been missing?" Rocco asked. His brain kept screaming, *hot guy, hot guy, hot guy,* and he couldn't seem to help the flirty comment.

Taylor gave him one of those blank-ish, stern looks with his light blue eyes, and Rocco shouldn't have been so into that, but he *was,* undeniably.

I just want to know how deep that ice goes.

"I'm not here for coffee," Taylor said.

Oh yes, please, Rocco's uncooperative subconscious purred.

"But surely I can persuade you to try *something.* I promise, I'll keep my goat cheese to myself," Rocco teased. *But that's all I'll keep to myself.*

Taylor flushed, and there it was. The first inkling of what lay beneath all that composure. "Maybe . . .uh . . .what doesn't have coffee in it?"

"Hot chocolate? Caramel apple cider?"

"I'm surprised you didn't take those off the menu, too," Taylor said, his voice calm and serious, but his eyes full of amusement.

He was teasing, just like he had last night, and Rocco liked it, maybe a little too much.

Well, at least if you end up faking it, it'll look really convincing.

"I'll make you anything you want, even pumpkin spice," Rocco said, leaning across the counter. Taylor stuck his hands deeper into his coat pockets. "Anything at all."

"How about uh . . .that apple cider? That sounds good."

"You got it," Rocco said. He didn't bat his eyelashes flirtatiously. After all, he was a goddamned professional.

Taylor watched him carefully as he grabbed the cider from the fridge under the counter and heated it up in one of his metal pitchers, then as Rocco swirled homemade caramel sauce into a cup. He didn't ask Taylor if he was enjoying his beverage here or taking it to go. Maybe that *wasn't* professional, but he wanted Taylor to hang around for at least the time it took for him to enjoy his drink.

"Did you mean what you said last night?" Taylor asked quietly.

It wasn't hard for Rocco to know which thing he was asking about.

But he wasn't against making Taylor work for it, a little.

"Which thing I said?" Rocco asked, feigning ignorance as he carefully poured the cider into the mug. He topped it with whipped cream and another swirl of caramel sauce. Setting it on the counter in front of Taylor, he gave in to the temptation and shot him a single smoldering glance.

"Uh, you know," Taylor said, stammering again a little.

"One sec. Let me make a coffee and I'll join you. That corner's quiet." Taylor looked like he was about to say something like, *all your corners look quiet*, but before he could, Rocco added, "And yes, I know. It's quiet today. But hopefully, we can fix that."

"That's the idea," Taylor said.

Rocco quickly made himself a latte and then joined Taylor at one of the tables.

"So you changed your mind," Rocco said.

Taylor shot him a look that promised he wasn't nearly as cold as he presented as being. "I never made up my mind," he retorted. Took a sip of his cider and gave Rocco an approving nod. "This is delicious. I had this probably half a dozen times before you bought this place and it never tasted this good."

"I know," Rocco acknowledged. "I changed a few things."

Taylor chuckled. "Are you incapable of leaving anything as it was?"

"Pretty much. I like to improve things. It's a personal strength and apparently also a failing."

"This town isn't big on change," Taylor said gravely.

"Believe me, I've learned that. The hard way."

"Well, I think you were right about one thing. We *can* help each other," Taylor said.

"Oh?" Rocco raised an eyebrow.

"Remember how I said last night there were no other serious, qualified candidates for my job? Well, scratch that. Someone applied this morning. Someone who was born here, is *not* young, and has a picture-perfect Christmas card family."

"Ouch."

"It doesn't make me a worse candidate, necessarily, but it does give me more competition. I'll need to work harder to look better in the city council's eyes."

"And that's where I come in."

Taylor nodded. "That's where you come in. You make me look settled and happy, because God forbid anyone could be settled or happy without at least a partner."

"Hey, sex makes a whole lot of people happy."

Rocco enjoyed watching Taylor choke on his cider. "That isn't . . .I didn't mean . . ."

"Chill," Rocco said. "I said *fake*, which means we've only got to convince everyone we're getting it on, not that we're actually getting it on."

Not that he'd be averse. In fact, the opposite was true. But Taylor's reaction to him even *saying* the word sex told him everything he needed to know. Taylor might be intrigued by him, but he wasn't even close to ready to tangle in the sheets.

"Right. Okay." Taylor cleared his throat. "You really want to do this, then?"

"Sounds like we both need to, now," Rocco said.

Taylor sighed. "I hate the thought that the council might vote for me and not for this other guy because of this, but I know I'll be better at the job. From what Mona said, I'm certainly going to be more committed to this town."

"Sometimes we do shitty things for good reasons," Rocco said. Shot Taylor a lopsided grin. The certified Moretti grin that never failed to reel anyone in within a ten-foot radius, and it didn't come close to failing now, either. From his pink cheeks to the tremor of his fingers as he gripped his mug, it certainly seemed to have some kind of effect on Taylor. "Besides, it might be fun."

"Fun?"

"You know what that is, right?" Rocco joked. "Or are you too buttoned up, too committed, too much of a workaholic—"

Taylor shot him a look, interrupting Rocco's recital, and this one wasn't just warm, it was downright hot. "I know what fun is."

"Alright." Rocco nodded, pretending that his throat wasn't suddenly dry.

He liked playing with fire, but only when he was sure he wouldn't get burned.

"We'll need to have a plan," Taylor said, all official. That shouldn't have been hot, either, but it definitely was.

"You don't want to just play it by ear?"

"Did you 'play it by ear' when you took pumpkin spice off the menu?" Taylor challenged.

Rocco wasn't surprised the guy had thought it. Taylor wasn't old, couldn't be more than thirty, and he was up for a promotion—a position that he was told was really the whole power behind the town—so he was hardly a slouch. But Rocco *was* surprised he'd said it.

"Fair. Ouch, but fair," Rocco said. "For the record, I *do* have a business plan. A good one, actually."

"I believe it," Taylor said, redeeming himself, slightly.

"Alright, so a plan. Like a dating plan?"

"I was thinking about this. First, you gotta get into the town more," Taylor said. "Let people see you as more than just the idiot who took pumpkin spice off the menu and tried to force-feed them goat cheese."

Rocco winced. "I think we either need to ban that phrase or . . ." He paused, an idea blooming in his mind. "We should actually make it your safe word."

Taylor's eyebrows rose, nearly to his hairline. "My safe word?"

"Well, *our* safe word," Rocco revised. "For example, if I ever do something that makes you feel uncomfortable. Too coupley. Or too romantic. Or too much like you want to drag me to bed? Just say *goat cheese*."

Taylor threw back his head and literally cackled.

Rocco had never seen him laugh like that and couldn't help but pat himself on the back *and* also let himself actually enjoy the sound of Taylor's laugh. The sheer joy in him, that he, from everything Rocco had seen, didn't let anyone see.

If that was why he wasn't immediately the front runner for the city manager job, that was probably why.

He kept this part of himself so restrained, so hidden, and *God*, it was wonderful. Rocco couldn't stop staring at him as he laughed.

"What about *your* safe word?" Taylor asked when he finally stopped laughing.

"You don't want to share goat cheese?"

"Gladly," Taylor said, still chuckling. "So that's *that* part of the plan, I guess."

"As far as I'm concerned, that's the most important part," Rocco pointed out.

"What else . . .well, we'll need to establish how we started dating?"

Rocco considered this. "Better to stick to the truth, right? The first time we met, I was intrigued, and then the other night, I deliberately sat next to you at Rudolph's. You were *also* intrigued and got my number. Asked me out on a date . . .we'll say, in a few days?"

Taylor leaned back in his chair. "You're scarily good at this."

"I am, aren't I?" Rocco would take the compliment, especially considering how fiercely his ego was smarting over the Jolly Java situation.

"Do I want to ask why? You said your cousin did this . . ."

"*They* weren't all that convincing though," Rocco said, not realizing he'd made a tactical error until a frown appeared between Taylor's eyebrows.

"You said it worked out, though."

"Well, *yes*, it did," Rocco added hurriedly. "In the end, they absolutely convinced my Auntie that they were dating. The rest of us? Well, it was a little bit of an over-the-top performance so we were less convinced."

"But she was the target, so it was okay?"

Rocco relaxed a fraction. "Exactly," he confirmed. That wasn't *entirely* accurate but it was accurate enough. And hopefully Taylor would never need to know the truth about the origin of his cousin Enzo and his boyfriend Will's very loving, very *real* relationship.

"Alright. So we stick to the truth as close as possible. We don't overact."

"Should be pretty easy, acting like you're into me," Rocco said, winking.

Taylor chuckled. "Does that work? Scratch that. Don't tell me. I bet it does. Ridiculously well."

"I don't kiss and tell."

"Maybe this time you should," Taylor joked.

"True. So, you're going to ask me out on a date. Where are we going?"

Taylor pulled out one of the flyers the festival committee had produced, all shiny and glossy, this year's schedule listed out in black and white, framed in curling red and green plaid ribbons.

"I marked a few possibilities. Like I said, I think the biggest thing is reminding the town that you're part of us now."

"Kind of like what you need to do," Rocco said.

Taylor nodded. "So we're going to stick to a lot of the festival events. Best way to be seen. Best way to look like we're a part of Christmas Falls. I'd be going to a lot of them anyway, as deputy mayor, but it'll be nice to not be alone."

Rocco wanted to ask if it would be nice to be less alone why Taylor *always* seemed to keep himself at arm's length, but he didn't. That was more of a third-fake-date kind of question.

"Alright, what do we have?" Rocco leaned in, scanning the flyer. Taylor did too, at almost the exact same time, and Rocco glanced up, only realizing a second too late just how close their faces were.

Taylor's hair was nearly as dark as Rocco's own, but his eyes were so crystal clear it was like looking deep into . . .

No. Snap out of it.

Goat cheese. Goat cheese. Goat fucking cheese.

"Uh, what about this one?" Rocco pointed at one of the events, not really bothering to read what it was. Did it really matter, anyway? As long as it was in the late afternoon or evening, he'd be able to attend.

"Oh, yeah, well I guess that makes sense you'd pick that one," Taylor said, and Rocco looked a little closer at what he'd just blindly pointed out.

Holiday Wine Tasting.

It was in three days, at six thirty on Monday night, and hosted at The White Elephant.

"What, because I'm Italian?" Rocco questioned.

Taylor nodded. "You like wine, right? Or is that—"

"Well, it is a cliche, sure. But yes, I do like wine." Rocco internally winced at how bad the wine was probably going to be. After spending a year in Indigo Bay, with his cousin Luca's cellar to pick from, it couldn't possibly compare, so he was just going to have to adjust his expectations.

Besides, it would be wet and contain alcohol. Something Rocco was sure he'd need if he was going to spend an entire evening faux-flirting with Taylor Hall.

"Alright, that's perfect then. Makes me look all thoughtful and shit," Taylor said.

"Are you not?"

Taylor shot him a look and his back stiffened. "It's not that I'm bad at this, I just haven't . . .not in a while."

"Ah."

"Not that it's been a *long, long* time or anything," Taylor said hurriedly. "I *do* date."

"Uh-huh." Rocco wasn't going to say anything. Just let the guy dig his own hole.

"I date," Taylor repeated in a very insistent tone.

"Sure." Rocco paused and grinned. "You wanna say goat cheese? I didn't even do anything."

"*No.* I'm fine. I don't need to say . . ." Taylor cleared his throat. "Goat cheese. Not even remotely."

"Okay. So the wine tasting it is. What else did you want to cover in this plan of yours?" Rocco finished his latte, glancing up as a few customers walked in. Rebecca could handle them, but he also liked to be present, front and center, for every visitor these days. Maybe it didn't mean anything, but it was something he could do.

Other than fake dating Taylor, that was.

"You need to go?" Taylor asked.

"Soon, but not right now."

"There's one big thing left." Taylor looked uneasy. "Are we going to tell anyone the truth?"

Rocco considered this. "I don't have anyone here that I'd care about knowing the truth." Rebecca was a friend and an employee, but she'd already guessed that he and Taylor were interested in each other, so it would be easiest to just let her continue assuming. As for his family, none of them were here in Christmas Falls. Would he tell any of them? He couldn't see it, considering how they'd want, in all their overdramatic Moretti-ness, to interfere.

"Me either. My dad's in Chicago and doesn't usually come for the holidays."

Rocco wanted to ask why not. It was on the tip of his tongue to ask, but before he could, Taylor said, "And as for my boss, she told me to take care of it. Maybe she guesses we're not legitimately dating, but I think better not to tell her directly. Plausible deniability?"

"Works for me," Rocco said, nodding.

Taylor looked at his watch again, and Rocco had a feeling that was his indication this "planning meeting" was over.

Trust Taylor to approach fake dating like it was a meeting at Town Hall.

Rocco resolved to help him loosen up a bit. Starting with right now.

"Well, I'd better make sure Rebecca doesn't need any help," Rocco said, standing up. Taylor followed suit, rising to his feet. "It was nice to see you again." He raised his voice a little more. "I'm looking forward to the wine tasting."

Taylor was looking everywhere but at him directly. "Me too."

"Remember," Rocco said, dropping his voice to a murmur, "that your safe word is goat cheese, okay?"

"Why—"

But Taylor didn't get the whole question out, before Rocco was reaching out and tugging him into a firm, affectionate hug. For a second, Taylor stiffened, maybe in shock, and then he relaxed into it.

If Rocco had anything to say about it, Taylor was *definitely* one of those clean-living types, with a hard body to match that attitude, deliciously firm against his own.

He was also the perfect height too—approximately four inches taller than Rocco himself—and bigger and broader in all the right ways.

Rocco didn't really want to let go, but he knew he should. After one last squeeze of Taylor's very nice shoulders, he released him.

"You good?" Rocco asked under his breath.

Taylor smiled. "I didn't say goat cheese, did I?"

"No, you did not." Rocco didn't add that he'd been feeling a little goat-cheesy himself. He didn't say it because it was just a hug, for goodness' sake. They were going to have to do a lot more than that if they wanted to convince Christmas Falls they were dating—though considering the town's gossip mill, maybe not *that* much more.

Rocco didn't know if he was excited or disappointed by that realization.

"Well, thanks for the cider. It was really good."

"Of course it was," Rocco said, patting him on the arm. That very firm, muscled arm.

He snatched his hand back.

Goat cheese.

"I'll see you around," Taylor said.

And then he was gone, the bell over the door tinkling as it closed behind him.

Freaking goat cheese.

CHAPTER 4

TAYLOR FORCED HIMSELF OUT of bed on Saturday morning, pretending he didn't understand exactly why he'd tossed and turned far too much the night before and a certain dark-haired, dark-eyed guy had taken up seemingly permanent residence in his dreams. He threw on his sweats and a Northwestern sweatshirt and went for his normal Saturday morning run.

Waiting for him as he swung by his house two streets over was Hayden Bradley, who did IT work for the city. They'd started jogging together six months ago when they'd discovered they kept running into each other on Saturdays—literally.

"Hey," Hayden said as he picked up speed next to Taylor.

"Hey back," Taylor said.

"Heard about the new applicant," Hayden said, the winter sun shining on his freckled face.

Taylor groaned. "You and everyone else. Was it too easy for me to just apply for this goddamn job and have nobody else serious apply?"

"Yeah, kinda," Hayden said wryly. "That was a pipe dream, dude."

"Ugh," Taylor said, groaning again.

"And what's this I heard from Murphy about you ditching Heath Kelly?"

Taylor groaned a third time.

"You okay? Eat something off?"

"No, no, I just . . ." Taylor didn't know how to say it. He'd told Rocco, just yesterday, that he didn't have anyone he felt he had to come clean with, but now, faced with Hayden, who'd first been a casual acquaintance but was now a friend, Taylor didn't want to lie.

"You're interested in someone else." Hayden said it matter-of-factly and then shot him a shit-eating grin.

"God, does *everyone* know already?"

"That you and Rocco Moretti had a drink together on Thursday and then you went to Jolly Java yesterday, *even though you don't drink coffee*? Oh, it's definitely making the rounds. When I ran into Arlo and Mrs. Lil last night at the rink, she was practically salivating when she told me all about it. How you're going to fall madly in love and Rocco's going to seduce you into drinking coffee."

Taylor gave a short bark of laughter. "Not likely," he said.

"Which part?"

He hesitated. He didn't want to lie. But he couldn't exactly tell him the truth either. Maybe he could stick to a *version* of the truth. "I don't think I'd ever like anyone enough to drink coffee, but if there was a chance, it would probably be Rocco Moretti."

Hayden shot him a knowing look. "So you *are* interested, then."

They turned down St. Nick Avenue, and sped up a little, both of them fully warmed up now, despite the chill in the air.

"He seems like a cool guy." Playing things close to the vest was too much of a habit, Taylor knew it. He should be more effusive. But he didn't know *how*, without giving everything away.

Hayden raised his eyebrow. "A cool guy?"

"Okay, a *hot* cool guy," Taylor admitted.

"Better," Hayden said, giving him an approving nod.

"I don't . . .I don't date much."

Hayden patted him on the shoulder. "Yeah, we know. If you want advice, you know who to come to."

"You?" Taylor said, his voice full of faux disbelief.

"I ended up with the guy, didn't I?" Hayden said, referring to Joel, who ran Ginger's Breads.

"You literally tripped and fell onto him," Taylor joked. "I'm not sure that counts."

"Hey, it definitely counts. Honestly, though, you're gonna do just fine. Rocco does seem like a cool guy. Pumpkin spice notwithstanding."

"God, not you, too."

"It wasn't me. Mrs. Lil was complaining about it. She wondered if maybe she could ask you to persuade him to put it back on the menu."

"Tell her it's already back. Not only that, he's part of this town now. Deserves a second chance, same as us all."

Taylor hadn't realized how insistent he sounded until Hayden laughed. "Oh, I can see it now. Your freaking enormous crush is visible from space."

He almost said, *no it's not, not remotely,* but 1) that was not what someone who'd be very publicly dating the guy would say, and 2) it sounded a whole lot like *he doth protest too much.*

"Uh, yeah," Taylor admitted bashfully.

"Aw, it's cute. I'm happy for you, Taylor. This is good."

Taylor sure hoped so.

Hayden peeled off two miles later, to visit Joel at the bakery, and instead of cooling down, Taylor did an extra mile to try to compensate for the visions of Rocco still insistently dancing in his head and then on his way home, stopped by the Arts and Crafts Fair to make an appearance.

It was the first day and that meant Murphy was in his booth, alongside Tasha who ran his carved gnome business.

Taylor waved to Murphy, talking earnestly to a customer, showing her all the different-sized gnomes. Tasha was hovering close by, a tablet in her hands, probably ready to show her all the available inventory.

Murphy's booth was the centerpiece of the festival every year, but it felt like each successive year, as the event grew, the waiting list for vendors who wanted to display their wares was growing more and more competitive.

Taylor walked through the narrow aisles, taking in all the sights and smells. Hand-dipped and hand-poured candles in dozens of holiday scents, hand-built birdhouses decorated in festive colors, and even a few decked out in professional sports team colors, including one in the Charleston Condors' signature red and orange. No doubt that vendor was hoping that Jem, retired from the Condors, might walk by and buy it for the new house he was building just outside of town with Murphy.

Knowing Jem, he might do just that.

Speaking of Jem . . .there he was, walking in the opposite direction, next to a woman with dark hair the exact same shade as his and a nose and cheekbones that Jem had been lucky enough to win in the genetic lottery. Sophie Knight he'd met lots of times before this, but Jem had only recently moved back to town.

"Oh, hey, Taylor. Out for a run this morning?" Jem asked, and they shook hands briefly.

He and Jem had worked together pretty closely over the summer with funding for the Holiday Hope Foundation, making sure there'd be enough money in the coffers for them to hire Mason and also for the foundation's move to better facilities that could support them year-round.

"Yep," Taylor said, nodding. "Hayden Bradley and I try to meet up every Saturday morning. Good to see you, too, Mrs. Knight."

"You, too, Taylor, and I always have to tell you to call me Sophie," she said, a small smile on her face. "Jem, you should join them."

Jem flushed. "I don't want to invite myself—"

"You'd be welcome to join," Taylor said. "Just don't expect too much. Neither of us are professional athletes. Not even close."

"And neither am I anymore," Jem said wryly.

Taylor shot him a look. "I'd still bet you'd run circles around us."

"I'll try not to," Jem said, "but it's not going to be a problem. I promise."

"I love a serendipitous moment," Sophie said.

"You here to see Murphy?" Taylor asked.

Jem grinned. "Per Tasha, if he makes a break for it, I'm supposed to drag him back to the festival by his ear."

"Ouch," Taylor said. He knew Murphy Clark was far, far more comfortable in his barn, carving his fanciful and whimsical gnomes, than selling them to an interested crowd.

"I told him I'd do it by the hair, instead," Jem joked.

"Jeremiah!" Sophie said, smacking her son on his arm. "That's my future son-in-law you're talking about."

Jem's expression softened. "Yeah," he said.

Taylor wanted to ask if this was a faraway future kind of expectation or a solid reality that would be happening soon, but before he could, Jem shot his mother a look and Sophie turned to Taylor, changing the subject. "And what's this about you and the new coffee shop owner, Taylor?"

"Uh, well . . ." Taylor stammered.

He was going to have to practice his answer to this question. The whole freaking point of dating Rocco was for it to be public knowledge, but right now, he couldn't even manage a simple question about him.

"Aw, you're cute," Sophie said, patting him on his arm. "You've got a real crush on him. I can tell. You look just like Jem did when he first came back to town last year. Walked around every day with his head in the clouds and hearts in his eyes."

"Mom," Jem said, flushing redder.

"You *did*," she said with affection. "And it was just as adorable then as it is now, with Taylor here. It's beautiful how much Christmas Falls loves *love*."

"That's a lot of love," Jem said. But he didn't look like he hated it. In fact, he looked happier and more relaxed, comfortable in his own skin in a way he hadn't been, when he'd first come back to Christmas Falls last year.

"And *you* love it," Sophie said, poking him in the arm. "Will we see you at the skating rink tonight, for the social?"

"Uh . . .sure," Taylor said. Mona had said, *get out and be present, remind everyone who you are, and that you love this town, even if you're not from it*, so he supposed that included wobbling around on the temporary rink set up in Sugar Plum Park and drinking lukewarm hot chocolate.

It would be better if Rocco was by his side, but he still had their date on Monday night to look forward to.

He wouldn't be alone, then.

And maybe before that, he'd practice acknowledging his interest in public without stammering or flushing an even brighter red than Jem Knight when his mom teased him about his boyfriend.

"Well, see you then," Jem said, patting him on the shoulder.

Taylor walked around for another few minutes. He bought a chai snickerdoodle candle that he hoped would make his house smell like he *actually* baked chai snickerdoodles and a cat ornament that reminded him of Meredith from the booths, and shook more hands. Greeted tourists and townspeople alike, until forty minutes later, purchases in hand, he headed home.

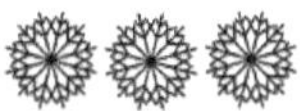

By Monday night, Taylor felt like the whole town not only knew about their date, but they'd gone out of their way to ask him about it.

Repetition helped him answer their questions better, but it was still undeniably awkward.

More than once, he'd been tempted to text Rocco and ask if he'd had a similar level of interest—and if they'd detoured to Jolly Java, buying coffee and scones and muffins, to do it.

Maybe just the *thought* of them dating had been enough to get Rocco back into everyone's good graces.

But then, that wouldn't fix Taylor's problem.

And you wouldn't get to hang out with him, and you want to. Even if you don't want to admit it.

He did.

He could barely think it without a blaring *goat cheese* accompanying the thought, but that had only turned into amusing punctuation, not even a deterrent.

By the time the wine tasting rolled around, he'd avoided actually texting Rocco, but Rocco had texted him twice.

Once to confirm they'd be meeting there, and another, just a minute ago, telling Taylor he was running slightly behind.

Taylor had read the first one—a fairly straightforward exchange—and the second, even though it had only just come in, more times than he wanted to admit to.

This is not a real date.

But it felt like a real date.

Then he heard footsteps behind him, and turned, and *yeah*, he'd felt this way the last time he'd been on a first date. That sharp wave of exhilaration and terror surging through him, though then it hadn't been nearly as strong as it was now, faced with a Rocco Moretti trying to make a good impression.

Or maybe he always cleaned up this good.

His hair was curling around his head in a dark halo, his cheekbones carved out of his face, brown eyes hot as they took in Taylor standing there, under the streetlight.

He wore a black wool peacoat, with a maroon scarf wrapped around his neck, and a pair of form-fitting black jeans and dark boots.

Goat cheese, Taylor thought dazedly. *All the goat cheese.*

"Sorry to keep you waiting," Rocco said breathlessly.

Taylor thought, *I'd wait a hell of a lot longer for you.* But he didn't say that, because nobody was here, and there was no point in saying anything sappy and romantic when they didn't have an audience. That was the whole idea behind this charade.

"It's fine," Taylor said. "You ready to go in?"

"Oh yeah," Rocco said.

Taylor gestured towards the door, and with his late mother's voice admonishing him in his head to be a gentleman, he pressed a palm to Rocco's firm, warm back.

Felt his muscles tense under his touch and then relax.

"So," Rocco asked under his breath as they walked in, "how does this work?"

"You're asking me? I've no idea. Never been to this event before."

It looked fairly straightforward though. The main dining room of The White Elephant had been rearranged, the tables in a half-moon shape, with different bottles of wine scattered across the surfaces.

"Hello," Elaine Watson said as they approached the main table. She managed The White Elephant for Kody Campbell, who'd taken over from his parents. "I didn't know you two were coming tonight."

That was a lie. He'd emailed her himself, making sure they were both on the list, and instead of merely emailing him back his confirmation, Elaine had called him up on his official line, asking half a dozen leading questions that she didn't really need the answer to.

He liked Elaine, had always liked her, but he discovered he *didn't* like the intense interest in what the two of them were doing here together.

Wasn't it *obvious*?

He shouldn't need to spell it out. Anyone who looked at Rocco Moretti had to understand exactly why Taylor had gone out of his way to take him out.

"Yep," Taylor said and gazed down at Rocco with what he hoped was a lovestruck expression.

Frankly it didn't feel that much different than it had when he'd turned a minute ago and seen Rocco walking up to him.

"Oh lovely," Elaine said. "Let me tell you how it works. Taylor's paid for your registration, which gets you each six tastes, which you can mark off on this card here—along with your impression and a score of each wine."

"Makes sense," Rocco said, picking up their two glasses and the cards Elaine had indicated. He handed one to Taylor, and if the deliberate way their fingers brushed when he passed the glass over was any indication, he was going to be a lot better at this than Taylor was.

Not very surprising.

"You can hang your coats over there," Elaine said, gesturing towards the rack they'd set up in the corner. "And feel free to start wherever, though the tables are arranged from light whites to medium whites to more light-bodied reds and finally, at the end there, the more full-bodied reds."

Taylor plucked the second glass from Rocco's hand and then set them both on the table, setting his fingers on the collar of Rocco's coat, helping him out of it.

Underneath, he wore a silvery gray button-up, open at the throat, showcasing a wedge of olive-toned skin and a thin gold chain around his neck.

Taylor's hand trembled as he hung up the coat and divested himself of his own.

"So polite," Rocco said, and there was another one of those eyelash flutters of his, the one that seemed unfairly designed to make Taylor's pulse stutter.

It would be both a lot easier and a lot harder to do this whole fake dating thing if he found Rocco less appealing.

"I . . .I'm trying," he said, settling on the least difficult response.

"You're doing better than that," Rocco said, patting him on the arm and shooting him a brilliant smile. His heart rate, not quite settled back to normal from the eyelash flutter, accelerated again.

If they kept this up for months, he was either going to have to get used to the potency of Rocco Moretti or go on blood pressure medication.

"Thanks," Taylor said.

"And for the record," Rocco said, his gaze sweeping from Taylor's feet to the top of his head, "you clean up real good, too."

Taylor flushed. He'd taken extra care with his appearance tonight, justifying it with the reasoning that if he was *actually* taking Rocco out on a date, he'd have approached it with not only some careful planning, but optimizing all his advantages.

His knit polo was a little clingier—*sluttier*, Joey would have called it—than he'd normally have worn to work, calling attention to his biceps and pecs and chest, and he'd worn it with his best pair of dark jeans. Maybe he wasn't a freaking smoke show, not like Rocco, but he wasn't hopeless, either.

From the way Rocco was looking at him, real or fake, he was pretty damn far from hopeless.

Well, the good news was everything was going to plan. Nobody would see the two of them and think they weren't definitely into each other.

"You good?" Rocco asked, leaning in closer. He still smelled like coffee—the best part of it, the rich deep scent of it—but like something woodsy and faintly floral too. Taylor had to remind himself that he was supposed to be doing the opposite of *hands off*.

He was supposed to be freaking hands *on*.

"Yeah, I'm good," Taylor said.

Maybe he should be *goat cheesing* all over the place, but he wasn't even tempted.

The truth was, it was easier than it should have been to put his hand on the small of Rocco's back, feeling the warmth of his body through the thin fabric of his shirt, and guide him towards the first table.

Rocco picked up their glasses and they approached the first station.

"Oh, this looks good," Rocco said, gesturing towards the bottles. "They've got a *cremant,* a prosecco, and a cava."

"You're speaking Greek," Taylor admitted.

Rocco raised an eyebrow. "You don't drink wine." He stated it, rather than asked.

"Not usually, no," Taylor said. Ironically enough, that hadn't even occurred to him as a problem during the time between Rocco suggesting this as their first date and tonight. He'd been too focused on doing this *right*, on convincing everyone he was crazy about the guy, and not painfully awkward, like he was trying too hard.

"It's alright," Rocco reassured him. "I do. One of my cousins, Luca, is practically a professional sommelier. I spent some time with him and his husband, during the last year, and what I didn't already know from working at my parents' restaurant in San Francisco, I picked up pretty quickly from him."

"So you're like . . .a wine expert then?" God, this was even worse. Not only was Taylor freaking clueless, but Rocco was the opposite.

"Not an *expert*, necessarily, but I know my way around. And don't worry, okay? I've got you." Rocco touched him on the chest, fingers lingering there, and his gaze was knowing.

Because he was playacting for everyone who was no doubt watching them, or because he knew how much Taylor enjoyed it—and didn't want to? It was unclear.

"If you'll help me, that would be . . ." Taylor cleared his throat. Mona was always telling him to be a little less competent and accept some help once in awhile, and he had a feeling this was one of those times. "That would be great."

"Oh, baby, I got you," Rocco repeated.

"Baby, huh?"

"Seems simpler, easier, than *holy hot hunk,*" Rocco teased.

Taylor swallowed hard. "Yeah?"

"Oh yeah. *Baby* it is, then."

Taylor let his palm, sweaty and damp, press even more firmly into Rocco's back, sliding it a fraction lower.

From the way Rocco looked at him—from Elaine's expression he caught out of the corner of his eye—he had a feeling they were being *extremely* convincing.

Excellent.

"So, what are these? Should we try them?" Taylor motioned to the bottles on the table with the hand that wasn't occupied with touching Rocco as firmly as he dared.

Rocco leaned in, and Taylor's hand slid lower still and sweat prickled under his arms. Rocco's back had been firm enough under his touch, but now he was edging closer to his ass, and it felt even better than it looked.

He half-expected Rocco to hiss *goat cheese* under his breath, but he didn't.

"Oh yeah, definitely this prosecco." Rocco lifted the bottle and tipped a taste into his glass. It fizzed as he lifted it to his nose, giving it a long sniff. "That's nice."

"It smells good?" Taylor had never really smelled wine before.

Rocco handed him the glass.

And it *did* smell good, like freshly baked bread and apple and sunshine.

"Now," Rocco murmured, "you give it another swirl. Just a little one. And then another sniff. Then, finally, you taste."

Taylor tried to do exactly as Rocco described and thought he got pretty close, the flavor of the wine exploding like fireworks against his tongue. "That's . . .that's really good, actually."

"Yeah," Rocco agreed, nodding after he'd plucked the glass from Taylor's hand and taken a sip of his own.

"Did I do it right?"

Rocco shot him a look that both reassured and challenged. "You don't have to get precious about wine. You want to taste something without doing all that? I'm not going to judge. Wine's good, and you should drink it, however you want."

"Huh."

Rocco tipped the rest of the glass back and they moved on. "I've never been at a tasting where they didn't pour *for* you," Rocco said under his breath as they approached the next table. "They're clearly not worried about me taking more than six samples—or what size those samples are."

Taylor had never been to a wine tasting before, so he had no idea what was normal. But then there was the way he'd felt his neck prickle, more than once, while they'd been sampling the prosecco.

Elaine had definitely been watching them. He'd assumed it was because of who he was with, but maybe it hadn't entirely been because of that.

"Don't worry, we're being monitored," Taylor said, leaning down a fraction, to whisper it into Rocco's ear. Hopefully Elaine would assume he was murmuring sweet nothings.

"Huh, yeah." Rocco flashed him a brilliant smile—though Taylor was beginning to believe that Rocco didn't own a smile that wasn't brilliant.

"You keep smiling at me like that, Elaine'll call Mrs. Lil and Marlene and every other gossip in town and tell her we're halfway to being madly in love," Taylor said, nudging him with his shoulder, the corner of his mouth quirking up.

"The smile is kind of a Moretti thing," Rocco said, a trace of apology in his voice, as they stood in front of the next table. These were supposedly the "light whites," per Elaine and also the discreet tented sign on the table, though Taylor had no idea what the hell that meant.

"There's more of you and they all smile all like that?"

"Oh, yeah," Rocco said.

"Geez." Taylor couldn't imagine. "Have you considered trying to take over a small country?"

There was another flash of white teeth, and this one was so potent Taylor swore he felt butterfly wings fluttering in his stomach. "We try to only use our powers for good."

"Us mere mortals appreciate it," Taylor said dryly.

Rocco elbowed him, not hard, but not exactly gently either. Taylor glanced up, looking the way Rocco had nudged him. "Is that a . . ."

Taylor laughed. "Uh, yeah. And weirdly, having some guy wandering around in an elf costume is not *that* surprising, at least in Christmas Falls."

"Wow," Rocco said.

"Okay, tell me about these," Taylor said, gesturing to the table.

This time, Rocco poured an inch or so of pale yellow wine into Taylor's glass. "If you're not a wine drinker, the sparkling stuff is good, like the prosecco we just tried, but this would be good too. It's a pinot grigio, from Italy."

Taylor tried just drinking it with only taking the barest hint of a whiff first and then a little sip. Yeah, it *was* good. Sharp and a little sour, but refreshing on his tongue, too.

Tried to ignore when Rocco sipped it too, putting his lips almost exactly where Taylor's had been.

Cleared his throat.

If he said *goat cheese* now, this would stop. And he *liked* having his hands on Rocco. He liked the way Rocco gazed up at him, that intoxicating mixture of faith and delight. Like there was nothing Rocco enjoyed more than watching as Taylor experienced something new that he happened to love, too.

"Next table?" Taylor suggested.

They worked their way around the half-moon, four more tables, and even though they barely took more than a sip, by the time they hit the "mature reds," Taylor felt a little light-headed and possibly intoxicated.

He wanted to blame the wine, but he had a feeling it had more to do with the guy he was with.

"You good?" Rocco said, licking his lips as he tasted the dark red wine he'd poured himself.

Rocco had lost Taylor around "damp asphalt" and "tobacco" notes, even though he insisted there was dark red fruit too, in the profile.

If Taylor wanted to taste asphalt, he'd go lick the freaking ground.

Still, even if he hadn't drunk the last round himself, he'd enjoyed watching as Rocco did.

"Yeah, I'm great."

Elaine approached then. Taylor had to give her full points. He'd felt her gaze on them quite a bit, but she'd actually left them alone. Until now.

"Feel free to pour yourself a glass of your favorite and stay awhile," she said, gesturing towards some of the empty booths. "I can tell how much you're enjoying yourself."

"It's an excellent list you've curated," Rocco said.

"Thank you. Nice to see it's being appreciated," Elaine said with a warm smile. "Have a wonderful evening."

"What are you thinking of having a glass of?" Rocco asked him after she'd gone back to the registration table. He was eyeing the second-to-last table they'd been at, and if Taylor had to guess, from the way he'd cataloged the miniscule differences in all of Rocco's delighted expressions as he'd tasted the wine, he'd be pouring himself a glass of the Sonoma County pinot noir.

Rocco had made a point of saying it was as good as anything he'd ever tried out of the famous Moretti cellars, and Taylor had a feeling that was high praise.

As for him? It was a no-brainer. Taylor broke off, hating to let go of him, but that was normal, right? Nobody was supposed to touch someone else the *entirety* of a date.

He poured himself a full glass of the prosecco. Watched as Rocco indeed picked up the bottle of pinot noir.

"All the way at the beginning?" Rocco sounded delighted. "Oh, I love a man who enjoys his bubbly."

"Yeah?" Taylor hadn't thought it was weird to pick the prosecco but maybe it was? Except he'd genuinely liked the way it had felt like fireworks on his tongue, like the way his blood fizzed every single time Rocco looked over at him.

"It's nice," Rocco said, patting him on the arm.

Taylor guided him towards one of the empty booths and decided it was the fault of the wine and also this whole ridiculous fake dating scheme that after Rocco slid in, he moved right in next to him.

"Aw," Rocco cooed, grinning, "you like me."

More than he was entirely comfortable with, if Taylor was being honest.

But instead of confessing that, he said instead, "Aren't I supposed to?"

Rocco patted him on the cheek. His touch fleeting and then gone, far too quickly, even though his whole side, including, *God*, his thigh, was solid and warm against Taylor's own.

"Yeah, and don't worry, I think that very nosy woman is going to tell everyone," Rocco said.

It seemed likely.

"They were already thinking you and me was happening," Taylor confessed. "I think I got asked about it a dozen times, since I went to Jolly Java last week."

"Same," Rocco said. "But did they come to Jolly Java to ask? *No*. Instead, they cornered me in the supermarket. In the hardware store. When I stopped by the Arts and Crafts Fair. Once, even when I was *outside* the coffee shop, but inside it? No way." He sounded a little bitter, but Taylor wasn't sure he could blame him for being frustrated.

"Well, maybe they will now." Taylor was trying to be optimistic. He already knew they'd be committed to this charade through the hiring process, which culminated in the April city council meeting where they made the final decision. But he'd hoped, maybe a little foolishly, that if they launched hard, they might not have to put much effort in after.

Maybe that assumption had been naive.

How are you gonna deal with Rocco smiling at you like that for four plus months and keep a level head on your shoulders?

Taylor didn't have an answer for that.

"We'll see. Though Remy from The Snowflake Shack came over and ordered some coffees. Even tried my marzipan latte. The *worst* part was that Luca's husband Oliver got the recipe from me and he said it's already a big hit in Indigo Bay." Rocco made a face. "Totally unfair. But then that guy could get a priest to drink all his communion wine."

"There's someone more charming on earth besides you?" Taylor realized a second too late he probably shouldn't have been *that* honest. He took a long drink of his wine.

Whoops.

"You should meet my cousin Lorenzo," Rocco said dispiritedly. "Though, maybe not. His husband Seth might kill you, and he's ex-military so that's something he's really good at."

Taylor didn't like it when Rocco felt bad. So he changed the subject. "Luca's your cousin too, right?" It was probably not part of the fake-boyfriend playbook to memorize Rocco's family tree, but most people didn't have a family like Rocco either. Taylor hadn't heard that much about them yet, and they already seemed memorable.

"Yep," Rocco said. "The one in charge of everything—Nonna's, and also married to Oliver. They live in Indigo Bay. Run the Italian deli there, and the Lowcountry Bistro, the restaurant they own together. And Oliver owns the bakery and coffee shop."

"A lot of cousins," Taylor said. It was hard for him to even conceptualize that much family. He only had his dad, and his mom had had a sister, much older, and she'd never had kids.

"God, so many cousins," Rocco said, the corner of his mouth tilting up. He sipped his wine. "And they're all terribly, terribly competent."

"A lot of pressure on you then, to live up to their legacy." Taylor didn't really have experience with that, but he imagined how it must feel.

Maybe bad, but also really, really great.

"Yeah," Rocco agreed. "How about you?"

Ugh. No. Let's not talk about my family.

"Uh, not much to say. Just my dad and me." Taylor changed the subject, because he really, really did not want to discuss why that was. Maybe the hurt had long since scabbed over and eventually healed, at least on the surface, but that didn't mean he liked talking about it, either. "So why didn't you settle down in Indigo Bay, it was, right?"

Rocco nodded. "You ever know *that* couple? The one that's absolutely fucking adorable and you know you should love them, and you *do*, but you also kind of want to scream in their face that their happiness is the *worst*? That it's a daily fucking reminder of everything you *don't* have?"

Taylor chuckled. "My old college friend, Joey, and his wife, Libby."

"Yep, you know. I just . . .I couldn't stay there. I love them, but I couldn't. And I wanted my own corner of the Moretti pie, you know? My *own* corner."

"I get that," Taylor said.

"I could've stayed. They'd have made room for me, because that's how Luca and Oliver are, and that's what Morettis do. Or I could have settled in LA, with my cousins, Gabe and Ren."

"But then it wouldn't have been *your* corner," Taylor guessed.

"Exactly." Rocco looked relieved that he understood, but it wasn't like this was a *real* date and it actually mattered if Taylor approved of the way he was choosing to live his life.

"When you brought up that we should do this, I thought you were insane," Taylor confessed.

"I know," Rocco said.

"But actually . . .I think it's a good idea." *I'm probably going to go out of my mind doing it, but that's okay. 'Cause it'll be worth it. The job'll be worth it.* "This has been fun."

Rocco elbowed him, grinning. "Don't sound so surprised. I'm a great time."

"I'm not sure *I* am, so maybe I should apologize for that," Taylor said. He didn't add that his reserve was so much a habit now it was hard for him to let it down, even on purpose.

"You're fine," Rocco said. Waggled his eyebrows ridiculously. Somehow even then he was hot, defying logic. "And *fine*. I don't mind the company or the visuals."

Did *he* mind the visuals?

No. No, he did not.

Taylor was even afraid that tonight when he returned home alone and lay in bed, as he stared unblinking at the ceiling, that it was going to be *this* visual he remembered—Rocco tucked up close next to him, his beautiful face tilted up towards his own.

"Good," Taylor said, nodding. "So we'll do this again?"

Rocco finished his wine.

Taylor nearly suggested he try finagling another glass out of Elaine, but then Rocco shot him a disappointed look. "I should really be getting home. The alarm goes off early."

"How early?"

"Four AM," Rocco admitted.

"Jesus, and I thought *I* got up early."

"Don't mistake me for a morning person. I just own a coffee shop and like to do the baking early in the morning," Rocco said. "And *do* the baking. I could still get my stuff from Joel, I suppose, but I . . .well . . ."

They slid out of the booth and headed to grab their coats.

"You wanted your own corner." Taylor did understand. Rocco wanted Jolly Java to be *his*, to put his own mark on it. Which was probably why he'd taken pumpkin spice off the menu and tried to convince Christmas Falls to give goat cheese a chance.

Rocco nodded. "You get it."

"We'll make it thrive, I promise," Taylor said, even though he could not possibly promise that. But he would, and he *would* make it happen. He knew that now, as surely as he knew he would work his hardest to convince the city council that he was the right city manager for Christmas Falls, not Steve Mills.

"And you're going to get the job," Rocco said. He slipped his coat on, and Taylor took advantage of his last chance to touch him, smoothing the fabric over his shoulders.

"I sure hope so," Taylor said.

"Goodnight," Elaine called out as they headed through the door, Taylor's hand brushing the small of Rocco's back.

"I should walk you back to your place," Taylor said as they stepped out onto the sidewalk. It was cold, now, and the sky looked like snow might be threatening.

"Well, it wouldn't be a proper date if you didn't," Rocco teased, wrapping his scarf around his neck. He shivered a bit, and Taylor didn't think, just grabbed his hand and tucked into his bigger one, squeezing it carefully to try to warm it.

He was cold, that was all. And someone *might* see, theoretically, and then they could say they'd watched as Taylor walked Rocco Moretti home after their date, holding hands.

Taylor told himself firmly that was what mattered as they walked down the city streets. What everyone else saw, not the firm pressure of Rocco's hand in his, warming him from the inside out, even though it was colder than his own.

"This was really nice," Rocco said quietly as they turned the corner, where Jolly Java sat, light glowing out from its lantern next to the door.

He stopped and tilted his head up. It was still early, and there were a handful of people wandering around, taking advantage of the festival time to get some last-minute shopping in.

Would it be anyone who'd recognize them? Taylor didn't know.

But he also knew if this had been a real date, he'd do this, no questions whatsoever.

So he leaned in, murmured, *"just say goat cheese,"* and brushed his lips quickly over Rocco's cheek.

He pulled back, hypnotized by the look in Rocco's dark eyes—the surprise, and the pleasure. Rocco's hand went to his cheek and he pressed his fingertips to it, like he wanted to feel it.

Rocco didn't say that he'd needed to *goat cheese*, and maybe he didn't need to. The fact that he hadn't wanted to was obvious enough.

Neither did you.

"Well, uh, have a nice night," Taylor said, trying not to stammer. Shoved his hands back into his own pockets so they wouldn't find their way back to Rocco's body.

"You too." Rocco flashed him one last of those smiles, and Taylor turned and walked off.

Telling himself the whole time that if he didn't leave right then, he wouldn't have wanted to leave at all.

Chapter 5

"And here I thought after your big date, you'd be on top of the world," Rebecca joked gently as she leaned against the big stainless steel prep counter running the full length of the back kitchen of Jolly Java.

"I'm not *not* on top of the world. Just trying to get these chai buns in the oven," Rocco said. He continued carefully rolling out the dough.

It was early morning, just after six, two days after his big date with Taylor.

And as many times as he had reminded himself that it *wasn't* a date, that Taylor had absolutely no reason to call or text him, that he had Taylor's number and he could certainly reach out if it mattered so goddamn much, he couldn't quite convince himself. Or that corner of his heart that was stuck on the fact that his evening with Taylor had been one of the best first dates he'd ever been on.

But it wasn't really a first date. It was a fake *first date.*

Rocco was tired of reminding himself of that fact.

"You waltzed in here the next morning like you'd just been swept off your feet. And then by closing yesterday, you were as grumpy as I've ever seen you." Rebecca was trying to be kind, he knew that. Which is why he didn't tell her to shut up or get out of the kitchen or leave him alone.

Rocco couldn't tell her that reality had come creeping in, along with silence from Taylor, bursting his happy bubble, and then there was the fact that it *hadn't* made a single bit of difference. By eleven, Jolly Java was still empty.

He'd known it would take time, but that didn't mean he wasn't still frustrated.

"Oh wait, did he *not* call you?" Rebecca continued.

No. No, he didn't call me. Or text me. Or send out any smoke signals.

Rocco pursed his lips and brushed butter onto his dough.

"But Elaine said you were—"

"Maybe it wasn't as good for him as it was for me," Rocco interrupted. *God,* why had he even said that? He added, in a rush, "And if that's true, then it's fine. I don't mind. I don't have time to date anyway."

Rebecca looked skeptical. "When the right person comes along, you *make* time."

Rocco sprinkled the brown sugar and spice mixture over the buttered dough. "It doesn't matter."

"Come on," Rebecca said. "It's the ornament party tonight. You'll really enjoy that. Griff said we're making little miniature Christmas Falls snow globes. You *need* one, for your first year here."

And that was the other thing that had taken his bad mood and plunged it off the cliff. Last night, in an attempt to cheer himself up, he'd decided to set up the little tree in his apartment.

Once he'd gotten the lights all strung, he'd started to hang all the ornaments—generic boxes of sets of twelve, red glitter balls and shiny gold bells and evergreen trees—but all Rocco had been able to think of was the tree his parents and he always set up in their restaurant foyer, cramming it in between the host station and the glass-fronted wine storage. It was an absolute mishmash of ornaments. Ones with crooked popsicle sticks that Rocco had made in school, ornaments that regulars brought them from their travels, ornaments from Italy and Scotland and Japan. The tree had told a story. It had weight *and* history. Rocco had always looked at it and knew exactly what it meant.

But last night, he'd looked at his new tree and realized the only story it was telling was that he was far away from home and didn't know what the fuck he was even doing anymore.

His black mood had only darkened even further.

Maybe he was becoming as overdramatic as the rest of the Moretti clan.

He'd woken up this morning and wished, more than anything, that he could just stay closed today, closely followed by the realization that being an adult and owning a business meant that he had to get up and tend to his responsibilities, even though the desire to pull his blankets over his head and pretend that none of this was happening was painfully strong.

"Rebecca, I know you mean well, but I'm *really* not in the mood for the ornament party."

"And what?" She raised an eyebrow. "You're gonna just go home, alone, and sit on your couch watching *Real Housewives of Duluth?*"

That sounded only marginally better than sitting on his couch staring at his meaningless tree. Or waiting for a text message that wasn't forthcoming.

What he should really do was meet Taylor and tell him this whole fake dating thing was off. That he'd miscalculated. That he couldn't do this.

But he *wanted* to do this. He wanted another date like the one they'd had. He wanted a lot more than one, if he was being very honest with himself.

"I like *Real Housewives of Duluth*," Rocco said stubbornly.

Rebecca grinned. "If there *was* a *Real Housewives of Duluth*, you probably would. Come on, come with me. Make an ornament. Felix over at Milton Falls farm told me you got a tree, a cute little one. I bet it needs some kind of ornament that doesn't come from the big box store."

It was annoying how perceptive his employee and friend could be. Because she had a point. How was he ever going to be able to replace his horribly generic ornaments with anything more personal if he didn't *try*? "Fine, fine. I'll go."

"Excellent." The doorbell tinkled and Rebecca shot him one last triumphant smile before walking out through the swinging doors to serve their first customer of the day.

Rocco finished rolling up his buns, deftly cut them with a serrated knife, and set them on a tray to do one last quick rise before baking.

By seven, the whole bakery would smell like fresh bread and spices. He'd even risk the heating system by opening the door—it was supposed to be a high of a brisk forty-two to-day—and hopefully wafting some of those delicious scents down the street.

If that wasn't inviting, he didn't know what else to try.

He ducked out from the kitchen and was pleased to see a second person in line, behind the obvious tourist.

"Hey, welcome to Jolly Java," Rocco said to them, "what can I start making for you?"

For the rest of the morning, Rocco baked chai buns, made coffee and hot chocolate, and even once, he got to make a caramel hot cider—but of course, it wasn't for Taylor, though he thought about him and the way he'd looked taking that first sip, as he'd made it.

By noon, his mood had improved—along with the visitors. He saw two old regulars, poured them *both* pumpkin spice lattes, and even convinced them to each take a chai bun to go, on the house.

"You're actually smiling again, and looking like you mean it," Rebecca said, as she cleaned tables and he re-stocked the glass-front case. "Did he text you?"

For a second, Rocco wasn't sure who she meant—then he remembered. But he was proud that he *hadn't* been obsessing about Taylor. That was progress, right?

"Uh, no, but it's fine. He will," Rocco said confidently.

With a trickle of regulars returning to Jolly Java, admittedly because they'd "heard that he'd brought pumpkin spice back *and* that you're dating Taylor Hall, that nice man at Town Hall," Rocco was newly committed to the plan.

Okay, maybe he liked Taylor a little too much, but that was normal right? They were both single, attractive people, and Rocco could admit that it had been awhile for him. He'd been too busy buying this place, remodeling it, and getting it up and running before festival season started. And Taylor's dry spell sounded like an eternity compared to Rocco's own.

Which really . . .that begged the question why that was?

Were they to the point in their "relationship" where Rocco could ask that question?

"That's the attitude," Rebecca said. "He's probably just busy. Obviously this is Griff's busiest time, but the mayor's office isn't exactly slacking either."

"I'd think not," Rocco said.

"You still want to go to the ornament party?" Rebecca asked.

Rocco was a little surprised she'd asked. He'd fully been expecting to get dragged there, whether he wanted to go or not. And he found he did kinda *want* to go. If only to make his tree slightly less depressing.

"Yeah, I do," Rocco said.

She smiled. "Awesome. Meet you there?"

"Yeah, sounds good."

"And after, there's a Grinch cocktail calling my name," Rebecca claimed.

"Is that the special this month? That bright green monstrosity?"

"It's like an apple martini, but *spiced*. With a caramel drizzle. It's freaking delicious," Rebecca argued.

Rocco nearly said, "Taylor likes caramel, I should have him try one," but at the last second, he kept his stupid mouth shut.

It was bad enough that Taylor was beginning to feel like an omnipresent force in his mind. He didn't need Rebecca *oohing* and *ahhhing* over how cute the pair of them were, too.

"I do like how they make an espresso martini," Rocco said.

"How you drink that much caffeine right before bed is baffling. I'd be awake for hours."

"We Morettis practically drink espresso in the crib. We're used to it by now," Rocco pointed out dryly.

Rebecca laughed. "Alright, if you think you can handle it."

"I can *always* handle it," Rocco said confidently. He did feel like he'd gotten a little of his normal swagger back. He *was* good at this. He just needed the town to see it, and they would. With a little time, and Taylor's help, they *would* come around.

"Good," Rebecca said and pulled him into an unexpected quick hug. "I hated seeing you all pissy and diminished. That's not you, Rocco. And he's going to text, he will. If he doesn't, well, that's his loss."

"He's gonna text," Rocco said. It was easy to be confident about this, because Taylor *would* text, eventually. He needed him, just like Rocco needed Taylor.

But by the time Rocco pulled on his scarf and was heading down towards Santa's Workshop, the toy shop where the ornament party was hosted, just down the street from Jolly Java, Taylor had not texted and his confidence had deflated a little.

Rocco was debating pulling his phone out and sending Taylor a text himself, something along the lines of *what the hell, dude*—but he told himself he'd do it after the workshop. Give him a little time to calm down, and maybe sound less outraged that Taylor hadn't contacted him after their (fake) first date.

But when he pulled open the door, immediately spotting Rebecca at one of the long tables dotted with craft supplies, there was a very familiar face next to her.

Taylor freaking Hall, in the flesh. Not too busy to text Rocco, not even close.

The only thing that made Rocco feel better was the shock on Taylor's face when he noticed Rocco approaching.

Taylor had *not* expected to see him tonight.

Rocco shot Rebecca a reproachful glance that told her they'd be talking about this later, because *surely* this was why she'd been so insistent he attend—she'd known Taylor would be here.

"Rocco," she said delightedly. "I'm so glad you came."

"Rebecca," he acknowledged, and then because it felt like the whole room was staring at the pair of them and how they'd greet each other, he turned to Taylor. "Hi, Taylor," he said, keeping his tone as neutral as he could. "Good to see you again."

Taylor cleared his throat, and then the idiot pulled him into a tight hug. Not even giving Rocco a chance to *goat cheese* out of it, even if he'd wanted to.

And that was the real reason his ego was smarting, wasn't it? Because he didn't want to *goat cheese* out of anything, not when it came to Taylor.

Tonight, he was wearing a T-shirt and another pair of jeans that hugged his long legs, cupping an ass that was completely, unfairly perfect.

Rocco was feeling a little punchy, so he let his hands drift lower as Taylor finally released him, giving that ass a little squeeze.

If Taylor looked surprised before, he looked shocked now. Well, Rocco hadn't exactly missed Taylor touching him all over during their wine tasting date, so as far as he was concerned, that squeeze had only been fair play.

"Imagine seeing you here," Rocco said dryly.

Taylor was still staring at him. Like he'd never seen his face before. God, he'd barely looked in the mirror before running out the door. Did he have a smear of pizza sauce on his face, from the frozen pie he'd thrown into the oven and eaten standing up by his miniscule kitchen counter?

"You okay?" Rocco said.

"Just . . ." Taylor cleared his throat. "Uh, glad to see you, honestly."

"Huh. And here I thought you might've forgotten all about me," Rocco muttered under his breath after he turned towards where Marlene was calling for everyone's attention.

"Never," Taylor said in a loud and clear voice that probably nobody missed, even anyone randomly passing by Santa's Workshop on the sidewalk.

Rocco did not roll his eyes. He was a grownup, wasn't he?

A mature adult who did not throw hissy fits like a child, beating their fists against the nearest convenient surface when they didn't get their way.

He watched as Marlene and Griff demonstrated how to fill the clear plastic globe with fake snow, and then miniature trees and buildings, finishing it off with glitter glue on the outside. There were also paint pens scattered on the tables, if they wanted to include a special message.

"Maybe I should paint my number on it," Rocco muttered under his breath.

"Are you okay?" Rebecca asked, looking concerned.

"Oh, just fine," Rocco said, just as Taylor also added, "He's just fine."

There was nothing worse than being told how you felt by a person who could not remotely have any idea.

Rocco decided this fake dating thing was actually *worse* than real dating. It had all the same potholes you could fall into, twisting your ankle or breaking your heart, without any of the associated benefits.

It was bad enough that he'd been thinking for the last two days what Taylor kissing him on his doorstep would've been like. It was terrible, heaped on top of complete shit, that apparently Taylor hadn't been thinking of it *at all*.

"Oh good," Rebecca said. "Hey, I'm gonna go ask Marlene something."

She left, even grabbing her purse, which probably meant she was permanently relocating.

Rocco huffed under his breath. They were going to have to discuss how transparent her efforts were. He picked up an empty plastic globe and began to carefully trickle in the fake snow, twisting and turning the sphere to make sure it was arranged in pleasant-looking piles.

When he glanced up from his work, he realized Taylor had not started his ornament and he was just standing there, staring at Rocco.

"Seriously?" Rocco asked. "Do I have tomato sauce on my face or something?"

"Do you *think* you have tomato sauce on your face?" Taylor countered.

"Yes. No. I don't know." Rocco set his partially filled ornament down. "You keep looking at me like I might."

Taylor shrugged, pretending now and smiling easy, like he hadn't just been staring like he wanted to catalog every nonexistent smear of tomato sauce along Rocco's jaw.

"Well, that's really helpful," Rocco hissed under his breath. It sucked they were doing this *here*, in public, because he couldn't even *act* mad. No, he had to look lovestruck.

Was it worse that he was actually, legitimately torn between berating him and gazing at the guy with heart eyes that didn't feel all that fake?

"Listen, I've never done this before," Taylor said. "And I'm shitty at dating, anyway, but fake dating? That's a whole other thing." He made a face. "I should've texted you, I know. I . . .well, if I'm being honest, I wanted to a little more than I felt comfortable with and that was weird."

Rocco felt that hard, anxious place inside him unwind a little. Like all it had needed to untangle was the right thread pulled, and Taylor's words had done just that.

"Oh." He cleared his throat. "Yeah, it is a little weird. Probably that I wanted you to, a little too much."

"Should we—"

Rocco imagined that Taylor was going to suggest they quit this whole stupid charade, and maybe he was right, because it *was* weird, but he didn't think Taylor would then suggest they date for real. The alternative was that they'd go back to being merely friendly acquaintances, and that was terrible. So Rocco interrupted him. "No," he said firmly. "I had a regular come back today. *And* it's a regular who I'm pretty sure is on the city council."

"Oh yeah?" Taylor didn't look disappointed by Rocco's interruption. In fact, he looked relieved. Like he hadn't even *wanted* to suggest it, either.

That soothed the rest of Rocco's ruffled feathers.

"Yeah," Rocco said with an emphatic nod. "I poured him the best goddamn pumpkin spice latte I've ever made. Maybe I even told him your inherent Christmas spirit inspired me."

"Thanks," Taylor said with genuine gratitude.

"I should..." Rocco didn't want to come clean, but he *should* tell the truth. Taylor deserved the truth. "I should be honest about something."

Taylor raised an eyebrow.

"My cousin?" Rocco continued. "The one who had the fake relationship and uh . . .I told you that it really helped? Well, it *really* helped. Better than either of them ever expected. They fell in love. They got together for real. They're *still* together, for real."

Taylor stared at him, and Rocco suddenly wished the floor would eat him up. Why had he brought this up? And *here*, of all places?

"You said it worked great," Taylor said slowly.

"Well, it *did*," Rocco said. And then added hurriedly, "It sure got his mom off their backs. And if you ever meet Giana Moretti, you know that's not an easy task. The rest of it was just . . .uh . . .coincidence. That doesn't mean it's going to happen with us."

"You seem sure about that." Taylor didn't sound so sure himself—or that he liked it. That took Rocco's ego down a peg. Maybe deservedly.

"You said you're not looking for a relationship. Neither am I. That hasn't changed. Sure, we had a great time the other night. But that doesn't really change that."

Taylor looked like he was five seconds away from *goat cheese*-ing out of this whole thing—the conversation, the Christmas ornament party, and maybe even their fake relationship—so Rocco forged ahead.

"Honestly, yes, maybe there's a little attraction. On both our sides. But if we just acknowledge it, then that doesn't mean it has to control *us*. We control *it*."

Taylor looked dubious at this claim, and frankly even Rocco wasn't that convinced. But the alternative was worse.

"I'm not sure that's how it works," he finally said.

"Sure it is," Rocco said breezily. "We just need to promise to be honest. And in worst-case scenarios, there's always *goat cheese*."

Taylor laughed then, long and loud, like it had been completely startled out of him.

"Right. Of course. That's true. I didn't think about that." He paused. "Well . . .uh . . .maybe we should take advantage of the fact we're both here and I'm pretty sure at least half the room is staring at us." Taylor's voice had dropped even more, and to make sure Rocco had heard him, he'd stepped closer, and now he was practically murmuring into his ear.

Rocco swayed closer, felt his side brush up against Taylor's.

It was funny, how everything—the doubts, the anxieties, the worries—seemed to quiet when he was with Taylor.

"I'm good with that," Rocco said. "I can be spontaneous."

"Not me, but I can try," Taylor said wryly.

"Hey, you're doing pretty good so far," Rocco said, even though he really wasn't. He handed Taylor an empty snow globe. "Let's make some ornaments."

"What am I supposed to do?" Taylor sent him a beseeching look. "I was too busy panicking that I fucked everything up, I didn't really listen to Griff."

"Panicking that you fucked everything up *and* staring at me like I had pizza smeared across my face," Rocco corrected.

Taylor laughed. "Yeah, yeah, uh, that's it."

"You're gonna fill your globe with snow," Rocco instructed, shaking his own. "Then we're going to make it look all cool."

"That I can do. Or at least I can try."

Rocco reached out and squeezed his forearm. Ignored how good it felt under his fingers. "You got this," he promised.

They spent the next hour finishing their ornaments, Rocco carefully writing the year and *Christmas Falls* on his, so he'd never forget his first ornament since moving to town.

"I can't wait to hang this on my tree. It's full of all these incredibly generic ornaments," Rocco said as he shook his snow globe and watched as the white flakes showered down over his buildings.

He'd attempted to construct a replica of Blitzen Street, with Jolly Java at the center.

"I love yours," Taylor said earnestly. "That's Jolly Java, in the middle, isn't it?"

Rocco nodded. "At my parents' restaurant, they had this old tree they put up every year, and it was full of ornaments they'd bought on trips, that I'd made in school, even ornaments our regulars brought us. It was full of memories. Looking at mine last night . . .it was just depressing."

"At least you have a tree up. I keep meaning to get out to the farm—Bruce set a tree aside for me, as a favor—but I've been so busy at work. It feels like there's always a hundred fires to put out during festival season."

Rocco felt guilty, instantly. Here he'd been all upset that it had been *days* since their first "date" and Taylor hadn't texted him or called, but of course he had big, important things he needed to take care of for his job.

Rocco might frame *his* job as important—after all, keeping people caffeinated was vital to the happiness of the town—but Taylor's job helped keep the town actually *running*.

"Oh yeah." Rocco felt so awkward. "Maybe tomorrow?"

"Yeah, I hope so. Have you heard about this Secret Santa?"

Rocco shook his head. "There's a real-life Secret Santa in town? Who is it?"

"Nobody knows. That's the problem. They're doing a hell of a lot of good, already, but I've gotten probably a dozen phone calls about it and even more emails. Everyone wants to know if it's something the town's doing and I have to keep telling them no."

"Let me guess, they don't believe you."

"*No*. Not after the graffiti last year. They just think we're pretending we're not involved, but honestly, we're just as much in the dark as everyone else."

"Well, if they're doing good . . ." Rocco trailed off.

"They sure are, but *ugh*, it's added some to *my* plate, that's for sure."

"What does the mayor think?"

"Oh, she loves it. Not surprisingly." Taylor chuckled. "Between that and fitting in more of these events because Mona thought it would be helpful, it's been crazy. But it *has* helped. I've definitely had an opportunity to talk to a few city council members."

"That's great, Taylor," Rocco said, meaning it. "Did you finally meet your competitor?"

"Ugh, *no*. I keep missing him. Maybe that's for the best." Taylor made a face. "Maybe I'd say something I couldn't take back. Something that isn't very advisable. But I keep hearing stuff about Steve Mills. How he fronts about how much he cares about Christmas Falls, but then turns around and does some shit that proves he couldn't possibly."

"That sucks." Rocco put a hand on Taylor's back and told himself he didn't enjoy how it felt—the way he tensed and then relaxed under his touch—and then let his fingers linger. Just because, damnit, he wanted to. "But we're going to make sure you get this job."

Taylor flushed, ducking his head a little. "You're kind of the best," he admitted in a low voice.

So low that nobody else probably heard him.

And Rocco realized, as he was walking home ten minutes later, that his comment hadn't been for the public; it had been just for Rocco alone.

Chapter 6

Taylor wasn't going to make the mistake again.

The next morning, he sent Rocco a text. **Some of us single folks are getting together for Thanksgiving at Rudolph's. Potluck dinner. They're providing the turkey and mashed potatoes and gravy. If you're at a loose end, you're free to come with me. Like a date. Or not, if you don't want to call it that.**

Rocco had texted back almost immediately.

That would be great. I was not looking forward to crashing Rebecca's mom's dinner.

If you have plans already . . . Taylor hoped that he'd say that *no*, he really hadn't wanted to go to Rebecca's mom's dinner.

No. Please. You're saving me. Really. Her mom doesn't get that I'm really not interested in her younger sister.

Ouch. Taylor chuckled out loud, in spite of himself, leaning back in his chair and ignoring the part of his brain that kept screaming that this was exactly why he'd not texted Rocco after their date.

Because he'd enjoyed him way too much, and he couldn't *goat cheese* out of this now.

But that didn't change that it had been a little shitty to *not* call or text. He should've, just to make sure they were still on, and to confirm when their next date was.

LOL. Well, maybe she'll believe you now. I'll swing by Jolly Java and pick you up around 1ish. Taylor didn't say it wasn't a date, or that it was. Frankly at this point, they could get there together and leave together, and the whole town would naturally assume this was just another date.

Sounds good. It's a potluck?

Yep. Any side dish.

What are you bringing? Rocco wanted to know.

That's a really good question. Not sure yet. Maybe a salad. I can do a salad. Taylor was never going to be a great cook. Or even a passable bone. But at least he could buy lettuce at the store and chop vegetables.

Hey, if we're coming together, we could always bring just one dish—I'm going to make a big lasagna, and that

should be good enough. Or you could always throw some bagged salad in a bowl?

How about both? And how about I help you?

Taylor didn't know why he'd suggested it—okay, *lie*, he knew exactly why he'd suggested it. Because when Rocco had walked in last night, he'd realized just how miserable he'd been making himself by *not* talking to him.

Rocco could be a friend. He could keep him in the friend zone . . . right?

And friends could make lasagna together.

You'd want to do that?

Of course. You're not a burden to hang out with. The opposite, actually.

Maybe that was being a little too truthful, but after how upset Rocco had looked the other day, he wasn't going to hide the way he felt.

Okay, he *mostly* wasn't going to hide how he felt.

And if he could fit those feelings into a friendly, platonic-shaped box, that would be even better.

Ditto. Come over about eleven, then.

See you then.

Taylor tossed his phone onto his desk as the mayor walked in.

"Hey," Mona said. "You're smiling pretty big these days."

He had not told her the truth about his burgeoning relationship with Rocco—though he'd assumed she'd guessed it wasn't one hundred percent legit—but then if she did believe that, why would she be looking so thrilled now?

It's because you're being way too fucking convincing.

"Yeah," Taylor said.

She shot him a conspiratorial look. "When I was throwing you at Heath Kelly, you could have just said you had your eye on Rocco Moretti."

"At that point, I didn't know if he'd *want* me to have an eye on him," Taylor said.

"Oh come on, you're a catch. You might pretend you're not, but you are. It's good to see some of your reserve melting. You've been locked up tight since you came to town."

Had he? Taylor supposed that was true. Right before he'd taken the job in Christmas Falls—a job he'd wanted, desperately, but almost hadn't gotten after all—he'd broken up with Michael.

Or rather Michael had broken up with him.

Between his mom and Michael, maybe he *had* been a little self-contained. But that was four years ago, now. A guy could change, right?

Surely, he *had* changed.

Mona smiled at him. "Also," she added, "I can't stay, but I want to say, Roger Knight stopped by yesterday, and said he appreciated how much of an effort you're making to be part of this year's festival. I reminded him that you're *always* part of it, but usually more behind the scenes, shying away from public recognition and he sounded surprised."

"You know I'm not always comfortable trumpeting my projects to the skies," Taylor said.

"I know, but you've got to tell people or else they don't know what you've been doing. And it's a lot of good stuff, Taylor. Better than anything Steve Mills has been up to."

"He's done jack shit except gladhand and run his candidacy like a freaking election," Taylor muttered.

"Exactly," Mona said, with an approving nod. "He'll expose himself."

"Hopefully not literally," Taylor said, deadpan.

Mona cackled. "God, I really, really hope not. That's a mess we don't need. We've already got this Secret Santa. I can't walk down the street or stop by the grocery or the hardware store without getting a ton of questions about it. You get anywhere on revealing the person behind this?"

"No, and I don't think we should dig into it anymore," Taylor said. "It's great stuff, for the people of this town and *for* this town. Let it lie."

"Alright." Mona sighed. "I trust your take on this. You're good at this."

"So are you, Madam Mayor," Taylor said with a grin.

"If you're free for Thanksgiving, you know you're always welcome at my house," Mona said.

Taylor knew if he even remotely revealed he'd have been alone, he'd have a half dozen invitations to dinner. But he'd been instrumental in putting together this Thanksgiving event for singles two years ago, and he wasn't about to miss it, even for Mona's famous stuffing.

"You know I always go to Mik's single mingle Thanksgiving," Taylor said.

"You mean *your* single mingle Thanksgiving," Mona reminded him gently. "Mik might host it, but it was your idea, and it's your execution. You bringing Rocco?"

"Yeah," Taylor said. Suddenly awkward at the idea of talking about him with his boss. Not because he was ashamed of the guy, but because he was ashamed of what it *really* was.

"Good." Mona stood. "I'm going to go with your gut on this Secret Santa thing. Not that we couldn't have dug into it more, but that we're going to choose not to."

Taylor nodded. "Have a good Thanksgiving."

"You too, Taylor." Her wink right before she ducked out of his office told him everything he needed to know about what her assumptions were.

The same as the rest of the town's.

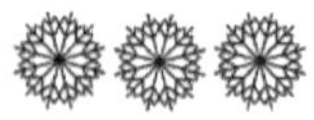

There was snow on the ground—the first significant snowfall of the year—when Taylor knocked on the Jolly Java door. Worried that maybe Rocco wouldn't hear him, in the back kitchen, he pulled out his phone and sent a text, too.

But before it even sent, Rocco was there, opening the door, shivering, even though he wore a beautiful burnt amber sweater and jeans, looking totally cozy and also like he'd just stepped off a runway in Paris.

"Hey," Rocco said, "just on time."

"That's me. Prompt." *God, I am so bad at this still.*

But Rocco laughed, like he was actually charming. "Come on, let's go to the back. I'd ask if you want a coffee, but you're a heathen who doesn't drink it."

"Someday maybe you'll have to attempt a conversion," Taylor suggested, even though he couldn't imagine changing his mind. But his suggestion made Rocco smile brighter, and that was all he cared about.

Rocco pushed open the swinging door to the kitchen and Taylor followed behind him. He stopped, taking in the rigidly organized system Rocco had spread across the long stainless steel counter.

"Lasagna isn't just a dish, it's a way of life," Rocco teased, gesturing towards the different stations. "You can make it without a plan, but then it's just chaos."

"What can I do to help?" He set down his bag of lettuce and already-chopped veggies onto the smaller counter next to the bank of very professional ovens he was fairly sure hadn't been here before Rocco had purchased Jolly Java.

"I'm just doing assembly, then we bake it," Rocco said. "You can keep me company."

"I meant to *help*," Taylor said, feeling bad that Rocco had made all these different parts. And there were a lot of parts. There was a white sauce, speckled with something green and herbaceous; mountains of shredded cheese, *not* from a bag; and three sheet pans full of what looked like roasted vegetables. Right next to where Rocco situated himself was a stack of pasta sheets, not the box kind that Taylor would normally assume anyone would use, and an enormous tinfoil pan.

"You're definitely gonna help," Rocco promised.

He watched as Rocco pulled on a pair of gloves and picked up the pasta sheets, carefully layering them into the pan.

"What kind of lasagna is this? It's not the normal kind, that's for sure," Taylor said.

Rocco shot him a teasing look full of heat. "Don't worry, I'm not going to terrify anyone with goat cheese again. It's just a roasted vegetable lasagna, and for those who missed their pumpkin spice, I threw some butternut squash in."

"Ah, well, it looks and smells amazing," Taylor said.

Rocco shrugged. "You haven't even started smelling it yet."

He moved onto the big batch of white sauce, ladling it onto the pasta sheets with an expert motion, like he'd done this hundreds of times before.

"You said your parents own a restaurant?"

"Yeah," Rocco said. "It's a great place, tucked away down a side street in San Francisco. I miss it, sometimes—we were always open for Thanksgiving, and we'd serve a version of this—but I'm glad I went out on my own. I didn't want to only work on the line for the next twenty years. That's not my idea of fun."

"So you've done this before."

Rocco laughed. "Hundreds of times. You're not a good Italian boy if you can't make a killer lasagna."

"Well, I can't wait to taste it. I definitely don't make a killer lasagna, but I can eat one."

"No?"

Taylor winced. "Uh, I buy the frozen ones, at the store?"

Rocco laughed. "No coffee and Stouffer's lasagna. You're trying to kill me, aren't you?"

He'd sprinkled the first layer of vegetables and cheese and was now repeating the motion with the pasta sheets.

Maybe, Taylor reasoned, it was better for him *not* to help, not when Rocco was so completely capable.

"Really, I'm not," Taylor said, chuckling. "But anytime you want to come over and bake me a lasagna, a *real* lasagna, I'm not gonna complain. I'll even pay you in wine." He didn't know good wine himself, but he remembered, because he couldn't forget, what Rocco had liked during the wine tasting.

"Sounds like a good deal to me. Good food. Good wine. Good company."

"You're sure I can't help?"

"I've got this. You're doing the important part, anyway."

"I am?" Taylor couldn't believe it.

"Keeping me focused, but not *too* focused."

Taylor opened his mouth to say it was just a lasagna, but he had a feeling that wasn't what it was to Rocco.

"This matters to you, doesn't it?" he asked.

Rocco glanced over at him, his hands still moving with those expert, quick movements. "Yes," he said. "I think of the couples who've celebrated twenty anniversaries at my parents' restaurant. Who, every single year, eat the same mushroom ravioli and it brings them back to the night they fell in love. The grandfathers who bring their families in, passing their love of food to future generations. How my cousin Luca and his husband Oliver put food on the menu of their restaurant that reminds them of all their best times. Food is a love language, you know?"

And the town had rejected Rocco's attempts to show them that.

"That's beautiful," Taylor said, because it was. More than ever, he wanted to make this right, not just for him, because it would be a terrible thing to destroy the hope in Rocco's eyes, the dream he held of continuing his family's tradition.

Rocco shrugged, but he could tell how much the rejection had hurt him.

"And," Taylor added, because he'd never known when to quit, "this town is perfect for that. I know they haven't all put their best feet forward, but they will, and you'll see. There's nothing more important to this town than tradition and nostalgia."

"That's why I bought this place," Rocco said. "And I hope you're right."

He sprinkled on the last layer of cheese.

"I am," Taylor insisted. He didn't know when Rocco's fight had become his, too, but it had.

"Now to get this in the oven," Rocco said.

Rocco was not particularly big or bulky with muscle, so Taylor watched with more than a little surprise as he hefted the huge, heavy pan effortlessly and slid it into the oven.

And he couldn't deny that Rocco's hidden strength, both inner *and* outer, was more of a turn-on than he'd anticipated.

Rocco closed the oven door with a firm thump and turned to Taylor. "Now I know you don't drink coffee, but I could use a latte. You can't approach a holiday without plenty of caffeine in your system."

Taylor's brain must still be short-circuiting over how much he wanted to feel those unexpected muscles Rocco was hiding under his sweater, because he said, "Why don't you make something I'd like."

A wide smile broke over Rocco's face, filled with so much delight, Taylor would agree to try coffee a dozen or so times, just to witness that look on his face again.

"You mean it?"

A better man probably would have *goat-cheesed* out of this, once he saw what it meant to Rocco, but Taylor nodded.

"I got you," Rocco said, rubbing his hands in excitement. Taylor followed him out of the back kitchen and behind the counter, watching as Rocco flipped switches and turned the enormous espresso machine on.

"You like sweet," Rocco stated, rather than asked.

"Yeah," Taylor said, blushing a little. Maybe he should've grown out of his sweet tooth, but he never had.

"Oh, I've got sweet for you, baby," Rocco said, shooting him a teasing look. He worked the machine like he'd done it a thousand times before, pulling levers and grabbing chilled ingredients from the fridge under the counter by feel alone.

Finally, he set a tall glass in front of Taylor, the top covered in a towering mountain of whipped cream, dusted with tiny flecks of spice.

Taylor picked it up, sniffing at it as Rocco made himself a coffee next. "It *smells* good," he said.

Carefully, he sipped, whipped cream smearing across his upper lip. To his surprise, the harsh acidity of the coffee he'd tried before didn't hit him this time. This was full and rich and mellow, somehow all at the same time. And sweet too, but with a bit of almond cookie taste, the cookies his mom had always baked for Christmas.

The ones he'd missed, like a gnawing toothache.

Rocco was watching him carefully, while trying to pretend he wasn't, as he worked the machine for his own coffee.

"So?" he asked. "Is it terrible? You can spit, you know. You don't have to swallow if you hate it."

"Maybe I should," Taylor joked. "God, it's absolutely fucking terrible, Rocco."

Disappointment flashed across Rocco's face. "It's okay," he mumbled. "And I'm sorry, I was *so* sure . . ."

"I'm *kidding*. It's really, really good." Taylor immediately regretted the joke. He hadn't anticipated how much Rocco would want him to like it, or how much he'd detest that look in his eyes.

"Really?"

It was banished in seconds, replaced by joy.

"It's different, somehow. Sweeter, yeah, but not fake sweetness, like . . .I don't know, a cookie my mom used to make. Her famous almond cookies. And it's not bitter or acidic. Just rich and full and yet super mellow."

"Well, *yeah,* I spring for the good beans," Rocco said. Then elbowed him suddenly in the ribs, laughing, and then Taylor was laughing too, because you couldn't hear Rocco make that sound of pure delight and not be seduced into joining in. "God, you're the *worst*. You had me going there."

"Yeah, I sure did."

Rocco smacked him again but this time his hand didn't move but lingered. Warm and firm against Taylor's chest. He swayed closer and *God,* Taylor would barely have to move to kiss him.

He'd just need to tip his head down and get lost in the magical pull of those passionate, dark eyes . . .

He jerked back. Holding the coffee between them like a personal shield.

It would be so easy to let himself have this. Rocco was a thousand times more attractive, inside and out, than Michael, and look how easily Taylor had let Michael lead him.

He couldn't let that happen again.

Especially not now, when what he'd worked so hard for was finally about to unfold—but only if he played his cards right.

"Uh, sorry," Rocco said. He gestured towards the kitchen. "You want a bowl to throw your bagged lettuce into?"

"Yeah, that would be great." Taylor took another drink of the coffee. It was *so* good, but really, he wasn't sure if it was the man or the actual beverage anymore.

Maybe Rocco could have poured him that wretched instant coffee crap and he'd have liked *that* too.

"That's the latte nobody wanted," Rocco said casually as he pulled a big metal bowl off one of the shelves stacked with gleaming equipment.

"What? Really?"

"Yep. I kept it on the menu, but God forbid, it's not pumpkin spice."

"I've never had pumpkin spice, but I can't imagine it being better than this. Anyone who doesn't want this is crazy."

Rocco shot him another one of those brilliant smiles. "Thank you for saying that."

"It's just the truth."

"Let's make your salad," Rocco said and Taylor knew he was changing the subject. Wondered if it was his version of *goat cheese*.

If it was, he was going to respect it. "Sure," he said, grabbing salad ingredients, pulling various things out of the bag.

"Oh, look at you with a fall culinary theme," Rocco teased.

"This is stuff the lady at the store said would be good," Taylor said, dumping it all into the bowl. Lettuce. Cucumber chunks. Pumpkin seeds. Dried cranberries. She'd also suggested adding goat cheese crumbles, and Taylor had barely managed to keep a straight face as he'd told her he'd better leave those out.

"It looks great," Rocco said.

"Yeah, it does," Taylor said, pleased with himself as he tossed it with the dressing. He hadn't wanted to slack, even if this was technically just a salad from a bag, not when Rocco was making something delicious from scratch.

"So, tell me who's coming to this thing," Rocco said, leaning against the counter, sipping his coffee.

"You know Mik, right?" Rocco nodded. "He hosts. And there's a few other singles who like to stop by. Griff used to, but now that he has Logan, he might not. I invited Mason, from the foundation, 'cause I know he's on his own. And Scott, who sells the baby blankets at the arts and crafts fair. Hank, I think his name is, told me he might stop by too."

"Oh, cool. Sounds like it's a good event."

"I've been happy I started it a few years ago."

"Wait, *you* did?" Rocco looked surprised. "Why didn't you tell me?" An alarm went off and he added, "I gotta check the lasagna, but seriously, you didn't mention *you* started it."

"I . . ." Taylor smiled. "I don't know why I didn't. Guess I'm used to being behind the scenes. It's what I'm good at."

"Trust me, you're good at lots of things," Rocco said.

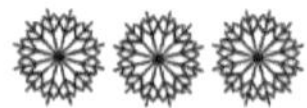

"Now this is so much better than Rebecca's mom's dinner," Rocco said, as he perched on one of the tall stools in Rudolph's, a plate of turkey and stuffing and about a hundred amazing looking sides on the table in front of him.

"Yeah?" Taylor looked happy, too. He'd greeted half a dozen people, including Scott, who made the baby blankets he was selling at the arts and crafts fair, Mik, and now Mason, and so many of them had said, offhandedly or pointedly, how great this get-together was for them.

"Yeah. These people would be alone or shoved unceremoniously onto an invite list, if they weren't here. That's special, Taylor."

Taylor was special, himself, and Rocco was just beginning to understand how much.

"Thanks," Taylor said, ducking his head, in between bites of turkey and mashed potatoes. "Your lasagna is amazing, and it's a big hit."

The foil dish he'd made was already half gone.

He'd been worried because it *wasn't* traditional, but more than one person had come up to him and mentioned how much they'd enjoyed it. Maybe the town wasn't willing to eat a turmeric and goat cheese scone, but if he wrapped up his different flavors in a more traditional wrapping . . .well, they might be willing to give it a chance.

Mason, who Taylor had said was new in town, too, and ran the Holiday Hope Foundation, stuck a fork into his mashed potatoes. "I'm so glad I came. Thanks again for inviting me. I felt . . .well, it's weird to spend the holiday away from my family, it turns out. Even when they make me a little crazy."

Rocco nodded. "Trust me, I know all about that. Mine is nuts, the quintessential Italian family that's too big, too nosy, too involved, but when they're not around . . .sometimes it's too quiet."

"Yep. Mine's not big, but it's still been weird to be away from them," Mason said. He turned to Taylor. "What about you? What brings *you* to the single mingle?"

"Uh . . .well . . .my dad's in Chicago. Doesn't get out here much. So it just made sense," Taylor said.

Mason nodded and they all fell to eating in earnest.

Rocco had noticed that twice now when family had come up, Taylor had been vague and/or changed the subject. There was a story there, and even if Taylor wasn't required to tell him, he still wanted to hear it.

Maybe in the next few weeks, he could convince Taylor to share more of his own history. After all, he'd gotten him to drink an entire marzipan latte, and *that* certainly hadn't been easy. But he'd been right; it was exactly what Taylor had needed to try coffee and even more, *enjoy* coffee.

It would be so easy to convince him to enjoy you, that uncooperative voice in the back of his head insisted. *You could do it. He'd like it. You'd like it.*

But now it wouldn't be uncomplicated pleasure. It would be more than that. Even when both of them had said they didn't want to date anyone. Rocco still believed that was true on his end. His plate *was* full, but would he have shifted some things around to make the time? Time for *real* dates? Sure, he might've, if the guy he'd be dating was Taylor.

But Taylor seemed more sure of not wanting it, even as he seemed undeniably interested. Maybe the reason for that was more of that history he didn't want to talk about.

"Mona approached me about writing a statement for your job application," Mason told Taylor when they'd finished cleaning their plates. "When she told me why you'd need it, I said, of course, no question about it." He paused. "But I did wonder why you didn't ask me yourself."

Taylor flushed. Rocco watched as the redness climbed up his neck and onto his cheeks. "Uh . . .'cause I'm really bad at asking for stuff like that?"

He was, Rocco was beginning to see that. Taylor was always working behind the scenes, making everyone's life in Christmas Falls better, but he never wanted to take public credit for it.

But he *should*. Everyone should know how hard Taylor worked.

"Well, I'm happy to do it," Mason said earnestly. "I'm glad she asked me."

"I didn't even know she had, but it makes sense," Taylor admitted.

"She's really trying to get you this job," Rocco said.

"Yeah," Taylor said.

Rocco could see the emotion flash across Taylor's face, and he glanced away, like he was afraid he'd be overcome by it.

"You've worked for her long?"

"Four years," Taylor said. "One as her assistant, three as deputy mayor. I almost . . .I almost missed out on the opportunity, to begin with, even though I'd really, really, wanted to move here, and work here. But I almost screwed it up, and she *still* moved heaven and earth to get me here."

"She's a good mayor. And you're a great deputy," Mason said, sounding like he meant every word. Maybe neither of them had been here long, but Rocco had seen the same thing, the first time he'd come here, to take a look at the coffee shop and sign the papers.

He'd known the moment he'd met Mona Grayson that she was the kind of mayor he wanted in the town where he built his new business.

Of course, then he'd met Taylor, and he'd felt the effects of *that* meeting long after Taylor had walked back out of his life.

"Thanks," Taylor said, shooting Rocco a grateful smile.

"Sounds like she's a great mentor, too," Mason said.

"The best," Taylor agreed.

As they finished up, grabbing a few slices of pie to go, Rocco realized that was another mystery to add to the ones he already knew existed in Taylor. What he'd done to potentially fuck up his position here, the first time around.

Rocco wanted to ask, and *almost* did, as Taylor walked him back to the coffee shop, but it was beautiful in downtown, the last leaves falling, mixing with the snowflakes dancing on the wind, the two of them walking in a silence that he'd never assumed would be so reassuring, but *was*, so he didn't.

Of course the moment after Taylor helped him get the food in his fridge and then said goodbye, gaze lingering on Rocco right before he turned to go, Rocco wished he'd done it.

As he walked up to his upstairs apartment, he pulled out his phone.

Thanks again for inviting me, he texted to Taylor. **I had such a great time.**

You're welcome. It was the best one yet.

Rocco wondered if it was because *he'd* been there, with Taylor, but he didn't ask that because how was Taylor supposed to answer? There was *no* right answer there.

But he hoped, anyway. Then a second text from Taylor came in. **You going to the parade on Friday?**

I wasn't planning on it, Rocco texted back, **but I have a feeling I'll be going now.**

I have great seats, and a plus one. Can't think of anyone else I'd rather invite than my fake boyfriend.

Rocco stared at his phone before tossing it onto his bed.

He wished Taylor hadn't added that *fake* to the boyfriend and wished that he hadn't wished that at all.

Because this was already complicated enough.

CHAPTER 7

"WHEN YOU SAID YOU had great seats, you weren't kidding."

Taylor glanced up and Rocco was standing there, a big grin on his face.

He was wearing that gorgeous peacoat again, with another luxurious-looking scarf—this time in green.

A knit cap of the same color was pulled down low over his head and his nose was already red from the cold.

Taylor felt his heart squeeze and then told himself to forget that feeling.

He didn't need this. Rocco was going to be a friend, while also being a convenient means to an end.

An end they both wanted and needed.

"Yeah, it's one of the perks of being the deputy mayor," Taylor said. He gestured to the seat next to him.

The VIP grandstand was not large—and you couldn't buy tickets, you could only be invited to sit up here, with its great view of the light parade, mid-route—but Taylor was one of the lucky few afforded tickets.

Technically he *didn't* get a plus one, but he'd finagled an extra ticket out of Griff, who'd softened considerably since his grumpy days. "But only if it's for Rocco," Griff had said, making his own position on Taylor's new relationship clear.

Frankly, he wasn't alone. *Everyone* was thrilled they were together now.

Taylor had never had so many people come up to him on the street or at the grocery store or at all the festival events he'd been attending. It was annoying and also gratifying. It turned out that Mona might have been right: the thing that had been keeping him on the outskirts of the town's acceptance had been his singleness.

"I'm going to get spoiled," Rocco joked, leaning in and nudging Taylor with his shoulder. "And I'm gonna have to be honest with you. I *like* it. I like it here."

"Yeah?" Taylor hadn't even realized that he'd been worried Rocco ultimately wouldn't until he'd laid that fear to rest.

"Do I love that the town got pissed at me? Not really, but I'm dealing. And it's getting better, slowly but surely," Rocco said. "Emerson Maxwell—you know, the writer who's with

Arlo?—stopped by three times this week. He's writing a book at *my* coffee shop. You know how exciting that is?"

Taylor didn't, but he was happy that *Rocco* was happy. "That's pretty cool," he said.

"And there's been a few new regulars too. Guys new to town, like Nova, the new wedding planner? And a few others. I want people to feel like my place is part theirs, you know? That they're welcome to come and hang out, meet up, and feel accepted."

"Like at your parents' restaurant, or your cousin Luca's bakery?"

"Yeah, kinda. Two of my other cousins run food trucks in LA, and one of them is permanently parked at this lot with a bunch of other food trucks—but it's so much more than just a place to grab something to eat. It's a community gathering place, with music and parties and these big long tables everyone shares. That's what I want too, someday."

"You're going to get there," Taylor promised. "If anyone is capable of doing it, it's you."

Rocco's dark eyes glowed. "You really think so?"

"There's nothing that this town loves more than an inclusive vibe," Taylor observed.

"Is that why this job is so important to you?" Rocco's question was casual, but Taylor could feel its buried pointedness. He'd been trying to be vague, making only offhand comments about his history, but of course Rocco wouldn't be placated or fooled by those. He'd want to know more.

"Yeah," Taylor said. He knew he *should* say more, but he didn't know where to start, or if he *could* start without unloading all his baggage. And surely Rocco didn't want all of that. Taylor barely wanted to hold it all.

Rocco stared at him expectantly.

But then a cheer went up from the crowd, and in the distance, after Heath in his decorated car, at the position of honor as the grand marshal, Taylor could see the first float coming—traditionally, and there was *nothing* Christmas Falls loved more than tradition, it was always Santa—and this year was no exception. Santa's sleigh and his reindeer appeared to float along the road, the edges picked out in strand after strand of lights, the rest of the vehicles dark to add to the illusion.

Taylor had seen a version of this parade probably two dozen times by this point, but the truth was it never got old. The thrill of the lights coming out of the darkness, each float elaborately lit and decorated, shining in the night, was something else.

He glanced over at Rocco and saw the beauty of it reflected in his eyes.

"This is . . .*wow*," Rocco breathed out.

"Yeah," Taylor agreed. "Just wait til you see the rest of it. But I agree, Cal's a highlight."

"Cal?"

"Santa, obviously," Taylor said, with a cute little shoulder nudge.

"He's a great Santa," Rocco agreed.

"We're lucky to have him. He's been doing this a long time."

Following Santa was the band and the color guard, their uniforms covered in brightly colored lights, the flags of the guard rippling with light and color as they spun them. The band played "Santa Claus is Coming to Town," heavy on the horns and the drums, the sound echoing through the whole town, and Taylor's heart throbbed with the beautiful nostalgia of it all.

He'd do anything to protect it. *Anything.*

Steve Mills might come in and want to make it more commercial. He'd cloak it in *bigger* and *better* but in the end, all it would mean was change.

Not all change was bad or destructive, but Taylor knew that *this* didn't need altered, not in any way.

"This is incredible," Rocco said, his voice full of wonder, the same feeling Taylor experienced every time he watched this.

"Yeah," Taylor agreed.

Rocco turned towards him and shot him a determined look. "This is what you want, *this* feeling, this is why you want that job."

"Partially, yeah," Taylor said. It was more complicated than that, but essentially, Rocco had nailed it.

"It's special. Special enough to need protecting. Special enough that I get why you're so determined," Rocco said.

It helped that Rocco understood it; but then, why wouldn't he? He was trying to build something *like* this. Without the fancy lights and the brass section, but the same kind of feeling.

That warm, cozy, protective, *protected* feeling.

If a town could wrap you up in a soft blanket, it would be Christmas Falls.

Rocco wanted the same feeling when you walked into Jolly Java as when you strolled through downtown Christmas Falls.

"I'm glad you see it," Taylor said, meaning it.

Not even flinching when Rocco reached over and took one of Taylor's gloved hands in his own, squeezing it. Maybe it was for the crowd around them but maybe it was also *just* for them.

If Taylor was better at lying to himself, he'd have claimed their dovetailing motives were why he'd agreed to this crazy fake dating plan in the first place. But the truth was more complicated. Yes, Rocco was ultimately good for the town, the same as Taylor was trying to be, but he was attracted, too. And not just to Rocco's undeniably gorgeous exterior, but to the whole goddamned package. His sly humor, his kindness, his creativity, his clear intelligence.

It had been a long time since Taylor had felt this kinship with someone. If he *ever* had. Michael had never understood Taylor's obsession with Christmas Falls. The one winter he'd brought him, he'd liked it, sure, but he hadn't felt the same.

It hadn't grabbed him by the heart and wouldn't let go.

At the time, Taylor had told himself it was because Michael didn't have the same history with the town he did. But it was more than that too.

Because Rocco didn't either, but *he* got it.

"You get it," Taylor said in a low voice, ducking his head so only Rocco could hear him over the echoes of the band.

"Yeah," Rocco said, eyes shining as they met Taylor's.

There was a part of him that was screaming *goat cheese, goat cheese, goat cheese,* but he pushed it away.

He didn't need that. Not tonight.

Tonight was perfect.

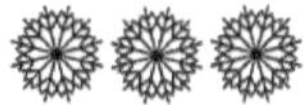

At least tonight was perfect, until after the last lights of the parade had disappeared, Rocco had sighed happily, said he wanted hot cider and didn't Taylor want some, too?

Taylor hadn't wanted to let the guy out of his sight—arguing with himself that if this was real, he certainly wouldn't, anyway—and so he'd walked with Rocco back to Jolly Java.

The inside was wreathed in holly, the windows edged in faux ice and snow, the doorbell tinkling above as Rocco unlocked the door and let him in.

It was still perfect, Taylor decided, lulled into complacency as Rocco heated up cider and poured it into two heavy white mugs.

"Here," he said, handing Taylor one of them and then leaning against the counter. "So are you going to tell me what else is going on?"

His question was still casual, but there was that steel edge in his eyes. A look that might not be demanding answers but asking very nicely to provide them.

"I . . .I'm not sure what you mean," Taylor stuttered, fingers clenching around his mug.

Rocco shot him a look. "I know we're not really dating, but we *are* becoming friends. And I shared why *I'm* doing this, but you didn't. You sort of did, but I know there's more you're not telling me. You wouldn't be so afraid of Steve Mills if there wasn't."

"I don't like the crap Steve Mills is going around saying," Taylor argued. "Mona doesn't either."

"You didn't even grow up here, right? So what gives, Taylor?" Rocco's voice was still smooth, still charming, but there was that undeniable will running through it, too.

"I used to come here with my parents," Taylor said. That was the rote answer he gave everyone. But didn't Rocco deserve more? *He's not going to want all that baggage*, that voice inside him insisted. *It's yours. Not his.* But Rocco was *asking*. He wanted to know. Most everyone else took his story at its face value, but not Rocco. "Every year," he added. Then kept going. "Even the year my mom died, we came here."

Rocco's eyes softened. "How old were you when she passed?"

"Fifteen. She had an undiagnosed brain aneurysm. One minute she was here, and the next she was gone." Taylor gulped a big mouthful of cider. It helped clear the lump in his throat.

Even seventeen years later, it still invariably appeared whenever he had to talk about her. And why shouldn't it? Just because that agonizing burn of grief had died out, it *still* hurt. He still missed her, every day.

He wondered, all the time, if she'd be proud of him. Proud of the choices he'd made, the life he was living.

His dad was, sure, but he'd always been more straightforwardly accepting. But Teresa Hall had always held him to a higher standard. Reminded him, always, that he was capable of anything he set his mind to so he shouldn't ever set the bar too low.

"Oh God, Taylor," Rocco said unsteadily, and a second later, he had his arms full of warm Italian man, hugging him tightly.

Rocco didn't let go quickly, and Taylor realized he didn't want to, either. The lump was still there, in the back of his throat, but with Rocco holding him, he could live with it a little better.

Michael had been the same, a momentary respite from his grief—still fresh, even years later, as he'd tried navigating being an adult without her—but the key part of that phrase had been *momentary*.

He hadn't stayed.

When it had come down to it, the only person Taylor could rely on was Taylor himself. He'd gotten used to that. Maybe *too* used to that.

He gradually disentangled himself, even though deep down, he didn't want to.

"I'm so sorry," Rocco said softly. His big dark eyes were full of empathy. Normally, Taylor would hate that; it was why he didn't share this story publicly. Not really, anyway. A few people, like Mona, knew because they'd been around when Teresa Hall had come to Christmas Falls every year with her family, and a few others knew because they'd gotten close enough to Taylor that they'd deserved to know the truth.

Rocco Moretti hadn't fallen into either of those categories, and Taylor had still told him.

"It's . . .it's been a long time," Taylor said. He was still bad at accepting condolences, despite how many of them he'd been given. "But yeah, that's why I want this job. I loved—*love*—this place, partly because of her, but also . . ." He trailed off.

"Partly because of who *you* are," Rocco finished for him.

"Yeah. Yeah, I guess so."

"Thank you for telling me," Rocco said softly. He was still staring at Taylor like he was seeing him for the first time. Like this knowledge fundamentally altered the filter he saw Taylor through. Every other time, he'd have hated that. But he was just curious what was different, now.

"I should've before, but I don't talk about it much," Taylor admitted.

"And your dad is back in Chicago?" Rocco said casually.

"Yeah, he moved to this new retirement community two years ago. Likes it there. Lots of friends. It's a good place. I think he's happy there."

"That why he doesn't come out here for the holidays?" Of course that was where Rocco had been going with this.

"I . . .I guess. Yeah." It wasn't like his dad hadn't ever come out to Christmas Falls, once he'd moved here. But he always had such a full schedule with the festival and his dad's calendar always seemed busy enough, when they talked on the phone.

In some ways they were too alike. Burying themselves in work.

In distractions.

Maybe it had become a habit, for both of them.

"Huh, well, I get it. I didn't want to drag my family away from each other at the holidays so . . .I'm on my own too, now." Rocco shot him a bit of a melancholy smile. "It's not so easy getting used to it."

"No," Taylor agreed. There was a part of him that wanted to say he'd never get used to his mom being gone, but then he didn't need to say that for Rocco to understand it.

Rocco's smile softened. "Thank you for telling me. I know you don't like to talk about it. You didn't need to say it, for me to understand that."

"You should know why we're doing this whole thing," Taylor said.

"I knew before but yeah, I understand it a little better now. And after being part of the festival, that's helped some too."

"I was thinking, tonight, that we don't want such different things," Taylor said.

"Yeah?" Rocco's dark eyes widened and he swayed closer, and for a second, Taylor was confused and also completely utterly thrilled. Rocco was going to kiss him. He wasn't sure why, but he couldn't be mad about it, even though it was probably the last thing they should be doing.

This thing between them was already complicated enough without adding kissing to the equation.

But Rocco must have seen the confusion on his face, because he pulled back. "You didn't mean romantically, did you," he stated, rather than asked. The openness on his face shuttered.

"Uh, no. Um. Professionally. We both want Christmas Falls to be the most welcoming, the warmest, the uh . . .best version of itself. You with your coffee shop. Me with the town as a whole."

"Oh." Rocco laughed, a little bitterly, and scrubbed a hand over his face. "I feel kind of stupid now. Yes, of course we do. That makes sense."

"Sorry," Taylor said. Meaning it.

"No, no," Rocco insisted, brushing his apology away with a quick hand movement. "It was . . .it would be foolish. Complicated."

"If it makes you feel better, I wasn't about to *goat cheese* out of it, even if I probably should have." Taylor shouldn't have said it, probably, because even though they'd admitted to a mutual attraction, this was him saying he wouldn't stop Rocco if he *did* attempt to alter this fake relationship to make it a little more real.

Rocco winced. "I . . .I shouldn't have, regardless. We talked about it. We're on the same page."

"Rocco," Taylor said, hating that he felt guilty, that he felt *bad.* That was the very last thing he wanted. He reached out and took Rocco's hand and squeezed it. "I consider you a friend. I wouldn't have told you about my mom if I didn't. We have that, and it's not nothing."

"No, it's not," Rocco agreed. But there was still a melancholy tinge to his eyes before he pushed it away and it disappeared before Taylor could ask about it. "I'm glad we're friends."

Taylor finished his cider and set the empty mug down on the counter. "I should get going."

"When are we meeting up next?" Rocco wondered casually.

Yeah, I want to see you again, too. Goat cheese be damned.

"Tomorrow night? There's a pretty cool ice carving demonstration. And then we could take a lap or two around the rink? I don't think you've been down there yet."

Rocco shook his head. "We could do that," he said.

"Alright, I'll meet you at the carving demonstration?"

"Yeah, that works for me," Rocco said.

But Taylor still hesitated, even though he knew he should go. Definitely before he changed his mind—changed his whole freaking paradigm—and told Rocco he'd changed his mind. That he wanted him, even if it was a bad idea, even if it was complicated.

"I . . ."

Rocco raised an eyebrow. Taylor was mostly getting used to the visual impact of him, but every once in a while it hit him viscerally just how handsome he was. How he'd have seen him walking down the street and done a double take. How he'd walked into Jolly Java to meet him for the first time and felt his tongue grow thick and uncooperative at the sight of him.

Kind of like now, actually.

"We're okay, right?" Taylor finally said.

Rocco nodded. "Of course. We're friends. That makes sense."

But as Taylor agreed, giving Rocco one last—very quick—hug on his way out of Jolly Java, he thought that maybe friends did make sense. The most sense.

But the heart wasn't always logical.

CHAPTER 8

THEY'D BEEN ON SEVERAL "dates" by the time Saturday night rolled around, but as he and Taylor walked towards Sugar Plum Park, Rocco's gloved hand tucked into Taylor's, it felt like this one was a big one, a *Date* with a capital D.

It seemed like most of the town was swarming around downtown, despite the snow that had fallen last night and into the morning, coating everything in a sparkling layer of pristine white. And many of them seemed to be out in pairs, holding hands the way he and Taylor were doing, gazing up at each other with the joy of the season and the joy of simply being together written all over their faces.

That is not you. You're just pretending.

But it didn't feel that way.

Rocco could at least admit that now. Especially after Taylor had finally let him in a little, let him see *him*, and why this job he wanted was so important to him.

Even though he'd done his regular routine this Saturday morning—pouring coffee and making lattes and cappuccinos and espressos, warming up cinnamon buns and scones, packing up to-go orders of breakfast sandwiches—his mind had been on Taylor's confession. Even Rebecca had mentioned how distracted he seemed, and he had been.

She'd assumed it was because of the growing regularity of customers coming in their door, but it was more than that.

Rocco had been pretty sure that after this was over, after they both had what they wanted, they could gradually shift down into a more casual friendship and he would be fine with it.

Maybe they could even have one last hurrah in bed, ending their fake relationship with a bang.

But now he wasn't so sure.

"Seems busy out here tonight," he said, breaking the companionable silence that had fallen between the two of them as they walked towards the park where the ice carving demonstration was being held. Next door was the temporary ice rink that was set up for the duration of festival season, and that according to Taylor, was where they needed to be seen on a Saturday night.

"Yeah," Taylor agreed. "But I'm not surprised. Carl's always a big draw."

"He's the ice carver?"

"Yeah, but I guess he and Murphy have been working together this year, and they're going to do a piece together. Might be why there's even more of a crowd than normal. Murphy kind of hates it, but he's incredibly popular here."

"I'd *love* one of his gnomes," Rocco agreed, nodding.

"Good luck with that," Taylor said wryly. "He's got a waiting list about a hundred miles long. I only got one for my dad last year."

Rocco nearly asked *then why is your dad not here?* But he'd already pushed Taylor hard enough on his history and his family situation. He knew Taylor hadn't wanted to tell him about his mom, and he understood why. Taylor presented a smooth, in-control front, professional and easygoing. But there was so much more to him—such a big heart and so much commitment and loyalty, buried deep underneath. And even deeper still, a secret, carefully hidden pool of old pain.

"Well, good thing I'm not planning on going anywhere then. Maybe in ten years I'll get one," Rocco said, shooting Taylor a grin and squeezing his hand hard. Ignoring how his own heart squeezed back.

What would it feel like if they were really on a date tonight? If this wasn't all just a front? If he had hope that in a year, in two years, in ten years, they'd still be walking hand in hand toward the entrance of Sugar Plum Park?

If tonight, Taylor didn't drop him off at the front door of Jolly Java, but came upstairs and they made their own heat in his big bed with its fluffy ivory comforter?

For a second, he lost himself in the vision, but then Rocco shook his head clear.

He didn't need these kind of distractions. Taylor being honest with him about his motivations had only made him more determined that he'd make sure he got this job. He not only deserved it, but he and the town needed each other. Rocco could see that now.

"Here we are," Taylor said, guiding them towards a good spot, near a stand of trees, a good ways back from the stage that had been set up with two huge, pristine blocks of ice. Rocco could recognize Murphy now, from his broad shoulders and distinctive red-and-green plaid jacket, talking to another man and his new fiancé, Jem Knight.

"We can get closer, if you'd like, but I think this spot gives the best view," Taylor added, glancing over at Rocco.

"No, no, this is perfect."

It was even more perfect when Taylor arranged himself behind Rocco, casually wrapping a hand around his waist and pulling him against his firm, warm body.

"You good?" he asked, dipping his head low.

Rocco guessed Taylor was worried that he'd *goat cheese* out of this particular snuggly arrangement, but at this point, he didn't think there was a single scenario in which those words were going to cross his lips.

Whatever Taylor was willing to give him, he'd take, *gratefully*.

"No, I'm good." *More than good*. He gestured towards the stage. "You hear about the engagement?" he asked, changing the subject.

"Hear about it?" Taylor was smiling, Rocco could hear it in his voice. "I feel like that's all anyone's wanted to talk about since Thanksgiving. But I'm surprised *you've* heard about it."

"Oh, well, Marlene came in for a late afternoon pick-me-up, right before we closed."

It felt good that he could say that.

Rocco had been pleased, because she was one of the first who'd come back, for her pumpkin spice latte, and she'd returned half a dozen times now. Doubly pleased, because she'd stood there with him, as she sipped her coffee, and inducted him truly into Christmas Falls by giving him all the good gossip.

And the biggest gossip was that last weekend, at the pie bake-off, Jem had gone down on one knee and proposed to Murphy. Murphy, who'd had his own engagement surprise planned.

"Part of the Christmas Falls gossip circle now?" Taylor teased. "You must be thrilled."

It had felt damn good, that was for sure. Maybe not as good as the way Taylor felt behind him, his warm body encircling his.

"I am. It's really beginning to turn around."

"I'm so glad for you," Taylor said, and it sounded like he meant every single word.

"Oh look, there's that movie star guy." Rocco gestured towards a spot in the middle of the crowd where the mayor was standing with Griff and Heath Kelly.

"I think Mona may never get over her disappointment that I ended up with you instead of him," Taylor said with a chuckle.

Rocco rolled his eyes. Not feeling jealous at all. Nope. No way. Morettis didn't get jealous. They were the ones who *made* everyone else jealous.

"But I'm not disappointed," Taylor said in a low voice, and Rocco swore his lips brushed his neck, and he had to restrain his resulting shiver. Or maybe he'd just imagined it. *Wanted* it so badly that he'd hoped it into existence.

"Good." Rocco could hear the smugness in his voice and decided that if Taylor heard it too that it didn't matter. He'd hardly made his attraction and affection secret.

But before he could point out that Heath Kelly wasn't all that handsome *or* that good of an actor—*really, you're not so hot yourself, Moretti*—Rocco could feel Taylor tense and then force himself to relax.

A second later, he was letting go of Rocco and coming to stand next to him. Rocco swallowed his disappointment and tried to figure out what had caused the change.

It was coming towards them now. A tall man, not quite as tall as Taylor, walking with purpose in their direction, blond hair, with maybe a touch of gray at the temples, and a complexion that said he definitely didn't usually spend winters in Christmas Falls. He was wearing a designer quilted jacket and a politician's smile, all empty charm.

"Hello, you must be Taylor Hall," he said, extending his hand. "Steve Mills. I'm glad we've finally met."

Ah. This was the guy who was Taylor's competition for the city manager job.

Rocco leaned closer, letting his whole side plaster against Taylor's, and this time it was his arm wrapping around *Taylor's* waist.

After they shook, Steve glanced over at Rocco and Rocco stuck out his chin and his hand. "Rocco Moretti. I own Jolly Java," he said firmly.

He had a weak handshake. Rocco hoped it was only one of many chinks in this guy's armor.

"Ah, the coffee shop. Looks charming."

But Rocco knew this guy had never been through its doors, and even though plenty had shunned him at the height of the pumpkin spice debacle, he took Steve Mills' absence more personally.

He wanted to run this town, he needed to *understand it*, and there was no way he could, or that he loved it even a fraction as much as Taylor did.

Taylor had made it a point to come by, and he didn't even drink coffee.

"Thanks," Rocco said dryly.

"I'm glad I ran into you, because I wanted to tell you what a great job you've done as deputy mayor. Everyone talks about what a great assistant you've been to Mayor Grayson."

Rocco wanted to roll his eyes. How did this guy make *great job* sound like the opposite? And relegating Taylor to an assistant to the mayor when the truth was he was a power in his own right?

But he didn't. Taylor's face was implacable, blank, and he just nodded. Rocco wasn't going to embarrass him, even if he wanted to tell this guy where he could put his backhanded compliments.

"Thank you," Taylor said stiffly.

"You do invaluable work behind the scenes," Steve said, and the insinuation was not even veiled any more. Taylor should keep the deputy job and continue to do all the work, unacknowledged while Steve got the public-facing job and took all the credit.

"He does more than that," Rocco said. He kept his voice smooth and even, but his point was clear.

"Ah, well, a partner always believes that," Steve said patronizingly. "And here's my own. My wife, Laura." She was just as blond and tan as Steve, and he was pretty sure she was wearing $5000 Gucci boots to mince around Sugar Plum Park's snow-covered landscape, which really said it all, didn't it?

She gave them each a nod. "Steve," she chided. "I want you to come and say hello to the mayor. She's with Heath Kelly, and you haven't met him yet."

"Sure thing," Steve said, sending the pair of them a cocky, knowing grin. "Gotta make friends, you know?"

A minute later he was gone, none too soon, and Rocco turned to Taylor, still feeling his tense body, his face equally as strained. "God, he's *terrible*," Rocco muttered.

Taylor laughed, but he didn't actually sound all that amused. "I know."

"You hadn't met him before?"

Taylor shook his head. "Could've done without it, too."

"You're going to get this job and send him back to Florida or wherever he came from." Rocco said it with certainty.

But Taylor's expression didn't echo Rocco's own belief. "I'm not sure I will. He's working the council like a fucking politician. Not surprisingly, considering that's why he wants the job."

"Well, he can want it all he wants, 'cause it's not happening," Rocco said. "We're gonna make sure of that. I can be just as good of a partner as his wife."

"I *would* like you to see you navigate all this snow and ice in high-heeled boots," Taylor joked, the tenseness in his face relaxing a fraction.

Rocco did roll his eyes then. "She was ridiculous. Also, someone should tell her that her Botox is showing."

"Same as his," Taylor said, and when he laughed this time, it sounded a lot more real.

"Please don't get Botox to win this job," Rocco said and reached up, smoothing away the creases on Taylor's forehead. He was still worried. Rocco could see it by the shadows in his eyes. "You're more qualified, you're more capable, and frankly, you're better for this town."

"He looks better, on paper," Taylor said.

"But in person? Oh, baby, you got him, hands down." Rocco hoped Taylor would laugh again, and he did chuckle.

"I'm glad you're on my side."

Rocco opened his mouth to say he was, for as long as Taylor needed, for *anything* he needed, even if that was probably a *goat cheese* kind of declaration, but before he could, Jem was stepping forward on the stage, clapping for everyone's attention, the demonstration beginning.

"Welcome to ice carving," Jem said, his loud voice carrying across the crowd. "You all know Carl Nicholas and you might also be familiar with this other guy on stage . . ."

There was a round of cheers and applause as Murphy stepped forward, his head ducked low, an embarrassed smile on his face that softened when he looked over at his fiancé.

"Murphy's been learning some from Carl, and he's decided he's going to give it a go this year," Jem finished. "Welcome them both and we'll do a quick Q and A after this, but in the meanwhile, enjoy watching them do their thing." He shot Murphy a flirtatious look. "I know I will."

Jem jumped down off the stage to another round of cheers, this time complete with a few catcalls.

"I wonder what they're going to carve," Rocco said, reaching over and grasping Taylor's hip again, trying to drag his attention, which seemed divided, back to the stage. Back to *him*.

He knew Taylor was worried about Steve and the job, but there was nothing he could do about it right now. In fact, he *was* doing something about it, already. Maybe Rocco wasn't wearing Gucci boots but he was still a Moretti. He could go toe-to-toe with that lady and confidently come out on top, designer gear or no.

"Not sure," Taylor said, relaxing a fraction.

"Carl's looks like an animal of some kind," Rocco speculated. "And Murphy's? Well, I'm not sure what that is." He shot Taylor a worried glance. "He knows what he's doing, right?"

"He wouldn't get up there if he didn't," Taylor said. "Besides, he told me the other day, ice isn't really that different than wood. A little easier to carve, he claimed."

"Well, I hope he meant it," Rocco said. Because what Murphy looked like he was carving was a building of some kind. Maybe? It was hard to tell. It just looked like one block stacked on another block, whereas Carl's was already taking noticeable shape, between his chainsaw and the different chisels he was employing to carve away chunks of ice, leaving just the design behind.

"Murphy always says what he means," Taylor murmured.

It wasn't a stretch that Taylor was still thinking of someone else—someone who might *not* mean every word they said.

Rocco nudged him. "I know he bothered you," he said.

Taylor just shrugged. "I guess," he said absently, but the truth was obvious.

"No, he bothered you, and frankly, I can't blame you for being bothered, because he was kind of a smug asshole, but don't let him ruin your mood or this evening."

Taylor looked over at Rocco and finally seemed to really be seeing him. "Sorry," he apologized. "It's just . . .I hadn't met him before, and I could pretend that I had a shot easier, before I had."

"I know," Rocco said. "But I meant it. You've got this. Definitely more than Murphy does."

"No, *no*, I know what he's making. It's a wedding cake," Taylor said, and he laughed, suddenly and pointed at the stage.

It *was*. There were the cake layers emerging now, Rocco could see them even across the expanse between them and the stage. And Murphy was using a little chisel to carve out flowers and trim on each layer, and finally, the crowning glory, two small figures on the top, holding hands.

The cheers were deafening as Jem jumped back on stage and pulled Murphy into a big hug and then kissed him, hard and wild, leaving him blushing a bright red.

"I know mine's not as exciting, but it's still a present for you two," Carl said laconically, smiling as he glanced at them. "They always say penguins mate for life."

And yes, Carl's penguin seemed to be gazing at Murphy and Jem with real affection in its icy eyes, congratulating them without words.

"That's so cool," Rocco said, looking over at Taylor. He was smiling, too, but Rocco wasn't naive enough to think even the loving display had banished Taylor's bad mood entirely.

He'd just have to try a little harder.

"You ready to take a spin around the rink?" Rocco said. "I could use some cocoa, to warm up."

"Even substandard cocoa?" Taylor teased.

"You didn't hear me say that," Rocco said. "I spent like the first month I was here trying to convince Joel that we weren't competitors. The last thing I need is for my opinion of his cocoa to get back to him."

"Joel's a cool guy. I think he knows he's serving it more for quantity than quality," Taylor said. "And yeah, let's get some and skate."

They walked over to the rink, where a lot of people had headed after the ice carving demonstration. The rink was full, on a Saturday night, even without an official "social" being hosted, and Rocco recognized probably a dozen or so of the people sliding across the ice and milling around the refreshment area, just chatting with other townspeople.

"It's busy tonight," Rocco said.

"This your first time here?" Taylor asked.

Rocco nodded. "Just don't ask me if I can skate." He was trying not to be apprehensive about it, but he also knew Taylor wouldn't let him humiliate himself.

"It's alright, I couldn't when I moved here, either."

"And now?" Rocco wondered.

"Well, it's practically a requirement of citizenship," Taylor said. "But if you're not ready—"

"No, no, we can, I just . . .I have *no* idea."

"You can hang onto me," Taylor said.

Rocco had been afraid—and also hoping—that Taylor might say that. "You're not worried about me dragging you down?"

"Not at all."

"So I guess that'll be two birds, one stone, then," Rocco said wryly.

Taylor shoved his hands in his pockets as they approached the stand that rented skates. "I guarantee if we were actually dating, I'd take you ice skating with the secret agenda of making sure I'd need to touch you as much as possible."

Rocco swallowed hard and tried to focus on the sign that gave the skate rental prices. This was either a very good idea, or a terrible one.

Dipping his head low, Taylor murmured in the vicinity of his ear, "As long as you're okay with that."

Rocco nodded because he didn't want to say there was no way he'd *goat cheese* out of this. Not with anticipation rushing through him in a thrilling wave.

"Well, let's get some skates then," Taylor said.

Ten minutes later, they were equipped and heading towards the rink—Taylor with confidence, Rocco with unsteady steps and wobbly knees.

"Just hang onto me," Taylor said. "We'll go slow. Careful."

"But nobody else is going slow," Rocco pointed out, trying to keep the hysteria out of his voice as he gestured towards the mass of people rotating around the rink, largely as confidently as Taylor seemed to be.

"Don't care what they're doing."

Rocco glanced over at Taylor and felt his knees wobble even more dangerously at the intent look in his dark blue eyes.

"Alright, if you say so," Rocco said as they approached the ice.

And it was not as bad as it could have been.

Sure, it was *ice* which meant it was inherently slippery and slick and he was only wearing a thin blade of metal that he was meant to *balance on*, but Taylor came through.

He balanced Rocco's unsteadiness and refused to let go of him, and when some teenage kids went racing by, bumping them, he gave them an appropriately intense glare.

"You *are* good at this," Rocco said as they made their second rotation. "And you were right, it's actually not so terrible."

"Maybe you might actually have fun?" The corner of Taylor's mouth quirked up and his grip didn't lessen. In fact, it seemed more solid than ever.

To the point of Rocco wondering, *even if we're not actually dating, would you still take me ice skating, to give you the excuse to hold on to me and not let go?*

"That might possibly be occurring," Rocco said, trying to keep a straight face.

But Taylor smiled. "Good."

They made two more rounds of the rink, and then Rocco tugged his arm. "Hot chocolate," he insisted, and Taylor led him off the rink, stopping to untie and return their skates before heading towards the refreshment stand.

And who else should they spot there but Steve Mills and Mrs. Gucci Boots?

"Oh, look at how cute you two are," she cooed as they approached the line to grab cocoa. "You actually went ice skating!"

"That is what people do at a rink," Rocco said dryly.

"Right, and oh, he's funny too," Mrs. Gucci Boots said with an annoyingly high-pitched giggle.

"It's why I like him," Taylor said, putting an arm around Rocco's waist and firmly tugging him closer. "One of many reasons. You ever tried his marzipan latte?"

"What's that?" she asked.

Steve turned away from the tourist he'd no doubt been attempting to charm and said, "Oh, honey, that's some weird foreign thing. You wouldn't want that."

Rocco stiffened. Wondered if they also thought of him as 'some weird foreign thing' even though his family had been citizens for four generations.

"There's plenty of that here," Taylor said firmly, quietly. "So better get used to it."

"Not when I grew up here, there wasn't." Steve's tone was still friendly, but casual, but Rocco knew neither he nor Taylor were particularly happy.

Rocco wasn't particularly familiar with this town yet, he'd only been here a few months, but he had a feeling Steve didn't really remember what Christmas Falls had been like, because for a town that celebrated nostalgia, it also embraced so many different kinds of people and traditions. And that didn't seem like a particularly new thing.

"We'll have to agree to disagree," Taylor finally said politely.

"Steve," Mrs. Gucci Boots whined, "I see Heath over there. Let's go over and chat."

He gave his wife an indulgent smile, sent a frostier one in Taylor and Rocco's direction, and thank God, they were gone.

"That freaking guy," Taylor muttered after he'd grabbed them two paper cups of hot chocolate. Rocco took one and sipped, not even minding the weak flavor because he was too preoccupied with how upset Taylor was.

"He's shitty, for sure," Rocco agreed. "But punching him in the face isn't going to get you the job you want, unfortunately."

"Unfortunately," Taylor grumbled. He glanced over at Rocco. "It's getting late. I know you get up early . . ."

"We can head back," Rocco said, hiding his disappointment that the evening had ended on such a low note. He took another long drink of his hot chocolate as they headed out of Sugar Plum Park.

Taylor didn't say anything as they walked down Candy Cane Lane. Stewing, Rocco assumed, in silence. He needed to do *something* to drag Taylor out of this angst. Because angsting about it wasn't going to change anything, and what he *was* doing, getting out into the town and showing them who Taylor Hall *really* was, was actually giving him the best chance to get the job.

A stray snowflake dropped down to his cheek, and Rocco brushed it away. But it gave him the idea. On the next block, he tossed his empty paper cup into the trash and then leaned down, gathering a handful of snow in his gloved hand and before he could think better of it, tossed it right at Taylor.

It glanced off his shoulder, spraying snow into his face, and his jaw dropped.

"What? Are you serious?" Taylor gasped.

Rocco laughed, the sound startled out of him by the shock on Taylor's face.

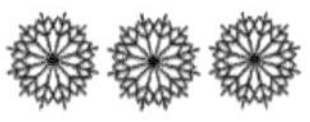

Taylor couldn't believe Rocco had just thrown a snowball at him and then *laughed* about it. But then, maybe he could. Because the look on his face was all playful heat.

Hot enough to melt whatever snow Taylor might toss his way.

Leaning down, he grabbed a handful of the softest snow and a second later, Rocco was still laughing but spluttering too as he wiped his face off.

"Oh, baby, it's on now," he called out and Taylor wasn't stupid. He ran, ducking back into the coverage of some of the trees on the edge of the park, Rocco right on his heels, pelting snowballs at his back. He chanced looking back and got a mouthful of snow that he hoped was at least clean-ish. Scooped up some more and hopefully gave back as good as he got.

But right after he did, Rocco shocked another breathless laugh right out of him by tackling him right to the ground, their landing softened by a snow drift.

Rocco was strong, but Taylor wasn't a slouch, and he turned them, flipping Rocco, and then letting Rocco wrestle himself back on top.

Taylor froze as Rocco leaned down, laughter spilling out of his mouth and mischief glowing in his eyes. He'd lost his hat somewhere, and his curls were messed up.

You could mess them up even further.

God, he wanted to.

Pulling together all his strength, he turned them again, and before he could think—or overthink—he tucked Rocco into the snowbank and kissed him.

The desire to do it was a fire in his blood, but doing it once, their lips finally meeting, didn't do anything to extinguish the need.

Instead, it flared hot and sweet between them, Rocco groaning as he pushed up into the kiss, his hands on Taylor's back, trying to pull him in closer.

He'd imagined it might be good. After all, they were young and attracted, and it had been awhile for both of them—a *long* while for Taylor, though he was under no delusions that Rocco's dry spell equaled his own.

Not when Rocco looked like he did.

He'd have a long list of men panting after him, and Taylor was just one in that line, but then, who was kissing him now? Kissing him so good that Rocco was making these hot, little desperate noises in the back of his throat.

But the kiss was so much better than anything his weak imagination could conjure up.

Taylor's fingers delved into his hair, deepening the kiss, his tongue brushing Rocco's, and he swore he heard his brain functions ticking off one after one.

Before this moment, he'd wanted exactly this, but he'd known it wasn't a very good idea. But now it *only* seemed like the best goddamned idea he'd ever had.

Rocco rolled them back, and the rest of the blood in Taylor's brain evacuated, heading down south, as he lay that perfect, compact, surprisingly strong body on top of his own. Sure, there were what felt like dozens of layers between them—coats and sweaters and jeans—but Taylor felt flayed naked.

Naked.

Oh yeah. That was what he wanted. To be naked and to gaze up, worshipping Rocco's no doubt gorgeously naked form above him.

He didn't thrust his hard cock against Rocco's ass, but it was a near thing.

He wanted . . .he wanted so goddamn badly, but it wasn't just the pulse of insistent desire that pulled him out of his fog and off Rocco's mouth, but the way the ice around his heart was undeniably melting.

Taylor wrenched his mouth off Rocco's, and a second later, Rocco slid off him and shot him a look that said a thousand things.

Why did you do that?

Did you know it would feel like that?

How are we not going to do that again?

Do you want *to do that again?*

It occurred to Taylor, then, that not only had he kissed him when he'd said he wouldn't, when they'd discussed *not* complicating their faux relationship this way, despite their attraction, that he'd not *once* been tempted to say *goat cheese*.

Shit.

"What the heck was that?" Rocco asked.

That underlying frustration in his voice might exist because Taylor had kissed him even though they'd established they wouldn't. Or it might be because he'd stopped and he wanted to keep going.

Yes. That. Lean over. Kiss him again. Let it carry you both away.

But Taylor pulled himself together.

"What was *that*?" he retorted, tossing a little bit of snow in Rocco's direction.

"I was just trying to pull you out of your head," Rocco said.

He heard what Rocco wasn't saying. *I wasn't the one who kissed you.*

"I . . .I'm sorry if I overstepped." Taylor lifted himself to his feet and held out a hand to help Rocco up.

Rocco shot it a vaguely suspicious look, but took it eventually, brushing off his jeans when he stood.

And *yeah*, the snow hadn't affected Rocco's situation below the belt either.

Taylor didn't know whether he should be flattered or horrified.

"You should have stopped me," he said, because apparently his brain-to-mouth filter was dead, gone, buried, truly burnt to a crisp by the heat in Rocco's lips.

"Are you freaking kidding me?" Rocco muttered.

"I should have stopped myself," Taylor said, apologetically.

"That was just you getting carried away by the . . .uh . . .holiday spirit then," Rocco said, and Taylor could acknowledge that the careful edge in Rocco's tone was both deserved and also absolutely terrible.

He'd done this. Taken way more than he'd ever intended to, and possibly ruined this good thing between them.

"Uh, sure," Taylor said. "That sounds reasonable."

He didn't want to tell Rocco about Michael. He'd already told him about his mom, yes, but Michael was different. Michael was humiliating, a cautionary tale that anyone with even a brain cell of common sense would have seen coming a mile away. Rocco never would've gotten ensnared and then dropped by Michael. He'd have seen right through him. Unlike Taylor, who'd really believed that, with him, things would be different.

Spoiler alert: not only had they not been different, they'd actually been worse. Taylor's mom hadn't wanted to leave him—she'd wanted to live, fiercely, not just for her own future, but for Taylor's.

Michael hadn't given a shit about Taylor *or* his future.

He wasn't ever going to be hurt like that again. Not even if he was *sure* Rocco wouldn't treat him the same.

"It's alright," Rocco said. "I get it. We did get carried away. It was probably inevitable, and honestly, it's fine."

But Taylor wasn't sure it was fine. Maybe he should say something about Michael. Not the whole embarrassing story, but enough of it that Rocco understood.

"I . . .I'm not in a place to have a relationship right now. A . . .uh . . .*real* relationship," he clarified. "At least for now, I have to put my career first. This town first. I didn't always, and I almost fucked it all up. I can't do that again. Can't take that risk."

He heard what he was really saying and was desperately hoping that Rocco didn't hear it, too.

I'm afraid.

Rocco's gaze narrowed. "But you can *fake* it for your career, huh?"

Taylor didn't want to bring up that this whole ridiculous scheme had been Rocco's idea. Rocco had ensnared both of them in it. Yes, Taylor had agreed, but . . .well. He could have stopped it at any time. He could have touched Rocco less. Could have distanced himself when he felt they were growing too close. Definitely not kissed him just because he wanted to so goddamn bad he didn't think he could resist one second longer.

"Yeah," Taylor said quietly. "And that's kind of shitty, isn't it? For both of us."

Rocco sighed and gave Taylor a soft smile. "Yeah. Maybe. It hasn't been easy for me either. Sometimes I think maybe we should just call it off, but then I see how it's working. How Marlene came in twice this week. How I have a guy writing a book in my coffee shop, like I'm *helping* him do that, even a little bit, and that's amazing. And that Steve guy? A complete asshole. You can't let him get that job, Taylor. You just can't."

"I know," Taylor said. He also knew if he was around Rocco, he'd want to kiss him again. That much was a guarantee.

And there was a part of him, tiny and buried, a hard kernel of desperation that hoped Rocco felt the same way.

"Maybe we should just . . . I don't know . . . take a little bit of space. Not see each other for a few days. Get some perspective." Rocco didn't quite look him in the eye when he said it, but that was okay. This was hard. Taylor was certainly struggling with it.

Hard enough he'd been sure Rocco would say, *no, it's all over*, and Taylor had been so sure he'd agree. But he hadn't, and Taylor discovered he didn't have the fortitude to force the issue.

It *was* working.

It's more than that, an annoying voice in his head reminded him. *You don't want to give him up.*

But he would.

He'd have to, eventually.

Someday, they'd have to shift things back into a friends-only zone. In public *and* in private.

"Yeah," Taylor agreed. "We could do that. We . . .uh . . .pretty much convinced everyone we were dating, so I don't see why we can't take a few days off."

"Yeah," Rocco said wryly, "we were real convincing."

Taylor could only laugh then. "I guess we were."

"Full points for authenticity. Ten out of ten. No notes." Rocco was smiling again, and he looked him right in the eye when he said it. Taylor let out the breath he'd been holding.

"And neither of us even *thought* goat cheese."

"Hey, I could have."

But they both knew he hadn't. Taylor shouldn't make him admit it, but there was a part of him, deep down and buried, that wanted to hear the truth.

That Rocco hadn't been tempted to say it either.

"Did you, really?"

Rocco sighed and smacked Taylor in the arm. "Damn you, *no*. I would say we could just hook up and call it good, but I know how *that* would turn out."

He didn't need to say it would be only a slippery slope to *more*, because Taylor already knew it was true.

Someday, you're gonna want it more than you're afraid.
Someday.

"Well, at least we're on equal footing," Taylor said.

"Is that supposed to make me feel better?" Rocco wondered.

Taylor didn't know. But it didn't make *him* feel better, either.

CHAPTER 9

AN UNEASY COMBINATION OF guilt and arousal lingered with Taylor for days.

The guilt should have been enough to stop him from thinking about Rocco's mouth on his, his body pressed against his own, but it wasn't.

In fact, if anything was winning out, it was the arousal.

More than once he woke up in a sweat, heart racing, cock hard, and after the second time, he gave up and wrapped his hand around it and let himself sink back into the dream. The dream was better than reality anyway. In the dream, Rocco's mouth was on his, his tongue sweeping into his mouth, his groans the best music Taylor had ever heard. His mouth slipped lower and then lower still, curling around a nipple, then nipping at his stomach, then finally wrapping around his dick, hot and wet, and after that Taylor couldn't think at all.

Maybe he should be ashamed, but while he'd initiated the kiss, Rocco's participation had been just as enthusiastic.

Taylor decided he'd make another appearance at the Arts and Crafts Fair. But first, he decided to take himself for a punishing run, even though he usually only jogged on Saturday mornings. He texted Hayden and asked if he was interested in fitting in another workout, but he was busy. Taylor figured he could go by himself, but then he remembered the last time he'd swung by the Fair, he'd run into Jem and his mom.

He sent Jem a text, asking him if he was interested in a run, and got an affirmative almost immediately.

Taylor changed into his running clothes in the Town Hall bathroom and ducked out, meeting Jem at the sidewalk.

"You doin' okay?" Jem asked as they set off, Taylor setting a pace faster than usual.

He and Jem had become friendly since Jem had moved back to Christmas Falls. At first, he'd been a little intimidated by the ex-pro football player, but he'd discovered that Jem was refreshingly down to earth, with no trace of ego, and seemed to want to be just a regular guy.

Well, Taylor was definitely just a regular guy.

"Uh, yeah," Taylor said as they headed down the street. He didn't really want to confess what was going on with Rocco was fucking him up, but it was.

"I ran into Steve Mills' wife *twice* at the store," Jem said. "One time, I could call that maybe a coincidence, but then she showed up the second time, when I ran out at nine, to grab ice cream 'cause Murph was craving it, and there she was." He shook his head. "I think she wants to be friends—or *God*, something else, which is crazy."

"A little. The whole town knows you're head over heels for Murphy. You just proposed to the guy, for God's sake," Taylor said sympathetically.

"I'm a rich celebrity—or so she thinks." Jem made a frustrated noise. "Heath told me she tried to pin him in the little hallway to the bathrooms in Rudolph's the other day. *Heath*. Who is most definitely famous for not being into women."

"Wow. Luckily the two times I've run into her, I was with Rocco." Taylor picked up speed again, breathing hard through his nose as his muscles warmed up.

Jem chuckled. "I'd love to see what Rocco Moretti would do if she put the moves on you in front of him."

Taylor didn't want to talk about Rocco, or how fierce he'd be if anyone threatened their (faux) relationship. Because he *would* be fierce. He'd call her Mrs. Gucci Boots to her face and he'd make every ounce of his disdain known, all while looking stupendously, brain-meltingly hot.

So hot that Taylor wouldn't be able to resist—

No. No. Do not go there. Do not pass Go. Do not collect two hundred dollars.

"He wouldn't like it," Taylor agreed.

"That why we're running so goddamn fast?" Jem wondered casually, but it was clear from both Jem's uneven breathing and his own, that yes, they were running fast.

He slowed down and Jem followed suit.

"I . . ." Taylor made a face. "We got into a little bit of an argument the other night."

"Ah, trying to punish yourself, huh," Jem pointed out dryly. "I get that. Or I do theoretically. I don't think Murph and I argued for months when we first got together. We were too busy in bed or uh . . .in the shower . . .or once . . ." He trailed off and cleared his throat. "You get the idea."

"I do," Taylor said wryly. Wondered what Jem would say if he admitted that all he and Rocco had done was kiss.

"So what happened?" Jem asked.

"I think we want different things out of this," Taylor said. Even though he wasn't sure that was really true. He knew *one* thing they both really wanted.

Jem frowned. "I don't know Rocco very well, he's too new to town, but surely, it's early to be having that argument?"

"I need to be focused on this job, and on the job I want. I can't let . . . Rocco's a distraction." It wasn't even a good lie. Taylor didn't even believe it.

And neither did Jem.

"You're the one who asked him out," Jem said wryly.

Apparently they *were* friends now, because Jem felt comfortable enough to call him out. Deservedly. Taylor could have left it alone. Could have never gone to Jolly Java and taken Rocco up on his offer.

Could have told himself and Rocco the truth.

You scare the shit out of me.

"I know, I guess I thought . . .I guess I thought I could keep my head." *And my hands to myself.*

"Keeping your head is overrated," Jem said.

"Not when I have this job on the line," Taylor objected. "I nearly fucked this all up once, and I can't do it again."

"How do you know having Rocco in your life is going to make that happen?" Jem's question seemed so reasonable.

Taylor didn't really make the decision to tell Jem. It just spilled out. "I had a boyfriend, a couple of years back, when I was still in Chicago. But I had befriended Mona, over the years, and she knew I'd always wanted a job in Christmas Falls. They were working on getting her an assistant, and when the funding came through, she offered me the job. But I . . ." Taylor let out a hard breath. "I thought I was in love. And I didn't want to leave Michael in Chicago. We'd been together about six months, and I thought, maybe this would be better. Maybe I should just give up on the whole Christmas Falls thing. That's the past, and maybe Michael's the future."

"He wasn't, was he?" Jem patted him on the shoulder. "Shit, man, that's rough. But you ended up here anyway?"

"A month after I turned down Mona's job offer, Michael got an offer to transfer to Seattle. He took it and didn't even *ask* me. Just laughed when I told him I'd thought we were going the distance. I was so stupid."

"Rocco wouldn't ever do that. He's in town to stay."

"Yeah, but I took my eyes off the prize, for a second. Thought I could have *both*, a professional future and a guy who'd stick, who'd *stay*, and . . ." Taylor didn't need to say it. He'd gotten screwed over when he'd imagined that might be true. Michael had fucking *laughed* at him for believing it. Called him naive.

And he'd ended up alone, again.

"He was an asshole. I don't know Rocco well yet, but I do know he's not an asshole." Jem cleared his throat. "Here's something else I *do* know, because I almost fell victim to it myself, last year. I didn't think I could have Murph, either. But the only person standing in the way of that? It was me. I was holding myself back, for no good reason."

"I want to believe that's true, because it would make everything a hell of a lot easier." He could go to Rocco right now, swing down Candy Cane Lane and walk into Jolly Java, tell the guy who'd been starring in his dreams for weeks now that he wanted him, *for real*. Beg, even. Would Rocco give him the cold shoulder? He'd never said it explicitly, but he'd been disappointed the other night, and speaking of the other night, there'd been the way he'd kissed Taylor back . . .

"Then make it easier. The risk is worth it, I promise," Jem said firmly.

"I'll think about it," Taylor replied, like he'd actually been thinking of anything else, lately. And with Rocco? The risk *would* be worth the fear. Taylor already suspected that was true.

"Good," Jem said, nodding. "You wanna swing by the fair?"

Taylor agreed. Ten minutes later, they arrived at the festival hall and he left Jem at Murphy's display, nearly empty now, since the fair was coming to a close.

He wandered the aisles, not sure what he was looking for—*liar, you know exactly what you're looking for and it's not here, it's at Jolly Java*—but stopping every so often to chat with a vendor or a Christmas Falls resident.

There was a cute booth with a comfy-looking nook, baby blankets with various fanciful designs, everything from princesses and castles to dinosaurs and spaceships, hanging on garments racks on each side.

Sadly he didn't know anyone who needed one of them, because he'd been sorely tempted to stop and hang out for a minute.

After another few minutes, Taylor wandered off to where the food stalls were. He bought a cup of hot cider and sat down at one of the picnic tables, currently occupied by an older lady with white curly hair a halo around her head.

"Is it okay if I sit here a minute?" he asked.

"Oh, darling, yes," she said brightly, looking pleased he'd come and sat down at her table, even though there were several empty ones available.

"I'm Taylor Hall," he said, reaching out his hand. She took it, shaking it firmly but delicately.

"The deputy mayor at my table. I'm honored," she said. "Marjorie Wagner."

"You're a resident or a tourist?" he asked.

"Resident," Marjorie said firmly. "A longtime resident. Almost fifty years. My whole family lives in upstate New York, near Syracuse, but I won't leave Christmas Falls. My husband and I moved here forty-eight years ago, raised our children here, and here is where I'll stay."

"That's beautiful," Taylor said. "I moved here four years ago and I can understand why you'd never want to leave."

"Not often young people want to move here. Often I see they're moving away." Marjorie frowned. "They think it's old-fashioned and believe that means it's backwards, even though we both know this town is anything but."

Taylor nodded. "I came here every Christmas with my parents when I was growing up. We're from Chicago so it was close enough to drive to. I always knew I'd come back here."

"You understand then. This town becomes part of your blood." Marjorie sighed. "My daughter keeps begging me to leave. Or to at least come up for the holidays, but I can't leave now. Won't leave now."

"I do," Taylor said. "My dad's still in Chicago."

"Not your mom, dear?"

"No, we lost her a few years ago," Taylor said. "But that's part of why I live here and work here. Her memory."

Marjorie's eyes filled with tears. "Oh, sweetheart. That's beautiful." She gripped his hands and wouldn't let go. "She'd be proud of you."

Even though Marjorie had never known Teresa Hall, he hoped she was right. Though he could theorize what she'd be thinking of how he'd treated Rocco.

"Thanks," he said.

"I hear you're up for a big promotion," she said.

"City manager *is* a big deal," Taylor admitted.

"But you're equal to it. I know what kind of good you've done for this town." She paused. "And now I know why. Unlike that dolt, Steve Mills, who thinks he can waltz back here and try to tell us how Christmas Falls is."

"He's wrong," Taylor said steadily.

"That he is, my boy." She stood, carefully, wobbling a little, and Taylor reached out to steady her. "I have no doubt you're going to get it, instead. The council might be difficult, sometimes, but they're not stupid."

"I hope so," Taylor said.

"You've got this in the bag," she said forcefully, and he imagined her going to each member of the council and insisting that they pick Taylor, now.

"Thanks. Couldn't imagine a better person to be on my side," he said.

After Marjorie wandered away, he toyed with his mostly empty cup and ended up dialing his dad. They talked once a week over the phone and usually more via text, but he *was* busy. Retired, but constantly staying busy.

This wasn't Taylor's normal time to call, so he wasn't sure he'd get him, but he did. "Hey, Dad," he said when his father picked up. "How's it going?"

"I can barely believe it," Walter Hall said dryly. "It's not Sunday and you're calling."

"I . . .uh . . .figured you might be busy," Taylor said.

"I don't have penuchle until five, so you've got thirty-five minutes," his dad said.

"You still going with that nice old lady. What was her name again?"

"Nina and no, she ended up moving to Florida with her daughter." But Walter didn't sound all that disappointed. "She was kind of a nag."

"Mom never nagged," Taylor said before he could snatch the words back.

"No, son, she didn't." Walter chuckled. "So what's the special occasion?"

"For my call? Uh, well . . .nothing special. Just was thinking about you. Met a real nice lady here, reminded me of you."

"Oh, yeah? Would I like her?"

Taylor laughed. "What would mom say if she could see you've turned into such a ladies' man?"

Walter chuckled. "She'd laugh and roll her eyes."

There'd been a time when they couldn't joke like this. When losing Teresa Hall had been debilitating and so painful that some days Taylor hadn't been sure they could move on. But they had.

They'd healed, because they'd had no other choice, but that didn't mean all that suffering hadn't left a scar.

"She would," Taylor agreed. "You have any big plans for the holidays?"

"Oh, you know the place here does it up big, and I'm right in the thick of it. Sometimes I don't know whether to rage quit or be relieved that it's me running the organizing committee."

They'd both dealt with those scars in different ways. Taylor had gone back to their shared past, burying himself in memories, in the uncomplicated rose-gold sheen of nostalgia. He'd searched for someone who'd *stick*. For awhile he'd believed that was Michael, and when he'd discovered he wasn't even close to the right answer, he'd returned to the one thing that always was: Christmas Falls.

His dad had gotten busy and maybe a tad bit over-involved.

Somehow, Taylor realized, that had put them at cross-purposes, only passing each other like ships in the night.

"You love it," Taylor reminded his dad.

"And so do you," Walter retorted fondly. "You're a chip off the old block, for sure, and I'm so proud of you. Any news on the job?"

"Not anything recent. I did finally meet the other candidate."

"He suck as much as you thought?"

"More, actually," Taylor said with a resigned sigh.

"Well, you're gonna get it over him. I know you, and you don't give up when the going gets tough. You'll do what needs done to make sure you're the best choice for the job."

"Thanks, Dad."

Of course Walter Hall didn't have any clue what he'd already done to ensure the job was his. Namely, Rocco Moretti.

What *would* he say about Rocco?

Taylor barely needed to give it a moment of thought. Walter would say, in that kind, patient, but spine-of-steel way of his, *You like this boy? Then you do the right thing by him.*

Taylor of a few days ago might've believed that "doing the right thing by him" would be dissolving this faux relationship and staying casual friends.

But now, he wasn't so sure.

No—that was a lie. He *was* sure. Terrified, but sure.

"You're awfully quiet today," Walter said. "You sure there isn't anything on your mind?"

"I . . .uh . . ." He didn't mean to say it. He really didn't mean to. But it came out anyway. "I met someone."

"Really? Oh, Taylor, that's great news. Who is he?"

"He just moved here, actually. Bought the coffee shop. Then changed everything. Kinda pissed off a lot of caffeine lovers in town."

"You're gonna rescue him, aren't you?" Walter sounded amused.

"Actually . . .Rocco's more the kind to rescue himself. I helped him see it, but he's on the right path. Forging his *own* path, actually. He's . . .*well.*"

"Speechlessness is always a good sign," his dad teased. "When I met your mother, I felt like I couldn't string together a sentence for months. But really, I'm happy for you. You work too hard. Could use a little more fun in your life."

Was Rocco fun? Well, he sure as hell wasn't dull.

Taylor always felt more alive when they were together, like he was seeing and tasting and smelling for the first time in a long time.

"I think so too," Taylor agreed. "Guess we'll see if it plays out."

"Just like that job you want, you give this Rocco kid that kind of attention, show him a real good time? He's going to love you, just the way I do," his dad said firmly.

"Dad," Taylor chuckled weakly.

"It's true. You've got this."

Taylor didn't think he really did, but his dad's confidence, like always, gave *him* confidence.

"I gotta get to penuchle," Walter said. "But it's the holiday season. Don't be a stranger, okay?"

"Okay," Taylor said, a sudden lump forming in the back of his throat. "Love you, Dad."

"Love you, too."

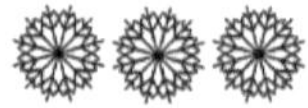

Rocco didn't know what the heck he was doing.

In this moment.

Or frankly, in general.

He'd not only *let* Taylor kiss him, he'd been a more-than-enthusiastic participant, and then he'd just let him—and himself!—off the hook.

What he should've done was tell Taylor to fuck right off and then insist it was off, their "relationship" was over.

But he hadn't done that.

Rocco huffed under his breath as he opened the door to the Christmas Falls Museum. It had been days and days since their last date and their kiss, and he still wasn't over it.

Still wasn't done thinking about it. Or Taylor.

To distract himself, Rocco had been doing some digging, trying to figure out the best place to get what he needed, and at the end of the day, it seemed that would be the Christmas Falls Festival Museum and its curator, Harvey Novak.

The floorboards creaked as he walked in, the big rooms full of old floats and display cases full of memorabilia. There was even an old mechanical Santa that Rocco gave a second look to, because he looked a *little* creepy.

"Hello?" Rocco asked, surprised at how empty the place was. Of course it was a Wednesday afternoon, so maybe that was why it felt like crickets echoing through the tall rooms.

"Oh, hey!" a man who had to be Harvey said, walking up to where Rocco was standing. "I didn't hear you come in."

"It's pretty quiet," Rocco pointed out.

"We're usually much busier on the weekends," the man said and extended a hand. "I'm Harvey Novak."

Rocco shook it. "Rocco Moretti. I'm new to town. Just bought Jolly Java in the summer."

"Oh! You're the one who took pumpkin spice off the menu," Harvey said.

"Don't tell me you're a PSL fan," Rocco joked weakly.

"Oh, no, no, I just heard some complaining about it. I just like my coffee black. And yours was *delicious* the few times I stopped by." Harvey paused. "But that's obviously not why you're here. What can I help you with?"

"I was wondering if you had any old records here? I know you have all this really great stuff, but I'm looking for something more specific. Like old recipes?"

"Recipes?" Harvey looked confused. Hopeful, but confused.

"I'm hoping to make some classic Christmas Falls recipes to add to my regular rotation. Marlene thought you might have some old records, maybe?"

Now, Rocco knew he'd erred with his enthusiasm on removing popular items people were comfortable with, but what he should have done was *add* a few things. Create some daily or weekly specials. And if he wanted *new* stuff, he needed to think about Christmas Falls and how it celebrated nostalgia. Surely he could find some old recipes and maybe punch them up a little? But everyone he'd talked to had blanked—finally Marlene had suggested that he try Harvey at the museum.

"Oh, recipes? Hmmmm, I'm not sure." Harvey frowned. "But I know we have a lot of old books. Historical texts and some such. I could look back there. See what I can find."

It had been a shot in the dark, but Rocco was disappointed, anyway.

"Sure, if you have time." Rocco shrugged. Nearly wondering if he should just tell Harvey to forget it.

"No, *no*," Harvey said, "come on. We'll look together. It's just back here." He gestured towards the back of the museum, and Rocco figured it wouldn't hurt to follow.

The room was small and packed to the gills with *stuff*. File cabinets on one side and a large bookshelf, rising nearly to the ceiling, on the other. "That's a lot of books," Rocco said.

"And I haven't spent much time cataloging them. There could definitely be something in here." The optimism and hope in Harvey's voice was catching, to say nothing of his enthusiasm.

For the next ten minutes or so, Rocco stood next to him and scanned book spines, looking for anything that could possibly deliver some kind of recipe.

He was even willing to settle for any kind of record of food that had been served in the town.

But Harvey had something so much better for him than that.

"Aha! I think I've got exactly what you're looking for!" Harvey sounded excited as he pulled it from the shelf and Rocco looked over at the book in his hand.

It was old, at least twenty or thirty years old, and an amateur kind of production, spiral bound, with a generic font announcing it was the Christmas Falls charity cookbook from 1997.

The laminate on the corners was peeling, but when Rocco took it and started to flip through it, he could see recipe after recipe, and many of them had names associated with them that he recognized.

There were two recipes from a Mabel Clark, who must be Murphy's grandmother, who Marlene had told him was famous for her pies.

"This is perfect," Rocco said, holding the book like it was gold. "Is there a copy machine somewhere where I can make a few copies or scans?"

"I can do you one better." Harvey put a hand on his shoulder. "I think this cookbook should go home with you."

Rocco looked at him, shocked. "I couldn't possibly—"

"No," Harvey interrupted gently. "You should. At least for now. Take it home. Study it. Then when you're ready, bring it back. But really, no rush. Nobody was looking for this. Nobody even knew it was here."

"I'll take good care of it," Rocco promised.

Harvey smiled. "Of course you will."

"Are you sure you don't want to put it in . . .some kind of protective . . ."

Harvey shook his head. "It's history, sure, but it's *living* history, Rocco. And I know you won't be careless."

"I haven't been here long enough for you to know that." But Rocco was smiling, too, Harvey's trust a balm for the remainder of the hurt he'd felt after Taylor had kissed him.

"You've been here long enough to know the town gossip mill is robust enough to tell us everything we need to know," Harvey said, winking. "Pumpkin spice notwithstanding."

"Well, that's really nice of you," Rocco said. "And if anyone asks, it *is* back."

"I'll make sure to tell anyone who asks," Harvey said with a firm nod. "Anything else I can help you with?"

"Nope," Rocco said. He couldn't deny it; he was excited to be able to look through the cookbook and see if there was anything he could use.

"Awesome. If you need anything else, don't hesitate to swing by," Harvey said.

"I definitely won't," Rocco said.

A few minutes later, he was walking back to Jolly Java, the cookbook burning in his hands. He stepped inside the coffee shop, made sure that Rebecca didn't need any help, grabbed a coffee and his notebook and then settled at a table in the corner.

He was about two thirds of the way through the book, deep into the dessert section, making notes and jotting down ideas and page numbers, when he saw it.

Rocco froze.

It could be a coincidence but he knew, deep down, that it wasn't.

The almond cookie recipe by Teresa Hall had to be from Taylor's mom, and these had to be the same cookies he'd talked about her baking. The cookies that had given him that sweet-pained look deep in his eyes when he'd tasted Rocco's marzipan latte.

Rocco looked up. Knowing what he should do, even though he wasn't sure he wanted to get his ass kicked again by the universe.

"If you really think so," he told it. "But I'm not so sure."

That was a lie though. He *was* sure. He wouldn't have been so fucking disappointed by the aftermath of their kiss if he wasn't sure. If he wasn't convinced, deep down, in a place he couldn't deny even if he wanted to, that Taylor was someone special.

That he wanted Taylor to be someone special *to him*.

"You talking to yourself out there?" Rebecca asked.

"Sort of," Rocco said wryly. "To the universe. To fate. Maybe even to Taylor."

Rebecca approached his table and made a face. "Are you finally gonna talk to him?"

He'd not been able to hide his post-kiss bad mood from her, so he'd admitted they'd had a little hiccup and he was giving himself some space from the guy.

She'd been supportive but also said that she thought she'd never seen him happier than when he was with Taylor.

And that was the kicker, wasn't it?

It was true.

"Yeah," Rocco said and picked up one of the schedule flyers he'd shoved into his notebook, noting next weekend's events, then pulled his phone from his pocket.

Up for some Carol-oke this weekend? he texted Taylor.

He didn't say anything about the kiss. What else was there to say about it, other than he desperately wanted to do it again? And this time have it mean something?

Maybe Taylor didn't agree, but how could he if Rocco didn't convince him to change his mind?

I am, Taylor texted back almost immediately. **I was thinking about you.**

And that, Rocco decided, was the universe telling him he'd made the right call.

CHAPTER 10

It had been a week, exactly, since Taylor had gazed at him like he held all the secrets of the universe, kissed him, and then confessed, *again*, that he didn't want a (real) boyfriend.

But this time, after a week of space and the universe giving him the nudge he needed, Rocco knew that Taylor was wrong *and* that he was going to prove it to him.

He walked in the door at Frosty's and immediately spotted Taylor, holding down the fort at one of the few booths.

"Hey," Taylor said, rising and Rocco had to swallow all his worries, because *damn*, after a week of only *thinking* about Taylor and not having a front row seat to all his deliciousness,

Rocco had forgotten how bright and hot the attraction flared between them.

It was flaring now, wild and undeniable, and Rocco swore Taylor felt it too as they hugged.

Rocco had intended to keep the hug short and sweet, but Taylor lingered, his hands tucking under Rocco's jacket and pressing warm and firm into his sweater.

Rocco swore he could feel every bit of that touch even through two layers of fabric.

How would it have felt if he hadn't been wearing a stitch? *Ugh. Focus. Goat goddamn cheese.*

Finally, he let go, but didn't drift away or sit back down. "I've been having to fight half the bar off. Everyone wants this booth, but I wasn't going to let anyone else take it."

Rocco smiled, pleased. "Yeah?"

Maybe he'd forgotten the visceral impact of Taylor, but he hadn't forgotten how kind and thoughtful he could be. How much he'd tried to do the right thing by his (fake) boyfriend, at least all the way up til he'd given Rocco a very real kiss.

And really, if he hadn't immediately regretted it, then everything would have been different. They'd have been inseparable, in bed and out, this last week.

That could still happen, Rocco promised himself.

"Maybe after a week off, I want to get as close to you as possible," Taylor said, his voice low and a little rough around the edges. Like he didn't want anyone else to hear it. Like it was a confession.

Rocco took a deep breath. He'd been the one to tell Taylor it was still on. He was the one who'd invited Taylor tonight.

It was just hard when it looked and sounded and *felt* like Taylor really meant it.

And maybe he does.

Well, they were going to find out.

"I'm not gonna complain about that," Rocco said softly, gazing up at him.

Taylor looked like he wanted to hug him again.

Or maybe more.

"Uh, okay, yeah," Taylor stammered. "Let's . . .uh . . .you want a drink? Do you want to see the song list?"

"Here I thought we were just coming out to remind everyone of our epic love, have a few drinks, and listen to the town humiliate themselves by singing Christmas songs badly?" Rocco teased.

"I . . .we can do that," Taylor said with a grin. "We can *definitely* do that. What do you want? An espresso martini?"

"Sure," Rocco said.

Taylor leaned down. "Don't let anyone take our booth. I'll be right back."

Rocco sat down, slipped out of his coat, and looked around at the setup.

He'd only been in Frosty's a handful of times since moving to Christmas Falls, but the few times he'd grabbed a quick meal or drink, he'd never seen the small stage set up at one end of the long room with a large screen behind it. Or the queue of festively dressed people waiting in line to sign up to sing their favorite holiday song.

"Young man, are you going to get up there or just sit there and listen to the rest of the town make fools of themselves?"

Rocco glanced over and Mrs. Lil was standing there, grinning at him.

"Uh," he hesitated. "I'm not much of a singer, to be honest."

"I vote for we listen to them make fools of themselves," she said.

Rocco chuckled as she sat down. He wasn't that disappointed. After waltzing in in her full glory two months ago and seeing pumpkin spice was not on his menu, he hadn't seen her grace Jolly Java since.

Mrs. Lil wasn't capable of a cold shoulder, but if she was, she'd have spent the last few weeks giving Rocco one.

But not now. Now, she was sitting across from him expectantly, her gaze roving over him with that appraising stare.

"That sounds like a great plan," Rocco said.

"Well, it's a plan of *some* kind," she said wryly. She leaned forward. "Now, Rocco Moretti, I hear you're seeing sense."

"Of some kind," Rocco said with a laugh.

She looked surprised, and he had a feeling not much surprised her. "Oh, I like you," she said.

"I like him too. Good evening, Mrs. Lil." Taylor slid in next to him, all graceful movements, setting a full martini glass in front of him and a beer bottle in front of himself.

Drinks delivered, he slung an arm around Rocco and tucked him in close.

"Oh, are you two here . . .oh, you *are*." She smiled. "You're on a date."

"Guilty as charged," Rocco said. "But you're welcome to stay."

"And be a third wheel?" Mrs. Lil shook her head and continued tartly, "I hardly think so. But thank you for the invitation. And Rocco? Expect to see me next week."

Rocco nodded as she slid out of the booth and headed over, ending up at the one two down with Griff and Logan.

"I guess she doesn't mind crashing *their* date," Taylor said mischievously.

"Guess we're cuter than them," Rocco said.

Taylor's gaze slid to him. Eyed him up and down. "Yeah, we are," he said. His fingertips skimmed over Rocco's shoulder and settled on it, his touch light.

"I . . ." What Rocco was going to say died in his throat. He swallowed hard. Taylor's eyes were so intent on him, his look so intense, it was like he could see right into Rocco. Could see all the parts where Rocco wanted this to be real.

"I should say I'm sorry," Taylor said.

"For?" But Rocco had a feeling he knew.

Taylor winced. "Pushing you. Pushing *us*. Then freaking out like that. That was . . .I shouldn't have done that."

Rocco wanted to melt like candle wax, but he stayed strong. If he got this wrong . . .well, that didn't bear thinking of. "To be clear, are you apologizing for kissing me?"

Taylor shook his head. "No, no way. For freaking out after. I . . .that was not my best moment."

"I don't think it was for either of us." Rocco could at least admit that.

"I'm glad we got that out of the way," Taylor said, and his grin was bright. "Now we can really enjoy listening to these people butchering Mariah Carey."

"They wouldn't," Rocco objected.

Taylor shot him a look. "Oh, there's a reason I told them to make your drink strong."

"Ouch. That bad?"

Something pulled Taylor's gaze from Rocco and then he made a face. "Worse, even." He pointed to the doorway. And sure enough there were Steve Mills and Mrs. Gucci Boots.

"Ugh, why?" Rocco questioned.

"Bad luck, I suppose," Taylor said.

Rocco nearly suggested they leave now. Find something else to do—*a bed*, his mind supplied, *and both of us in it, naked*—but before he could, Taylor turned to him and said, "I'm not letting them chase us out, okay?"

It was a good reminder that the lines between him and Taylor might've gotten blurred, but half the reason they'd started this relationship in the first place was to get Taylor the job he wanted.

"You got it," Rocco said, taking a sip of his martini. "What other artists should I expect to be butchered tonight?"

"Oh, expect at least two off-key renditions of 'Little Saint Nick' by the Beach Boys and at least a few Brenda Lee and Jackson 5 copycats."

"Sounds great," Rocco said weakly. He liked Christmas music, but he liked it done *well*. Why had he suggested this? Well, truthfully, he'd just picked an event from the list. It hadn't mattered to him what they were doing as long as he could see Taylor again.

The mayor stepped on stage to a loud cheer. "Good evening," she said into the microphone. "I hope you're all excited to hear our town's vocal stylings." There were additional cheers and a few boos.

"Now, now, none of that," she said with a grin. "We're here to have fun. Our first caroler tonight is . . ." She paused, looking at the paper in her hand. "Is this right?" she asked the man running the karaoke machine, pulling the microphone away so the whole room couldn't hear her. But it wasn't a very big room and after so long in office her voice just naturally carried. "This can't be right."

"It's right. I'm definitely up first." Steve Mills' wife flounced onto the stage. That was the only way Rocco could describe it. She was dressed in a short, tight red velvet dress and sure enough, those same Gucci boots.

They were hot boots; Rocco could give her that at least.

But the mayor just stared at her incredulously, finally handing the microphone over as her song began to play.

It was, as Taylor had foretold, Mariah Carey's seminal holiday hit, "All I Want For Christmas is You."

It was not a song for an amateur, and unfortunately, from the first wobbly notes, it seemed Laura Mills was not of Mariah Carey's caliber.

In fact, as the chorus hit, it got worse, and Taylor winced, taking a long drink of his beer. Rocco heard a few boos begin in the audience.

"Is this normal?" he asked Taylor, who shook his head.

"No. It's not. Mona usually stops it if it gets too heated, or too mean, but she doesn't look like she's stopping it now."

No, it didn't. In fact, the mayor's lips were set in a grim line, and she'd made no move to stop the song, or Laura Mills' increasingly deranged and off-key wailing.

But apparently if the mayor wasn't going to stop her, someone else would.

Rocco's jaw fell open as Steve hopped onto the stage, a forced smile on his face, and tried to wrangle the microphone away. "Come on, honey, you told me you had this," he hissed, loud enough and unfortunately for him, directly into the microphone. "You gotta stop. You're making us all look bad."

She vamped harder and then, pulling the microphone back, sang loudly, "All I want for Christmas is Heeeeaaaaaath."

Rocco found Heath Kelly in the back of the room, and he was visibly wincing.

Either at how terribly Mariah Carey was being emulated or at Laura's insistent attempts to interest him when he was clearly *not* interested in her. It was hard to say. Rocco was going to vote *both*.

"Come on, you're making a fool of yourself." Steve tried to grab the microphone again, and his voice had gotten hard. Unrelenting. Nothing like the smooth, charming facade he normally wore.

"Oh shit," Taylor murmured. "I should—"

"Yes," Rocco said. "Go up there. *Now.*"

The mayor also had the same idea, because she was climbing back on the stage, watching with trepidation as Steve tried to wrestle the microphone out of his wife's hands.

She segued into an off-key, off-melody version of Carly Simon's, "You're So Vain," which was a transition that Rocco hadn't seen coming, but one he could at least get behind.

"Mrs. Mills," the mayor said loudly, "it's time to stop. You shouldn't even be up yet. The signup is first come, first serve, and you *just* showed up." She glared at the guy running the karaoke machine, and sure enough, he looked guilty.

Had Steve slipped him some money to make sure his wife went first? Or had she done that?

It was hard to say, but the whole thing was playing out publicly, and in a town like Christmas Falls, where the gossip mill was incredibly active, the retellings of this evening were going to spread like wildfire.

Rocco watched as Taylor approached the stage. The mayor leaned down and whispered something in his ear. He nodded.

Finally, Steve successfully yanked the microphone from his wife and said into it, apparently unaware of how microphones worked, "Goddamn it, you made us look bad."

She crossed her arms over her chest. "You do that well enough on your own."

"I was doing just fine without your 'assistance,'" he retorted.

"Let me give you *both* some assistance," Taylor said, intervening by stepping between them and neatly plucking the microphone from Steve's hand. "You're both done. Time to get off the stage."

Steve made a face, turning him ugly, and he lunged for the microphone, but Taylor just stared at him. Not engaging, but clearly not permitting him to continue. It was a perfect line to walk, and there were a few cheers from the audience.

"Time to go," Mona repeated firmly.

"We should get *all the turns* if we want them," Steve retorted. "We're practically Christmas Falls royalty!"

Mona shot him a venomous stare. "There *is* no such thing as Christmas Falls royalty. That's what you don't get, Steve. That's not what this town is. It's not what it's ever been. We don't stand for that kind of superior attitude here, even if your family's lived here forever."

Taylor looked between the mayor and Steve. "Ma'am," he said, so polite, so perfectly Midwestern that Rocco wanted to cry with it, "should I take out the trash?"

Mona chuckled. "Yes, please. Let's go."

Wrapping a hand around Steve's arm, Taylor tugged him off the stage, as Mona escorted Laura off.

"And uh, now up," the karaoke guy said, stammering, his voice nearly drowned out by the cat calls and the applause, "is Mrs. Lil singing 'Rocking Around the Christmas Tree.'"

Mrs. Lil took the stage to an absolute *roar* of approval, and a moment later, Taylor slid back into the booth next to Rocco, wearing a shit-eating grin and a lightness around him that Rocco loved to see.

"Well," Taylor said, "I guess that's that."

Rocco reached over and gave his arm a squeeze. "You were brilliant, baby."

"Was I?"

"You know you were. You just let him have enough rope to hang himself. And Mrs. Gucci Boots, too."

"I guess we did," Taylor said, but his smile said it all. By tomorrow, this story would be on everyone's lips and Rocco would be surprised if the council even considered Steve Mills' application, once the truth of his feelings came out.

"She's actually pretty good," Rocco said a moment later, listening to Mrs. Lil in the background. "And here I thought she wasn't going to actually participate. She told me we were going to listen as everyone made fools of themselves."

"She always sings this and only this," Taylor said. "And Mrs. Lil is incapable of making a fool of herself."

Rocco smiled, nodding. He understood it now. She hadn't included herself in that assessment because she knew she had the pipes to sing this song.

Taylor lifted his beer and tapped it against Rocco's glass. "Cheers to a great evening in Christmas Falls," he said.

Unlike last Saturday's run-in with Steve Mills and his wife, *this* Saturday night, Taylor was in a great mood by the time they exited Frosty's.

He'd been flirty and charming all evening, touching Rocco as much as he could, and Rocco hoped, even though he knew the danger in it, that maybe *this* Saturday night, things might end differently.

Maybe Taylor would kiss him again and this time not regret it.

Or maybe . . .as they walked out the front door of Frosty's, Rocco toyed with the idea of being the one to initiate, even though Taylor hadn't actually said a word about a redo.

But he had to be thinking it, didn't he? Because Rocco sure was.

It felt like he'd barely stopped thinking about it, during the last week.

"Well, uh, I guess I should walk you home," Taylor said.

"But I'm not tired," Rocco said flirtatiously, letting his body sway a little closer to Taylor's. And sure enough, his breath caught and his pupils dilated.

Yes, he definitely wanted Rocco.

The only question was, did he *want* to want him? Rocco didn't want to go through this again only to end up back in the same place.

His heart couldn't take it.

"Me either, honestly," Taylor said, shoving his hands into his pockets like doing that might keep him from reaching for Rocco.

"I think it's come time in our dating relationship for you to show me your house," Rocco said, giving Taylor *that* Moretti look, the one that always guaranteed they'd ensnare whoever was on the receiving end.

He didn't add *and your bed*, but he knew they were both thinking it.

Taylor looked appropriately blown away by it. "Uh, yeah? You think?"

"A good night calls for one last drink, don't you think?" Rocco asked persuasively.

Shooting him a questioning look, Taylor just nodded. "It's this way."

They walked down Dasher Street in silence. It was late and the only sound was the crunch of the snow underneath their boots.

Rocco was wondering if he'd overstepped his bounds when suddenly Taylor stopped in the middle of the sidewalk.

Just fucking stopped. Right there.

Rocco turned, suddenly worried that he *had* pushed him too hard. He hadn't meant to, really, he just wanted the guy so much it was hard to practice much restraint.

"Everything okay?" Rocco asked, worried at what Taylor's answer was going to be.

But Taylor didn't say anything, just lifted his cold fingers to Rocco's face and traced the lines of it, his touch soft but intent. "I can't do this," he said.

Rocco felt his heart crack. He swore he fucking *heard* it. He couldn't say anything. He never struggled with words but he had nothing to say. It was ironic how he'd thought last Saturday was bad enough, but this was so much worse.

But then Taylor kept going. "I can't keep pretending, I don't even *want* to keep pretending," he continued and before Rocco could respond, he shocked him by kissing him.

Taylor's mouth was firm and confident and *God*, so real. Rocco groaned and kissed him back just as fiercely, and they stumbled a bit as Rocco plastered his body against Taylor's. Wanting his warmth, but more like *needing* it.

Taylor pulled away but it wasn't like last time. It wasn't at all. He was happy, practically glowing with it, and he said, "You—"

But that was all Rocco let him get out of his mouth before he was kissing him again, needier this time, pouring everything he'd felt over the last week, over the last *few* weeks, into the kiss.

Taylor's hands reached under the hem of his coat and pressed into his sweater, as hungry and needy as Rocco felt.

"You," Taylor gasped again, pulling away.

Rocco was a little disappointed, but only in the *not* kissing. He wasn't even close to disappointed at Taylor's expression, which was a heady combination of awe and arousal.

"Me," Rocco said, pressing his body fully against Taylor and feeling *all* his arousal.

"I just…I don't know what to do with you," Taylor said, but he sounded like he felt the exact opposite.

His cock, hard and hot, pressing into Rocco's thigh, said the exact opposite.

"Yeah, you do," Rocco teased. He leaned in and brushed a gentle kiss against Taylor's mouth. "You want to take me home to your place, undress me, and stop fighting this thing between us."

Taylor looked surprised. In fact looked *poleaxed*.

"You can't be surprised that I want to get you naked," Rocco said. "Or that you want to get *me* naked."

"No," Taylor said, chuckling. "I'm shocked that you'd be willing to let me, after I was such an ass last week."

"It's 'cause you're cute," Rocco said playfully. *And hot. And sweet. And kind. And so charming it's a freaking miracle I didn't goat cheese out of this the first time you touched me.*

Taylor grinned. "Just cute?"

"Come on, *hot* stuff, take me home," Rocco said.

"I can do that," Taylor said. Leaned down and gave him one last searing kiss.

When they broke apart, breathless, Rocco couldn't help but say, "Please tell me your house is close."

"Really close," Taylor promised.

It turned out he was right; Taylor led them down Dasher Street, stopping at a quaint little blue bungalow trimmed in red and white lights.

"This is your house?" Rocco asked as Taylor unlocked the door.

"No, I'm gonna fuck you in a stranger's house," Taylor joked and then hesitated, the door shutting behind them. "But uh, we don't have to—"

"Shut up, just shut up," Rocco said and pressed him against the door, kissing him hard. For a second, it was easy to get lost in it. To want to start and never, ever stop.

"I . . . uh . . . take it you like that idea," Taylor said, and Rocco had to pull back from his lips because he was laughing too hard to stop easily.

"Do I *like* that idea?"

Taylor chuckled. "Clearly *I'm* a fan, since it was my suggestion. But we don't have to—"

Rocco pressed his fingers to Taylor's mouth. His breath stuttered when Taylor's lips slid down them, sucking on them insistently, tongue teasing their edges.

"Fuck," Rocco groaned. "Come on."

"Come on how?" Taylor teased, and then his expression grew more serious. "Honestly, we can do whatever you want. I'd be happy to just keep kissing you."

"Why don't we start here?" Rocco said and unzipped Taylor's coat. Then lifted up his sweater, his hands leaving goosebumps in their wake as they coasted down Taylor's chest and abs. "The real question is how does a guy who works behind a desk look like this?"

Taylor was breathing heavily now as Rocco's fingers slid lower, working at his belt. "Uh, well, it's been awhile for me. So I uh . . .spend a lot of time in my garage—uh, my *gym,* we'll say working off the excess energy. I have it set it up with a few things. Uh . . ."

Rocco patted himself on the back (metaphorically, of course) when Taylor's breathing got harder, and he trailed off right when he began to unbuckle the belt on his jeans.

He hadn't touched him yet. Not really. Not where Taylor really wanted to be touched. Rocco could feel the heat coming off his dick, clearly outlined in his jeans.

"I don't think you're gonna need that gym, anymore," Rocco teased and went to his knees, right there in Taylor's tiny foyer, taking his jeans with him, tucking his fingers under his navy blue boxer briefs and tugging them down, too.

And was very pleasantly surprised by the cock that bobbed out. It wasn't super thick, but it was long and flushed red, precome already wetting the head.

Rocco licked his lips and then leaned in, licking it, enjoying the way Taylor's breathing seemed to stop entirely.

"Oh, *oh.*" Taylor exhaled sharply. "You—you know what, nevermind. Nevermind what I was about to say. Everything I was about to say. Do whatever you want. Anything you want."

"Yeah?" Rocco asked casually, like he wasn't on his knees, *this close* to sucking Taylor's cock.

Like his own wasn't throbbing in his pants, as turned on by the thought of pulling Taylor to the edge as he was by the thought of Taylor doing the same to him.

"God, yes, please, though . . ." Taylor gasped as Rocco leaned in and licked again, this time a long stripe up the underside. Acquainting himself and just plain enjoying his taste. The weight of him against his tongue. "I'm definitely not going to last that long."

"Not worried about that," Rocco said. Glanced up. "Unless you've decided this is a one-off."

"It's not," Taylor said, and that was all the reassurance Rocco needed. He leaned in, slid Taylor's cock into his mouth, and sucked hard.

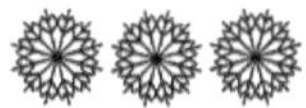

Taylor was pretty sure he was going to hyperventilate. Any moment now, the hot suction of Rocco's mouth was going to make him die in the best possible kind of way.

He'd tried not to think about his cock in relation to Rocco's mouth before tonight, but who was he kidding?

He'd thought about it. Extensively. Exhaustively.

And the reality dwarfed every imagined fantasy he'd had.

Taylor sank his fingers into Rocco's curls and tugged, Rocco groaning around his cock as he took him even deeper still. Pleasure was hot and thick in his system, short-circuiting anything but basic thought.

And his thoughts were pretty freaking basic: after this, he was going to take Rocco to his bedroom and fuck him so good he'd never stop coming back for more.

At the thought of sinking into something even tighter, even hotter, than Rocco's incredibly talented mouth, his balls drew up, ecstasy so fucking close, he could nearly taste it. But he held off, enjoying this moment so much that he never wanted it to end.

"Fuck," Taylor ground out, barely holding on to his self-control. Rocco slid a saliva-slick finger back, behind his balls, pressing right up against him as he swallowed him whole again.

"That's the idea," Rocco said roughly as he pulled back.

Taylor glanced down and nearly lost it then. Rocco's mouth, red and wet, his tongue flicking out to lick his head, curling around it confidently. Like he knew that would bring Taylor to *his* knees.

And sure enough, it only took one more long suck, before Taylor was moaning, sliding off the edge, his orgasm going on and on, unloading into Rocco's waiting mouth.

Taylor's head thumped against the wood door. "Oh my God," he said, Rocco licking him clean. "I think I just died and went to heaven."

"You want more?" Rocco asked, and that wasn't even a question.

He still felt drunk with the pleasure of that incredible orgasm, but Rocco wouldn't be desperate to come back if he didn't give as good as he'd gotten.

And *God*, he wanted to get his hands on this man.

He summoned his strength and lifted Rocco up and then up even farther, picking him right up and unsteadily taking them into the bedroom.

After he deposited Rocco on the edge of his bed, Rocco gazed up at him with reverence crossed with arousal, the look in those dark eyes mesmerizing.

"Shit," Rocco groaned. "That was hot."

"Good," Taylor said and then got down to business, which was taking Rocco's clothes off, unwrapping him the way he'd unwrap a present. Slowly, with anticipation growing inside him.

And Rocco was a fucking gift.

No question about that.

With each inch of skin he revealed, Taylor felt his own arousal—which shouldn't have been spiking again so soon, not after the blowjob of a century—grow.

But first, he'd make it so good for Rocco.

When Rocco was down to just his briefs, cupping his hard dick, and that chain around his neck, Taylor leaned in and his lips slid over it, tasting metal and something that was sweet and salty that he knew could only be Rocco.

Rocco's hands gripped his shoulders, shuddering under him. "Shit," he groaned. "I need you. I need you so fucking bad."

"You got me," Taylor promised and then slid his briefs down.

Rocco's cock was as gorgeous as the rest of him. Shorter than Taylor's, but thicker. Clothed, he was gorgeous. Naked, he was a work of art that Taylor couldn't wait to worship.

He reached out, gripping Rocco's upper thigh, feeling the muscles tremble with his touch, then slid his hand up and up farther still. Wrapped his hand around Rocco's gorgeous cock, Rocco shuddering underneath him.

Taylor gave his cock a gentle stroke and then another, loving how responsive Rocco was. Was so focused on every single one of his reactions that he nearly missed Rocco opening his legs. Luring him in further.

And Taylor wasn't stupid enough to resist that unspoken invitation.

"You want this?" he asked him. Afraid he'd say no. Afraid he'd say yes.

"Yes," Rocco hissed. "Come on."

Taylor scrambled for the lube in his dresser drawer, also pulling out the box of condoms he'd bought three weeks ago in a fit of optimism he hadn't been sure he understood at the time.

He understood it now and was fucking grateful for it.

Arousal burned in Rocco's dark eyes as he rubbed a lube-wet thumb around his hole, going as gently and carefully as he could. Rocco didn't urge him on further or faster this time, just tilted his head up and said softly, "Kiss me, okay?"

An easy directive Taylor could follow.

He kissed him deep just as his finger slid inside him, burning from just how insanely hot and tight Rocco was.

He didn't think he'd ever fingered anyone this slowly before, this intently, and the intensity of it was mind-blowing. How Rocco wrapped around his fingers, how his body pulled him in and didn't want to let go.

By the time he slid a third finger in next to his other two, he was flushed and as hard as he'd ever been in his life. And Rocco? Sweat dotted his forehead and he was straining, even as he lifted his mouth and his body up, for Taylor to take.

He gave him one last fierce kiss, loving the way Rocco clenched around his fingers before he pulled them out, hands shaking as he rolled the condom on.

"Keep kissing me," Rocco pleaded, and Taylor had never been asked to do anything easier in his whole goddamn life.

He tucked Rocco underneath him, tilted his hips up and kissed him as his cock snubbed up against Rocco's loosened hole.

Even through the layer of latex, the heat of him burned Taylor.

Taylor felt his limbs shake, lips trembling against Rocco's, as he slowly slipped inside.

He cradled Rocco's head with one of his hands, fingers slipping between his silky-soft curls, and finally slid home. Fought the urge to move with every ounce of his self-control. And yeah, he'd just come earlier, but it had been a *long* time since he'd done this—since Michael, and Taylor hadn't even thought he'd wanted to do this again, not until Rocco—and he was balancing on the knife's edge of just losing it entirely.

"You feel," Rocco panted against his mouth, "so freaking amazing."

Taylor tipped his forehead against Rocco's and thought, *I've never had sex like this. Not ever before.* "Not as good as you feel," he murmured.

"Come on," Rocco said encouragingly.

Taylor didn't need him to keep begging. He needed to give Rocco everything he craved.

One unsteady thrust turned into another, then another, and finally, he remembered how he used to be good at this. Used to make Michael shake apart with pleasure. But right now, he wasn't thinking of Michael—his brain and his heart and it felt like every freaking molecule in his whole body was full of someone else.

Rocco had somehow snuck his way in and he wasn't going to leave—and truthfully Taylor never wanted him to.

"Oh, God," Rocco cried out as Taylor built up in speed, aiming his thrusts at exactly the spot that was making him shake the most. "That's so fucking good."

The one positive of spending so much time burning off excess sexual energy with exercise was that he had the stamina to give Rocco exactly what he needed. Long, steady strokes just where he craved them.

"Do you need—"

But Taylor was interrupted by Rocco shoving a hand between them, giving his cock one single jerk, and he was crying out, coming between them and clenching around Taylor in a way that he'd be dreaming about for a real long time to come.

His orgasm hit too, and he rode it out, trying to be as careful of Rocco as he could as the waves of pleasure finally subsided, and he gently pulled out, collapsing next to him.

Rocco rolled over, and his eyes were glowing with happiness and remembered pleasure. He grinned. "Goat cheese," he said.

Taylor was still enjoying the tail end of his orgasm but his laughter chased it right away, and he couldn't even be sad about it.

"You jerk," he teased, smacking Rocco in the arm. But he knew neither of them meant it.

"If I'd known you were this good in bed," Rocco said with a happy sigh, laying an arm over Taylor's chest, clearly not disturbed by the mess, "I'd have seduced you ages ago."

"Oh, *you* seduced *me*, huh?"

"Didn't I?"

Taylor considered this. "We'll just say that by the time tonight rolled around, I was very willing—even *eager*—to be seduced."

"Fair," Rocco said.

They didn't talk about what this meant, but Taylor was pretty sure they didn't need to. At least not yet. Their fake relationship had been so natural, it seemed as easy as breathing to fall into something more real.

CHAPTER 11

On Sunday morning, Rocco reluctantly left Taylor's warm bed and left a note next to Taylor's unconscious form and slipped home, grabbing a quick shower before heading downstairs to get the morning's baking started.

He'd hated to leave Taylor but the sheer joy he felt overrode any disappointment and by the time Rebecca walked in at eight, he was still smiling so hard his cheeks hurt.

When he got a text an hour later—a selfie from Taylor, shirtless, his face adorably scrunched up with disappointment—his smile only grew.

"Aw," Rebecca said, pinching his flushed cheeks, "you're adorable. And in love."

Rocco didn't know if he wanted to be in love.

He and Taylor were so newly on this different path of *this might be something more than just a fake relationship we're playing at.* What would really dating look like?

If it's anything like last night, really fucking good, Rocco's subconscious supplied.

"It's a crush for sure," Rocco admitted.

A *strong* one.

He ignored Rebecca's knowing wink when Taylor popped in just after noon, a smile on *his* face that equaled or maybe even exceeded Rocco's, carrying a takeout bag from The Snowflake Shack.

Rocco made them a pair of marzipan lattes, and they shared sandwiches at the corner table, knees knocking together and feet brushing up against each other, before Rocco totally let Taylor lure him upstairs.

His mouth tasted like almond and *Taylor*, and Rocco didn't complain one bit as Taylor pushed him up against the door and then went to his knees.

On Monday, an enormous poinsettia arrangement arrived at the shop, just when Mrs. Lil was there, grabbing her favorite pumpkin spice latte, and she oohed and ahhhed over the flowers.

Rocco knew the news would be all over Christmas Falls by sunset and decided he didn't mind. They'd wanted everyone to know when their relationship was all fake, and now that it had morphed into something true, why wouldn't the same apply?

At four, when Taylor stopped by, ostensibly to grab a coffee, but really, Rocco was beginning to figure out, to take full, glorious advantage of the fact that he had a bed upstairs, he decided he should say something. Make sure Taylor knew what he was getting into.

Sure, Taylor had lived here for four years, but maybe he'd lost his mind, right alongside Rocco.

Lying on Taylor's naked chest, his fingertips sweeping up and down Rocco's bare back, he said, "The flowers were gorgeous. Thanks."

"You're welcome." Rocco could hear the smirk in Taylor's voice. "And here I thought you already thanked me."

The way Rocco had blown him this afternoon—slow and wet and deep—had had nothing to do with the flower delivery and they both knew that, but Rocco still smiled against Taylor's skin. "Mrs. Lil was here when they showed up."

"Ah, so the prodigal daughter returns," Taylor teased, but Rocco could hear the deep pleasure in his voice, and he knew it was all for him.

"Yep," Rocco said. He knew he should keep going and say, *so if you were wanting to keep this under wraps, it's not gonna happen. And by the way, what are we doing here?*

Rocco's heart thought it knew the answer, but his brain was working overtime, worrying that maybe he didn't.

But before he could figure out how to phrase the question less bluntly, Taylor's phone dinged, and he disentangled himself, rolling over with a groan.

"Shit, I gotta go," he mumbled.

Rocco stared at the ceiling, the bubble of happiness inside him too solid to burst, even if the questions peppering it threatened its integrity.

"Sorry," Taylor added, with a little bit of a wince as he slid out of bed. "I wanted to stay, but Mona wants to meet last-minute with Harvey about something."

"No worries." Rocco shifted his focus to where Taylor was pulling on his work clothes. "Watching you get re-dressed is *almost* as fun as undressing you."

Taylor flushed. "Maybe one of these days I can make it twenty-four hours before I *have* to have you again."

Rocco smiled. "Ditto. But it's alright. Rebecca only gives me a little bit of shit about holding down the fort during our 'community development meetings.'"

"Is that what you told her we're doing?" Taylor laughed as punctuation.

Rocco groaned a little, sliding out of bed and sorting through the clothes on the ground, looking for his briefs. "She knows the truth. I think the pretense is more for me than for her," Rocco said. "We're friends but not good enough friends for me to say, *by the way, I really need Taylor's dick. Like right fucking now.*"

Taylor straight up cackled as he finished buttoning his shirt. "I was pretty sure the flowers were a pretty obvious example of that."

Rocco had thought so too—but he'd also thought they were a statement that also said more, like *I was thinking about you and I hoped you were thinking about me, too.*

And maybe Taylor *had* meant that, but *ugh*, Rocco thought as he headed downstairs, lips still flushed from the last deep kiss Taylor had given him before he'd left, why hadn't he said so?

Nothing stopping you from asking. Rocco ignored this voice that sounded too much like his cousin Luca for comfort.

Because yes, that *was* true.

But Rocco was *so* goddamned happy. Every moment with Taylor pure perfection that he was increasingly worried about bursting that bubble.

On Wednesday, he took the afternoon, after Taylor had texted that he couldn't make it over—there'd been another emergency, this one about the upcoming holiday lights tour that required his intervention—to test the almond cookie recipe that Rocco was sure had been Teresa Hall's.

He wanted to surprise Taylor with them. A personal gift that he hoped might express how much he was feeling these days, maybe without actually saying the words.

Say the goddamn words, Moretti. This voice sounded suspiciously like Oliver's, and Rocco wanted to ignore it, like he'd ignored all the others, but it was becoming harder and harder.

Especially when Wednesday evening, as he was just coming back from Rudolph's after eating a chicken salad wrap for a quick dinner, Rocco saw Taylor leaning against the closed and locked door at Jolly Java.

"Wondered where you'd gotten to," Taylor said, greeting him with a warm arm wrapping around his middle, tugging him close enough to kiss.

Rocco tilted his head back and pressed his lips to Taylor's. Taylor didn't hesitate, just leaned right into the kiss. It got intense fast, Taylor groaning in the back of his throat as his arm tightened around Rocco.

"You could've texted." Rocco was breathless when they finally broke apart, his fingers trembling as he pulled his keys from his pocket.

"I didn't mind waiting for you. Knew you'd be back sooner rather than later. And maybe," Taylor added with a grin that made Rocco's heartbeat accelerate even further, "I was hoping to surprise you."

"You accomplished your goal," Rocco admitted. He unlocked the door and Taylor followed him up the stairs. He'd considered grabbing a decaf cappuccino when it had been just him, but the almond cookies were cooling on the kitchen counters downstairs, and he still wanted to preserve *his* surprise.

Taylor nuzzled into his neck as he unlocked the door to his apartment, at the top of the stairs. "Missed you this afternoon," he murmured into Rocco's skin.

Rocco's heart skipped another beat, and he swore it tumbled right out of his chest and into Taylor's waiting hands.

Okay, maybe Rebecca wasn't wrong, after all.

Rocco had had crushes before. Rocco had been positive he'd been in love before, too, but it had sure never felt like this.

Like he'd *die* if he didn't get skin-to-skin with Taylor as soon as possible.

Taylor seemed to be on the same page, because he was already pushing Rocco's jacket off and tugging up his sweater.

"God," he groaned after they kissed again. "You smell so good. Like sugar. Like cookies. Like *fucking magic.*"

Taylor smelled like pine and fresh air. Like he'd spent all afternoon outside, doing the wrangling that he was so good at. And from how cold his nose and cheeks were, against his newly exposed warm skin, it seemed like he probably had.

Rocco pulled back. Trying to find the brakes, even though he didn't know if he actually *wanted* to slow down.

"So do you," he murmured, reaching up and cupping Taylor's cheek, slightly rough with the scruff that had grown in since the morning. "I missed you, too."

Taylor seemed to get that he wanted to slow things down and flopped down onto the couch, his jacket and shoes off, digging his socked toes into the rug.

Rocco settled down next to him. "Did you get the light tour all figured out?"

Taylor sighed. "Yeah. Mostly. It's like wrangling a whole bunch of naughty cats."

"Aren't all cats naughty?" Rocco wound his hands around Taylor's shoulders and his neck. Maybe he'd wanted to take a breath, but he also didn't want to stop touching Taylor either. His heart craved him, worse than any drug. Worse even than his highly developed caffeine addiction.

"I'm going to tell Meredith you said that," Taylor teased, leaning in again, cold nose brushing against Rocco's neck. "And you know, she likes you."

She hadn't been sure of him, at first. The first time he'd spent the night—the first night they'd slept together—she'd eyed him suspiciously. But then two days ago, he'd woken up with a mouthful of fur and a single disdainful eye as she'd given him a look like *how dare you jostle me from my chosen throne?*

"I like her, too. Her *and* her owner." It was the most Rocco could say without confessing everything, without letting himself word-vomit out, *Actually, it's so much worse than that. I think I'm in love with you. Please be in love with me, too.*

"Like you, too. I thought I'd go nuts this afternoon." Taylor's voice was hushed. Intimate. "Every time I leave, I think, I can go twelve hours without kissing you, and I can't. I'm—"

Maybe Rocco should've let him get the rest of the sentence out. Maybe Taylor would've said what he himself was struggling *not* to confess, but instead, he leaned in and kissed him, hard. Taylor's lips lush on his, his heart racing as their kiss deepened.

"I want you," Taylor murmured into his mouth as one kiss slid into the next, one after another in a never-ending chain. "Want you so bad."

Rocco, sliding into Taylor's lap, could feel just how much he did, his cock hard and throbbing in his slacks.

"I want you too," Rocco said, even though that was hardly a surprise.

"I just don't want you to think I'm only here for—" Taylor's voice broke into a gasp as Rocco's hands slid down, palm pressing against his erection. "For that. Don't get me wrong. I love that. But we can . . ."

Rocco applied more pressure, in a way that he knew Taylor liked, and Taylor's words devolved into groans.

"How about this," Rocco said, undoing Taylor's belt and then unzipping his pants, "we do this *first*, and then we can pretend to watch some TV while I'm thinking of how to lure you to my bed?"

"No luring necessary," Taylor said with a gasp as Rocco's hand closed around his bare cock. He gave an experimental twist of his fist and then let go, guiding his fingers into Taylor's mouth. He sucked them deep, eyes fluttering closed, cheeks hollowing out, and Rocco's heart gave another feeble gasp of complete surrender.

"God, that's so fucking hot," Taylor groaned as Rocco wrapped his now-wet fingers around Taylor's erection.

He stroked him tight and firm, the way he'd learned Taylor liked. He wanted to be overwhelmed. Then to be edged, until he couldn't take it anymore and begged to come.

"Honestly, everything you do is so fucking hot," Taylor continued, babbling now, in that loose, uncontrolled way that meant he was already reaching that place, the one where Rocco liked to lead him to and then pull back, *just enough*.

Rocco slid down off Taylor's lap and took Taylor's spit-slick cock into his mouth, tonguing at the head, gratified at how it twitched in his mouth. Then he slid it deep, sucking hard.

"God, yes, please," Taylor said with a long drawn out groan.

But that was always the cue to Rocco to pull back. He did, and Taylor groaned even louder. "I hate it when you do that," he complained, fingers deep in Rocco's hair now.

"No, you don't." Rocco teased the head with a few light licks. Keeping Taylor right there on the edge.

"No, I don't," Taylor agreed breathlessly. "Every time you do it, I want to bend you over the nearest flat surface and make you scream."

"Exactly why I do it," Rocco said and then sucked him deep again.

He repeated his actions a few more times, until only nonsense pleas were falling from Taylor's lips, his chest was flushed all the way up to his chin, and his fingers dug hard into his skull.

"You wanna come?" Rocco teased. He took one of his hands and pressed it against his own erection, feeling Taylor's desperation.

Taylor's only response was a broken moan.

Nevermind how hot Taylor thought *Rocco* was, he couldn't be even close to as hot as Taylor was like this.

Rocco gave him one last long suck, letting his dick slide even farther into his throat, and Taylor pulsed down it, his hands clamped hard around his head.

"Fuck," Taylor said as he finally stopped shuddering and his cock slipped out of Rocco's mouth. "That was so good, I think I almost died a little there at the end."

"Yeah?" Rocco had thought so too.

And as good as it was for Taylor, it was nearly as good for Rocco.

Just seeing him like this . . .well, he was more and more convinced he was in deep enough in this that he couldn't have gotten out even if he'd felt the inclination.

And he didn't. Not even close. Especially not after Taylor roused himself, never one to leave Rocco unsatisfied, and led him into the bedroom. Did exactly as he'd promised too.

Taylor sucked cock differently than Rocco did, but that didn't mean his technique left anything to be desired.

Especially not when his long, perfect fingers were buried two-deep inside him, hitting him in a spot where Rocco could only hang on for the ride.

When he came, it felt like it went on forever, pulse after pulse of come falling onto Taylor's tongue.

And Taylor thought *he* was hot, but could it be any hotter when Taylor tugged him into a hot kiss, sharing his own load with him?

After, they curled up on the couch, just as Rocco had suggested, the TV playing at a low volume, some holiday movie that Rocco didn't recognize, but probably the rest of the town had memorized.

"So, you wanna talk about what went wrong this afternoon?" Rocco asked. "Or are you allowed? Are you bound by town secrecy?

Taylor chuckled, his arm warm and firm around Rocco's shoulders. He dropped a kiss against Rocco's bare collarbone. "Just a homeowner who's unhappy at the specified order for the holiday light tour. They think their street should be first on the flyer, because it's, according to him, 'better decorated' than the one that *is* first."

"That sounds annoying."

"Hey, you gotta deal with the anti-goat cheese contingent, I gotta deal with the jerks who believe because they'd spent *all year* planning and collecting lights and putting them up, that they deserve more recognition than the other guy."

"I guess they take it pretty seriously." Rocco should know that by now, but every time he thought he understood the intensity Christmas Falls residents brought to the festival, he was surprised.

"You're beginning to get it," Taylor said with a chuckle. "Seriously is an understatement."

"But you got it all worked out?"

"Yep. I listened to them and then told them, very nicely, to take a seat." Even though his eyes were on the TV, Rocco thought he could *feel* Taylor smile in satisfaction of a job well done. Was that taking care of the residents? Or was that taking care of Rocco? Maybe it was both.

"You're good at that. Steve Mills wouldn't have done nearly as good of a job."

"Oh, did you hear? He's moving back to Indianapolis. Withdrew his application for city manager today." Now Rocco *could* feel Taylor's smile.

"Good," Rocco said.

"But I guess *Mrs.* Steve Mills will not be accompanying him," Taylor said.

"Uh, that's awkward."

"Guess she likes it here."

"Or she likes it away from him."

Taylor shrugged. "Maybe both? Anyway, I'm not worried about the job anymore. I think I'll be a shoo-in."

"As you deserve," Rocco said and yawned deeply.

"Come on, we'd better get you to bed," Taylor said.

Caught between sleep and consciousness, Rocco murmured, "Stay."

And the last thing he remembered was his head hitting the pillow, Taylor's body warm, cuddled against his own.

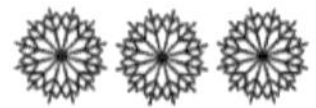

Thursday morning, Taylor dodged the walk of shame by heading out the back door of Jolly Java, detouring to the kitchen for a moment to give Rocco a quick kiss goodbye.

They'd spent every night together this week, without him even meaning to.

Liar. You totally meant to.

When he let himself into his house, Meredith gave him the stink eye from her perch on the sofa, and despite her prickly look, he went over and gave her a quick rub, apologizing without words for his absence last night.

Somehow, without attempting to, they'd spent about half their nights tucked up in Rocco's little apartment above the coffee shop, and half of them here.

They'd fallen into this routine without even discussing it, even though as Taylor fed Meredith and then headed to the shower, he knew they needed to.

But it was *so good*, he didn't want to.

What if he was imagining the look in Rocco's eyes just before he fell asleep? The one that proclaimed trust and affection and something deeper, too. Something that resonated inside Taylor too, a truth he kept shying away from. Not because he was afraid of it, but because it was too big, too bright, too hot for him to touch.

If it was just him, too? *Ugh*, Taylor didn't know what he'd do if that was true.

Make him fall in love with you, the way you've fallen for him.

Taylor braced a hand against the shower wall and wanted to ignore it, wanted to deny it, but there was that truth again.

It followed him all the way into work, through the morning staff meeting, and there was no question of it not following him to lunch, because he was meeting Griff, the festival organizer, and if there was anyone who'd been transformed by that bright light, it was him.

Before last year, Griff had been gruff and short-tempered, the festival always seemingly winding him tighter and tighter, but then he'd met his boyfriend, Logan, and he'd changed.

He was *still* Griff, but he was softer. Sweeter. Less prone to frustrated outbursts. Even given to smiling sometimes.

And though he'd always been gossip-averse, he'd even begun to indulge in Christmas Falls' second favorite thing.

"So, I hear you're spending a lot of time at the coffee shop these days," he said as the waiter at The Snowflake Shack finished taking their order.

"I thought we were here to talk about the cookie exchange," Taylor pointed out.

Griff laughed. "We can do that. But I know why you wanted to. And I don't know if I can swing it."

"Listen, he's *not* going to put goat cheese in the cookies," Taylor said, chuckling. "He promises."

Griff shot Taylor a knowing look. "I gave up lunch with my boyfriend for this, and we're going to talk about goat cheese?"

"Oh come on, you and Logan are inseparable," Taylor said. "Besides, you owe me a favor for defusing that ridiculous light tour issue."

"True." Griff leaned back in the booth. "So you wanna talk about it?"

"No."

Yes.

But Griff seemed to understand that he'd actually meant the opposite because he just sat there, waiting him out.

Taylor gave in, saying in a rush, "Okay, fine. I guess I didn't expect this to happen. I didn't *intend* for this happen. Rocco and me, it was just supposed to be a means to an end."

"And now you're wondering how you got in this deep?" Griff chuckled. "Yep, sounds about right."

"I don't know if he feels the same way. We barely know each other but . . ."

"But it feels like you've known each other forever?"

"Ugh, you get it," Taylor said.

So much for being afraid. He was all freaking in, now. Heart *and* soul.

"You need to talk about this," Griff said.

"I know, but . . ." Taylor grimaced. "I feel stupid and I'm worried. What if I'm wrong, what if it's just me? What if I've miscalculated this whole thing? I did that once before, and that really, *really* sucked. And as bad as that was, this would somehow be even worse." He'd have to see Rocco all the time in town, a constant reminder of what he'd wanted and had never really had.

"You gonna let some dickhead in your past impact your future?"

"You suck."

"I just tell it like it is," Griff said reasonably. "Now, tell me what you want."

"An invite for Rocco to be featured at the cookie exchange."

"He gonna want to murder you for giving him all this extra work at the last minute?"

Taylor considered this. But then thought about the way Rocco's face lit up every time the little jingle bells over the door at Jolly Java sounded. How much he craved a spot in this community. How dejected he'd been when he'd believed he was being pushed out. He remembered how upset Rocco had been when he hadn't managed to win the festival committee over and return to providing the cookies at the tree lighting.

"Honestly, I don't think there's much Rocco can't do," Taylor said, knowing it was true.

Griff smiled. "Spoken like a man in love."

And Taylor didn't think he was wrong.

After lunch, his afternoon was packed with meetings, but he managed to duck out of his office just before five, when he thought he might be able to catch Rocco before he headed out to the cocktail hour he'd said he was going to attend with Rebecca and a few of the other regulars he'd met at Jolly Java, including Emerson, the writer.

Sure enough, when Taylor peered into the windows, he could see the faint light emanating from the direction of the kitchen.

Pulling out his phone, he shot Rocco a quick text, asking if he had a minute to talk.

A few moments later, Rocco appeared at the front door, wiping his hands on a flour-dusted apron. "Hey, you," he said as he unlocked the door and ushered Taylor in.

His curls were rumpled, and there was a smear of flour on his cheek, and Taylor couldn't do anything else but lean in and kiss him. Sweet and hard, pouring all the passion he didn't know how to deal with, all that bright light that terrified and enchanted him, into the kiss.

"*Really*, hey, you," Rocco teased as he finally pulled back. "What's the special occasion? Thought you had meetings this afternoon." *Thought we were meeting up after the cocktail hour.* Rocco didn't say it, but Taylor didn't need to hear it for him to know it was true. But for the first time, he felt like maybe he *should* say it.

"I do, but I ducked out of one of them a bit early, 'cause I had some exciting news."

"Yeah?" Rocco's eyes sparkled.

"I got you an invite to the cookie exchange," Taylor said.

Rocco looked floored. "You mean, the cookie exchange that I've been trying to get invited to for weeks now? For a freaking *month*?"

"Yep, that one," Taylor said.

"Really? You got me in?" Rocco waited a second until Taylor nodded, and then he threw his arms around his neck, hugging him tightly.

But it wasn't tight enough for Taylor, who pulled him in even closer, until their bodies were pressed together.

"God, you're amazing," Rocco murmured into his neck.

Which really was ironic, because the amazing one was Rocco.

"I just asked—well, begged, really—Griff. And he owed me one, 'cause I handled that issue with the light tour." *And I think he took pity on me because he sees just how crazy about you I am.*

"Well, he's amazing. And *you're* amazing. Even more amazing. For thinking of me."

It would be so easy to just say, *I think about you all the time.* With Rocco gazing at him like this, his dark eyes full of affection and gratitude, it should be easy. After all, it probably wouldn't be news.

But he'd been afraid for years, and even though he didn't *want* to do what Griff said and let his past ruin his future, it was hard to get past that lump in his throat.

Then it didn't matter, because Rocco was kissing him fiercely, and if their kiss a minute ago had been passionate, this one topped it easily.

Taylor groaned into Rocco's mouth and they stumbled backwards, Taylor's hip hitting one of the stools in front of the big bay window.

Rocco's tongue stroked his, insistently, and a second later, he pulled back. "Do you have time to . . ."

Taylor's cock was pleading that *yes*, he had time, and he really kind of did, and it wasn't like they didn't want each other. They had barely been able to keep their hands off each other all week.

But he also wondered if this sex was about more than just wanting each other.

It killed Taylor, but he took a breath and then another. "Not right now," he said.

Rocco pouted. "But I wanted to give you a—"

That had been exactly what Taylor was afraid of. "Yeah, and believe me, I'm not ever going to turn you down, but that's not what this is. A . . .favor for a favor."

"It's not?" Rocco frowned.

Taylor's heart started beating a little faster. "No," he said firmly. He was still afraid, but he cared about Rocco enough that he couldn't let him believe that was true. They weren't just doing a favor for a favor. They were having sex, they were goddamn *together*, because they liked each other.

Because you love him. And you hope he might love you back, someday.

"Okay," Rocco said, smiling, and his eyes were full of that same feeling Taylor was full of, pressing against his breastbone. "I like the sound of that."

It wasn't everything Taylor should say, he knew that much, but it would be enough.

For now.

Chapter 12

Rocco was nervous.

Okay, if he was being honest, he was completely freaking terrified.

There was a lot riding on this afternoon.

His cookies were all packed—dozens of the almond cookies from Taylor's mom's recipe, and even a few dozen more gingerbread biscotti, which was something his own mom made every year, for the holidays at the restaurant.

In five minutes, Taylor would be here to pick him up for the cookie exchange, and before they left, Rocco was going to hand him a second box. Smaller, packed with just a dozen of the almond cookies, and wrapped up in festive paper, topped with a bow.

An early Christmas present.

A present that tells him exactly how much he means to you.

Rocco saw Taylor's tall form outside the door and he took a deep breath, standing and heading over to it, opening it for him.

"Hey," Taylor said, dropping a quick kiss against his lips. "You ready to go?"

"Yeah. But before we go, I have something for you." Rocco picked up the box, trying to ignore how his fingers were trembling.

"What's this?" Taylor asked, smiling down at him.

"Just something I thought you might like. Something I thought you might recognize," Rocco said as Taylor ripped open the paper.

Rocco's heart stuttered as Taylor lifted the top of the bakery box, gazing down at the cookies nestled so carefully there.

His face was totally blank and for an awful moment, Rocco wondered if he'd made a horrible miscalculation.

"These are . . ." Taylor's voice was deep and rough with emotion as he reached out, gently tracing the edge of one cookie with his fingers.

"Yeah." Rocco found his own voice wasn't too steady. "They're your mom's recipe. I hope I got it right."

When Taylor looked up at him, his eyes were wet. "You found her recipe."

Rocco squeezed his arm. "Yeah. I think so. You've got to try one to make sure, though."

"How'd you even do this?" Taylor had made no move to actually pick up a cookie and eat it, like he wanted to just stare at them forever. Like he couldn't quite believe they were real. That he could actually reach in the box, pluck one out, and take a bite.

"I went digging for some old recipes, something new-but-old that I could serve, but in the community cookbook Harvey over at the museum found, I discovered this recipe. It was contributed to the project by a Teresa Hall, and based on the name and the cookie I thought it might be hers."

"Yeah." Taylor's voice cracked. "They look just right. They *smell* just right."

"I think it's time to try one, make sure it tastes just right."

Taylor gazed at him. "I don't know if I remember what they tasted like. I thought I knew, but now, suddenly I'm not sure and what if I don't . . ."

Rocco reached down and took his hand into his own and squeezed it. "All that matters is if you like them. And honestly? If you don't? We'll fix the recipe. They're just cookies."

"I'm sorry." Taylor gave him a watery laugh. "I don't know why I'm so weird about this. I *am* so grateful. Honored and grateful. It's one of the best presents anyone's ever given me and I'm still being neurotic about it."

"Hey, you're allowed."

"I really do . . ." Taylor swallowed hard. Rocco could see his Adam's apple bobbing. Then he reached his other hand up to cup Rocco's cheek. "God, you're incredible."

Rocco knew he was staring at Taylor with his heart in his eyes and maybe he should say something now. Because they were dating, for real, now, clearly. But they had *just* started doing that. It was maybe too early to say, *by the way, I'm head over heels for you. Are you right there, too?*

"Alright," Taylor said, taking a deep breath. "I'm going to try one now."

He picked up a cookie and didn't hesitate—one of the things Rocco loved about him, once he committed, *he committed*—and bit into it.

Chewed. Swallowed.

Rocco thought he'd never been so anxious in his life. And over a cookie!

But then Taylor's face broke into a huge grin, a smile that enveloped his whole face. "God, I *do* remember what they tasted like, and these are exactly the same. Just . . .so perfect. The most perfect."

Rocco unclenched and let himself enjoy that smile. The way Taylor curled around him.

"Yeah?"

"Better than perfect. Is there something better than perfect?" The way Taylor was gazing at him now, Rocco wondered if that could be *him* Taylor was referring to. But before he could drum up the courage to ask, Rebecca popped her head in from the kitchen. "Oh, you two haven't left yet. Sorry."

"We're leaving right now," Taylor said. "We can't be late and let everyone miss out on these amazing cookies."

He squeezed Rocco's hand one more time, and then they were grabbing the boxes and heading out towards Dancing Sugar Plums.

They were quiet on the walk there, even though Rocco still hoped that maybe they could recapture the moment they'd had earlier. But it was good, too, to be able to walk like this, together, on their way to do something that Rocco had wanted to participate in so badly, that Taylor had made possible.

Couldn't that be enough?

It's going to be enough, Rocco told himself firmly.

When they entered the shop, it was set up with a dozen or so tables, little signs at each one identifying the participant, with a blank space underneath for description of their cookies.

In the middle was one big long table, piles of blank sugar cookies cut into holiday-themed shapes, and three bins of red, green, and white frosting bags. Dotted up and down the table were bowls of sprinkles.

"Let's get you set up," Taylor said, leading him by the hand towards his table.

And yes, he had his own table, with *his* name on it, a marker sitting next to his sign, so he could fill in the names of his cookies.

While Taylor set up his boxes of cookies, Rocco carefully wrote down his two cookie types, and underneath where his recipes had come from.

Teresa Hall and Beatrice Moretti.

When he finished, he set the sign at the front of the table and took a step back, gazing at it. Taylor joined him, wrapping an arm around his waist, tugging him in.

"That looks . . ." He trailed off.

Rocco knew what he wanted to say and he *said* it. "Right. It looks right."

"Yeah," Taylor agreed, giving him one last squeeze.

"What a beautiful display," Marlene said, approaching them. "And are these your *mom*'s cookies, Taylor? I remember these."

"I found them in an old cookbook Harvey at the museum helped me dig up," Rocco said and felt a warm thrill as Marlene smiled, nodding approvingly.

"What a beautiful gesture, Rocco," she said.

"Yes, very much so."

An older lady with curly white hair approached.

"Marjorie, good to see you here," Taylor said, disentangling from Rocco and reaching over to shake her hand. "Have you met Rocco Moretti, who bought Jolly Java this summer?"

Rocco greeted Marjorie, who he figured out Taylor had run into at another one of the festival events.

After she'd gone to a different table, Marlene turned to Taylor and Rocco. "Did you know she's all alone at Christmas?"

Taylor nodded. "I met her the other day and she told me, about her family, and how none of them live here. It's too bad."

"Even worse," Marlene said, "did you know her birthday's December 23rd?"

"Really? That feels appropriate for living here," Rocco said.

But Marlene shook her head. "I suppose, but I think it would be lonely too, and difficult because nobody worries about celebrating it. It's just Christmas, you know? And here, Christmas is *everything*."

"That's actually kind of sad," Taylor said quietly, his gaze following Marjorie as she greeted Mrs. Lil on the other side of the room.

"I agree," Marlene said. "Alright, I've got to make sure everyone else is situated. And *oh*, Heath just got here."

She ran off to get their grand marshal situated at the main decorating table, and Taylor turned to Rocco. "Are you thinking what I'm thinking?"

"What are you thinking?"

"I think we should do *something*," Rocco said. "But what? I'm not sure."

A few minutes later, Marlene came back, along with a shorter guy, with blond curly hair and wide blue eyes. "Rocco," she said, "have you met Milo Montgomery?"

Rocco shook his head as he extended a hand. "Nice to meet you, Milo."

"Rocco bought Jolly Java this summer," Marlene explained and then tilted her head towards Milo. "Milo's running Jingle Bites, the little chocolate shop in town."

"Oh, *oh*, I know where that is. I've passed by it a few times," Rocco said, remembering the cute storefront with its festooned holly and old-fashioned painted sign.

"And I keep meaning to stop by your coffee shop," Milo said with an apologetic shrug. "I've just been so busy this fall and winter."

"I know how that is," Rocco agreed.

"I was just telling Rocco and Taylor about Marjorie Wagner and how she's on her own here," Marlene said in a quiet voice.

"I've had a few customers mention her too," Milo said. "They were saying they wanted to do something for her, but they weren't sure what."

"Well, with her birthday falling on December 23rd, what would you guys think of me throwing her a surprise birthday party at Jolly Java?" Rocco asked.

"I love that idea," Taylor said, nodding enthusiastically.

"It's a great idea. Very Christmas Falls. Why I wanted to move back home, because people do things like that, even if they're practically strangers," Milo said.

"I'm discovering that," Rocco said. "We were planning on closing early anyway, so no reason I can't just hold it in the afternoon. The only issue . . ." He hesitated. "I'm not sure anyone's going to show up if I invite them."

"You've got so many more regulars coming back, though," Taylor reminded him.

"Hey, I didn't have an issue once pumpkin spice was back," Marlene said. "And you've made some other good changes."

"I heard you had a really delicious new drink. Some customers came in talking about it," Milo said.

"Oh, the marzipan latte. It *is* good," Taylor agreed.

"Thanks," Rocco said dryly. "But I know business isn't quite the same as it was under Holly and Joelle. I have all their records. But maybe they'll show up for Marjorie."

"I'm sure they will," Marlene said, patting him on the arm. "I'll talk about it and we'll see what we can do."

"Make sure it stays a secret though," Taylor reminded her. "And I'll take care of getting Marjorie there. I'll ask her to meet me for a coffee."

Marlene frowned. "But everyone knows you don't like coffee, Taylor."

"I don't think anyone's going to be confused why he's changed his mind," Milo joked.

Taylor looked over at Rocco and smiled. "You're probably right."

"I guess I should have made more cookies," Rocco said as they walked down Dasher Street, towards Taylor's house.

Before they'd left the cookie exchange, empty boxes in hand, Taylor had suggested ordering takeout and cuddling up in front of his wood-burning fireplace. Rocco had been reluctant at first—"I've got to be up early, to bake, and Rebecca starts late on Sundays" —but Taylor had volunteered to get up early and help him out.

Did he have to? No. But he found himself *wanting* to.

"Honestly, I don't care where we're staying, but I did think on this cold night, cuddling up by the fire with you would be nice."

"Yeah, that YouTube channel with the fireplace isn't quite the same," Rocco said. "Let's do it."

Rocco tipped his head towards Taylor's as they waited for a car to turn before crossing the street. Snowflakes dotted his dark hair and dusted his lashes. "I'll make you a marzipan latte to drink in the morning with your cookies."

"That sounds perfect," Taylor said, pressing a kiss to the side of his head. "If I didn't say it enough, I *love* them. I love that you baked them for me. And for the town. It's like my mom's back, with me."

"I'm glad. I worried you might think I was overstepping, or even worse, that it might make you sad."

Taylor unlocked the door and they headed inside, shedding their coats, scarves, and boots.

As he crossed to the fireplace and bent over, getting the wood arranged and lighting the fire starter, he considered Rocco's worry.

"Yes, and no," he said, giving Rocco a smile that made it clear which of these answers mattered more.

"I think I understand that," Rocco said and flopped down on the couch. "This fire thing was a good idea, I'm freezing."

"Give me one minute, and it'll be up and running—and until then, I'll keep you warm."

Rocco waggled his eyebrows. "You'd better," he said.

As he worked on the fire, he thought about the way he'd answered Rocco.

And yes, when he'd first seen the cookies, he'd missed her the way he always did, like a punch to the solar plexus. But like always, there was joy in that memory, too. It wasn't the first time he'd experienced a mingling of the two, but maybe for the first time, Taylor felt like the giddy happiness of having her back, even as a flavor on his tongue, overrode the bitter sadness.

And he'd be lying to himself if he claimed it didn't have anything to do with the man behind him.

Rocco made him feel lighter than he had in years, so much lighter than Michael had. And it was because, always in the back of his mind, he'd worried about the other shoe dropping with Michael, but now, with Rocco, he was beginning to trust in this connection they were forging.

The wood was finally catching and he leaned back on his haunches, poking one of the logs with one of the set of fire irons his dad had sent him two Christmases back.

But before he could stand and head over to the couch, to do his very welcome duty in keeping Rocco warm—which he assumed, probably correctly, was kissing him until they were both too hot to keep their clothes on any longer—he felt a touch against his back.

"Couldn't wait?" Taylor teased, leaning into Rocco as he wound an arm around his waist.

"I'm impatient," Rocco murmured, kissing his neck, and Taylor understood, because when it came to Rocco, he wasn't interested in waiting either. Only if it led to some very good delayed gratification.

"That feels . . ." Taylor let out a contented sigh as Rocco nibbled down the tendon, to the collarbone his shirt exposed, his fingertips digging into the cotton.

"Good, I hope."

"Everything with you is . . ." Taylor wanted to say more. Say, *I thought I'd been in love before, but it's never been like this. Every day I keep discovering new ways to fall in love with you.*

But before he could summon the courage, Rocco curled his body farther around Taylor's and kissed him.

It was so easy to keep going, to let his tongue brush against Rocco's and to press him down to the rug in front of the fireplace.

Rocco pulled back, chuckling, clear affection in his eyes. "Oh, so it's okay if *you* do it," he teased.

"What do you mean?" Taylor wasn't thinking very clearly—still too lost in the feel of Rocco's mouth moving against his, in the feel of Rocco's hard cock pressing into his thigh.

"You didn't let *me* thank you with sex the other day." Rocco grinned.

"How about this . . ." Taylor leaned in, trailing kisses down Rocco's neck. He arched into his touch. "We thank *each other*, for just how goddamn awesome this is."

"I like the sound of that."

"How about the sound of, I'm going to strip you down right here and enjoy every goddamn second of how gorgeous you look in the firelight before making you scream?"

It was gratifying how quickly Rocco's pupils dilated even further. His cock a hot line, even through his jeans.

"I . . .uh . . .*yes*. That. Please."

Taylor leaned over, kissing him fiercely before pulling back to strip him out of his sweater.

"God, you're so . . ." Taylor trailed off as he leaned back even farther, because the light from the fire danced across Rocco's olive skin like it was made for it, outlining every shadow and curve, every muscle as they flexed under Taylor's gaze.

"I could just eat you right up," Taylor confessed roughly.

"Then what are you waiting for?" Rocco asked.

Taylor didn't know. But the touching and the kissing was even impossibly better than the looking, a fact he could hardly deny as he bent down again, capturing Rocco's mouth with his own.

He tasted like sugar and spices, like the almond cookies he'd never forget the flavor of now.

Taylor tried to pour all his gratitude, all his love—because that's what it was, he knew that now—into the kiss. He didn't rush. Told himself firmly to take his time as Rocco groaned into his mouth, his hands roaming across Taylor's back, slipping up under his shirt so they'd be touching skin.

Only when he'd gotten his fill, for now, of Rocco's mouth did he venture lower, his lips nipping at his collarbone, and then lower, curling around one nipple and then the other. Then lower still, drifting down, every kiss he pressed to his skin a repetition of the feelings he hadn't found the courage to say out loud yet.

Rocco's abs tensed and then relaxed as he kissed down his stomach, tongue drifting in and out of every ridge of muscle.

"How are you so hot?" Taylor mused.

"A question—" Rocco gasped as his mouth found a particularly sensitive spot. "A question I ask myself all the time. Basically from the first day."

"Really?"

"I nearly dropped the cappuccino I was making when you walked in. Don't you remember that?"

Taylor might, but his brain was currently full of *Rocco-Rocco-Rocco* and it was hard to do any critical thinking.

"No, but it was definitely mutual. I think I walked around in a Rocco-inspired fog the next ten minutes," Taylor admitted.

Rocco laughed, the sound abruptly cut off when Taylor reached for his belt, palm brushing against his hard dick.

"God, *please*," Rocco begged.

Taylor decided that would never, ever get old. Especially when he glanced up and saw the plea mingled with the arousal and affection in his dark eyes.

"You want me to suck you off?" Taylor got rid of Rocco's jeans and pulled down his briefs, too, exposing his cock.

It was as hard as Taylor had ever seen it—flushed red and leaking at the tip.

He couldn't resist a little taste. Leaning forward, he gave it a lick and loved how Rocco babbled out how good it was.

They'd have to go into the bedroom if they did more—Taylor wasn't so desperate that he'd started hiding lube in the living room, but now that he thought about it, maybe that wasn't so much desperation as it was prudent preparation.

But before he could lean down and take more of Rocco's cock into his mouth, he reached down and pulled Taylor's shirt off, tugging it over his head.

"If you'd lie down, we could make something work for both of us." His voice was rough, a dark entreaty, leading Taylor deeper into an already bone-deep arousal.

"Yeah," Taylor agreed. Reached down and with trembling fingers shed his own jeans and boxer briefs. He'd barely finished undressing when Rocco was leaning up, pressing him down to the blanket with a hot palm to his chest.

"Stay there," Rocco ordered, his lips curving into a seductive smile. Like Taylor was going anywhere. Especially when Rocco perched above him like that, looking like a fucking masterpiece in this light.

Like *Taylor's* masterpiece, in this light.

Taylor's cock twitched, hard and needy, against his thigh, as Rocco settled on top of him, that perfect peach of an ass and his balls, tight up to his body, settling above Taylor's face.

Taylor groaned, unsure which was hotter. That view or the way Rocco's hot, lush mouth swallowed his cock whole.

He had to remind himself to give back as good as he got, but the good news was that he'd learned now what wound Rocco up, and what made him lose it.

His tongue swept over Rocco's balls, and back further, tracing his hole with it, before he pushed the spit-slick pad of his thumb against it.

Rocco choked a little, and *yeah*, that was what Taylor was looking for. For him to lose it, to lose himself.

He pressed his thumb in, even as he situated his head a little better so he could suck the head of Rocco's cock in, curling his tongue around the head.

But the pleasure Rocco was feeding him back was addicting, long, slow sucks of his cock, in the incredible suction of that mouth.

Taylor felt keyed up and ready to blow almost immediately, but it was too good to give in, too good to not enjoy every single dirty second of it.

He dragged it out, and he was sure that Rocco was too, slowing down, even as he clearly employed every trick he'd ever learned.

Taylor's thighs were trembling with the effort to hold himself back and not just give in to the incredible pressure of Rocco's mouth, even as he moved from one thumb to one finger, to two, pressing right against the spot he knew made his guy wild.

He *would* make Rocco come first. Make him come in the kind of orgasm he thought about, long after this night was over.

Maybe he wasn't balls-deep in Rocco right now, and he did want to be, desperately, but he could make it just as good.

Better, even.

Angling his head better, he took Rocco's cock deeper, as he pressed those fingers inside him, shifting them around just enough that Taylor could feel him clench back.

Rocco lifted his own head, groaning as he leaned his forehead against Taylor's thigh crease. "Fuck, fuck, *fuck*," he cried out, and Taylor braced and swallowed his load as he clenched down hard on his fingers.

He finished shaking, Taylor drawing his orgasm out as much as he could, but before he could ask Rocco if he was okay, he was sucking him deep again. So deep, Taylor cried out at the unbelievable pleasure of Rocco's throat fluttering around his cock.

Rocco coming had been hot enough, but this was too much—it pushed him right over the edge.

After swallowing around him, Rocco collapsed onto his body, and Taylor decided that wasn't a bad spot to lie for awhile—tucked between Rocco's incredible thighs.

"Give me a sec," Rocco mumbled, "and I'll turn around."

"If I suffocate," Taylor said quietly, "it'll be the best way in the world to die."

Rocco smacked him lightly on the side and then groaned, turning his body around until he lay back down, head pillowed on Taylor's chest.

"Fire's going," Taylor said a minute later, glancing over at it. "You warm enough?"

"I'm perfect," Rocco said, slurring a little, and *yeah,* he was.

CHAPTER 13

ROCCO WOKE TO HIS alarm blaring, and for a second, he didn't know where he was, disoriented in the dark, only the embers from a banked fire giving him enough light to see.

They were still on the couch, cuddled up together, even though it was barely large enough for one.

He and Taylor had landed back here after they'd shared a late dinner of delivery pizza, and they must have eventually fallen asleep here.

"Shit," Taylor groaned underneath him.

"I gotta get up and get to the coffee shop," Rocco reminded him. "Sorry, I'll try not to—"

But Taylor put a hand on his arm. Squeezing it firmly. "Remember," he slurred, voice soft with sleep, "I said I'd come with you. I don't want to let you out of my sight. Not yet."

Rocco's heart twinged. Maybe they hadn't said the words last night, but they'd been there, in every breath he'd taken. Surely it wouldn't feel like this if he was in love alone. Taylor *had* to be right there with him.

And then there was all that incredibly romantic stuff he said—like what he'd just said, without batting an eye—that made Rocco's heart practically melt right out of his chest.

"Alright, well, we gotta get going."

"Okay," Taylor said with a groan. "Let me get up, feed Meredith, and I'll throw some clothes on."

Rocco pulled on the jeans and sweater he'd worn last night, and a few minutes later, they were out the door, walking through the frosty cold dawn towards Jolly Java.

"I can't believe you do this all the time," Taylor said after Rocco had unlocked the door. But he didn't sound judgmental or incredulous, but awed.

Rocco flipped everything on but the open sign—lights, ovens, and most importantly, the espresso machine.

He was going to need a *lot* of coffee to make it through this day.

"It's not easy getting up so early, but after a few years doing it, I'm used to it now. Same way I got used to late nights when I worked for my parents."

Taylor yawned. "You're a wonder and a marvel, Moretti."

Rocco grinned at him. "That's what all the cute boys say."

"You gonna fix us some coffee and then show me some of your magic?" Taylor asked, and as Rocco passed by on the way to the espresso machine, now fully warmed up, he caught him around the waist and tugged him in, Rocco leaning in between his long legs.

"I thought I showed you plenty of magic last night," Rocco teased and leaned in for what he'd imagined in his head would be a quick kiss before he was on his way. But the moment their mouths met, he didn't want to move. He just wanted to sink into Taylor's warmth, into the feeling of his arms wrapped around him, so secure and safe, and *stay*.

You should really say something.

Rocco nibbled at Taylor's bottom lip and then swallowing his groan, pulled back.

"I . . .this is really good," he said.

Not that.

Taylor nodded, expression serious. "Really, really good," he agreed.

Stop talking in fucking circles.

"I . . ." *Just do it.* "I don't think I've ever been so happy with someone. Not . . .not like this."

Taylor nodded again. Still looking so freaking solemn. Maybe if he smiled, Rocco could find the little bit of additional courage he needed to say the three words echoing in his heart.

"I definitely wasn't looking for this, but I found it," Taylor said. And there it was, that smile. The one that made Rocco's heart plain fucking *sing* with joy. "Found *you*."

Rocco opened his mouth and before he could say, *Yes, yes, yes, me too. I love you, too,* a sound broke through his consciousness.

A loud sound. Like someone knocking—no, *pounding*—insistently on the door.

His front door.

Then they were yelling. *Crowing*, actually.

Rocco squeezed his eyes shut and hoped when he opened them he would not see the same glimpse he'd gotten right before closing them: a whole passel of Morettis, leaning against his front window, catcalling and pounding on the door, wanting to be let in for coffee and hugs and well . . .since they were Morettis, to hear all the hot gossip.

Namely: who Rocco had been making out with only a moment ago.

"What *is* that?" Taylor asked, mystified.

Rocco opened his eyes. Grimaced, even as he *was* happy. He hadn't expected to see his family for Christmas—any of them, in fact—but unless his eyes were deceiving him, a *lot* of them were right here, in Christmas Falls.

Unexpectedly.

"Please don't freak out, but I think . . ." Rocco took a deep breath and disentangled himself, though they'd already gotten an eyeful. "I think that's my whole family. Surprising me. For Christmas."

Taylor's eyes grew big. Huge, really.

"Your whole family?"

Rocco nodded. The pounding increased. He was fairly sure that was either Gabe or Ren, maybe even Enzo, whooping, now.

"Oh—"

But Rocco needed to get this out first. "They're a little bit loud and maybe a touch insane, but they honestly mean well. However, they're a lot to deal with, regardless, and if you want to escape out the back door before I let them in . . ."

Taylor's back straightened and he shot Rocco a look that meant business. Rocco liked to think of it as his "future mayor of Christmas Falls" look.

"As if I would *ever* be that cowardly. If I feel this way about you—" Taylor smiled knowingly, like he was acknowledging they'd just been on the cusp of confessing their feelings before they were interrupted. "Then I can meet your family. Then I *want* to meet your family, no matter how wild or crazy they might be."

"And that," Rocco said, the words falling out of his mouth without forethought or panic, "is exactly why I love you." He leaned in and kissed Taylor's cheek briefly, enjoying the pleased surprise on his face. "I know, but don't say it yet, okay? We'll talk, later, I hope."

"Yes," Taylor said, nodding firmly. "A lot. And more."

"Talking *and* more than talking are both good," Rocco said, babbling a little. Was he procrastinating letting the Morettis in? Oh, a little.

The thumping grew even louder.

"I think you'd better let them in before they break down the door," Taylor said. "I'll stay here. And when the initial cacophony has finished, you can introduce me."

"You're thinking they won't want to meet you the very first thing, and you're wrong. You're all they're going to want to talk about." A boyfriend that he hadn't told a single Moretti about. They were all going to be salivating.

"No," Taylor said, squeezing his hand. "They're here for you, Rocco."

They were. Rocco realized they'd all come. Dropped their own holiday plans to fly to Christmas Falls and see *him*.

His heart felt so warm, so full, he thought it might burst.

"Go on, then," Taylor said, squeezing his hand one last time.

Rocco went. Unlocked the door with trembling hands and then opened it a fraction, bracing it against his foot.

"Good morning, who are you?" he teased.

Gabe, who was in the front, stuck his tongue out. "Some surprise this was!" he exclaimed, elbowing their cousin and his business partner, Lorenzo, who held out his hands in welcome.

"Rocco! It's so good to see you. Also, it's *freezing*. Let us in!"

There was Luca, too, and Oliver, standing in the back of the group with Enzo and his boyfriend, Will. And his parents, smiling at him like he hadn't seen them in forever, and maybe it did feel that way, now that Rocco considered it. It had been a long six months since he'd seen them, right before he'd flown to Christmas Falls to finalize the purchase of Jolly Java. And Luca and Gabe's mom and dad, Nicoletta and Matteo, were rubbing their hands together, clearly cold in the chilly early morning.

"Come on, come in," Rocco said, widening the door.

And suddenly, he was caught up in a blast of cold air and a mob of excited, loving Morettis.

He lost track of how many tight hugs he was given—and gave back—and how many pairs of cold fingers were pressed to his cheeks and how many people exclaimed that he looked too skinny, that he needed some meat on his bones, did Rocco need them to bake him a lasagna? But mostly, everyone wanted to know 1) how he was doing and 2) who the really cute, tall guy behind the counter was.

"Uh, yes," Rocco said, gazing over the crowd of Morettis surrounding him to meet Taylor's amused gaze. "This is my boyfriend, Taylor. It's new so—"

Someone—it might have been Nicoletta, or maybe even Giana—let out an excited screech, but before the stampede towards Taylor could begin, Luca held up a hand and bellowed in that *I'm Italian and I will take no prisoners* voice. "Not everyone, not at once! Let Rocco introduce him to his parents, and the rest of us can go sit down. You'll get plenty of chance to talk to Rocco's boyfriend." Luca turned to Rocco. "Sorry, I told them they didn't need to *all* come, and so early, too, before you even opened, but I got out-voted."

Rocco shrugged. "Of course you did. But uh . . .thanks. And I *do* have some work I need to get done before we open. A few things that need baked—"

Oliver popped up next to his husband. "Did I hear my favorite word?" he asked mischievously.

Luca rolled his eyes. "You did. And it was naive of me to think we'd actually get a vacation coming here. You'll be in Rocco's kitchen the whole time and I'll be wrangling almost twenty Morettis."

"*Almost twenty*?" Rocco exclaimed.

"Everyone wanted to come and see you, darling," his mom said, greeting him again, with a big firm kiss against his cheek. "Now, introduce me and your father to your very cute boyfriend before he runs away."

"He's made of stronger stuff than that," Rocco said, even though he was a little afraid of how terrifying this might be for Taylor. Taylor who only had his dad . . .who apparently was not coming for Christmas. Or if he was, Taylor had certainly not said so.

But then, Rocco hadn't expected *his* parents—or a whole van-full of his relatives—for Christmas either.

"If he's dealing with you, yes," Luca said dryly. "I hope you don't mind, I think Dario and Gabe have just commandeered your espresso machine to keep this brood caffeinated."

Rocco just shrugged. He knew how much the Morettis loved their espresso.

"Let me know what I can help with," Oliver said. "Do you need me to—"

"*Yes*. A few batches of scones? I use your recipe, of course. And get the sweet dough mixed up for chai rolls?"

"Got it," Oliver said. "I'm sure I'll find everything well-organized."

Rocco threw his arms around him, hugging his friend tightly. "Thanks. Someone taught me well. I'll join you in a minute?"

Oliver grinned. "Maybe ten minutes."

Rocco winced and then nodded, taking his mom's hand and leading her over to where Taylor was still leaning up against the back counter. He didn't look apprehensive at all, only interested.

"Mom, Dad, this is Taylor. Taylor's the deputy mayor of Christmas Falls, and uh . . ." Rocco hesitated, but Taylor tilted his head, smiling, like he was very curious what Rocco was about to say. "And my boyfriend."

Taylor's smile made it clear that Rocco had said exactly what he'd hoped he might.

"It's so lovely to meet you, and a politician! Well." Beatrice looked thrilled. "I don't suppose you're Italian in the bargain."

Taylor grinned, extending his hand to shake, but Dante pulled him in for a hard hug, instead. Taylor just went with it, hugging Bea right after. "Sadly, no. I'm sorry."

"That's alright, Rocco has enough hot blood for both of you," Bea said.

"I think he's just perfect the way he is," Taylor said, wrapping an arm around Rocco's shoulders. He nudged him. "Do you need help with any of the baking? I'm not much of a cook, but I can follow directions."

"No, no, Oliver's already in there, probably revolutionizing the way I organize my spices. He'll help. And after this lot is caffeinated and fed, Luca will get them out."

"Alright. I can stay to help, if you want . . ."

"No, no," Rocco said. Pressed a quick kiss to his cheek. Ignored the *ooohing* and *ahhhhing* from the gathered Morettis. "You do what you need to do. We'll meet up later?"

"You sure you can?" Taylor eyed the group with a bit of trepidation.

"Yes," Rocco said firmly. "We've got a *lot* to talk about."

"And not talk about," Taylor teased.

"Well, I think Oliver's got you pretty well situated," Luca said from across the bar as Rocco finished up a latte and a cappuccino, placing them on the counter and calling the name on the ticket.

"More than well situated. The man's a genius. Also threw some ham and cheese hand pies in that sold out basically the minute he put the tray in the case. I'll be adding those to the regular menu."

"That's my husband for you," Luca said warmly. "But really, because you haven't been asked enough times already this morning, how *are* you doing?"

"Good," Rocco said firmly. "And surprised."

Luca grinned. "You really weren't expecting us to descend *en masse*? It's your first Christmas away from your family, and on top of that, we *did* miss you."

"I missed you guys too." He hadn't even realized how much until they were all here, so bright and vibrant in their inherent Moretti-ness. Talking over each other and hugging and laughing and teasing. Sharing a new recipe. Congratulating each other on another great year in the restaurant business.

They were a force. A wild, slightly insane force, but a force nonetheless, and he loved them.

"A lot of them are very excited about the festival events, so I'm sure we'll see you, but for the most part, we're not going to be in your hair twenty-four seven. I promise." Luca shot him a grin. "You're welcome."

"How did you manage that particular miracle?"

Oliver emerged from the kitchen doors, wiping his hands on a paper towel. "When he heard the plan to descend on you for Christmas, Luca found the festival flyer and emailed it to everyone. Told them to pick four events they couldn't miss."

Oliver kissed his husband. "Would you believe me if I told you there's a color-coded spreadsheet?"

"Yes," Rocco said. Because that sounded exactly like Luca. "So what's on the docket this afternoon?"

"I think most of us are heading to the brew and cider fest this afternoon, so if you'd like to join us, you're free to. Or . . ." Luca waggled his eyebrows. "You can always spend time with your very attractive boyfriend instead."

Rocco remembered, a few years ago, when Luca had been incapable of jokes. Or smiling. Or generally human behavior.

Oliver had not only done wonders for Rocco's kitchen, but Luca's humor.

"I think maybe I can work out a bit of both."

"And then there's the *Santa Crawl* tonight," Oliver said with excitement. "I know my mom and Giana are wanting to come with us to that. Enzo and Will, too."

Luca groaned a little, but he was still smiling. He'd used to herd Morettis because he felt obligated too. Now Rocco thought he did it mostly because he loved them.

"Well, have fun with that. I'll already be tucked in bed," Rocco said.

"And not alone either, I'd guess," Ren said, sauntering over. "You guys staying or heading out? Seth and I wanted to get some breakfast at this Snowflake Shack."

"Are you taking anyone?" Luca said. "Remember the group chat. I don't want anyone getting left behind."

Ren gave Luca an ironic salute. "No, sir, yes, sir, we're taking Gabe and Sean. And uh . . .oh, Nicoletta too. And Matteo."

Luca rolled his eyes. "Don't lose them, okay?"

"Would I ever, sir?"

Luca smacked Ren in the arm, but he hadn't stopped grinning the whole time.

"You are a pain in my ass, Lorenzo," Luca said.

"And you love it," Ren retorted back teasingly.

Luca sighed. "God help me, I think I do. But you're going to be okay here?" He directed this question to Rocco.

"Golden. I'll text you later. Taylor and I will probably meet you at the brew and cider fest."

"Sounds good." Luca reached out and pulled him in, grasping him close. "It was good to see you, little cousin."

Taylor did *something* from eight to two, he didn't know what it was, but it had to be something.

When his watch finally read 1:55, he looked around and realized he'd scoured the kitchen and the bathroom until they shone, dusted and vacuumed, and done several loads of laundry which he'd actually folded and put away.

Meredith had given him several very grumpy looks, probably because for Taylor, Sundays were usually for relaxing on the couch, football on the TV, and maybe he might fit a few chores in, during halftime and between games. But in the fall and winter, Sundays were for *nothing*.

But this Sunday it felt like his whole life had changed.

Rocco had told him he loved him. He'd met Rocco's parents—well, not just his parents, what felt like his whole extended family. And like Rocco had said, they were a lot. Noisy, boisterous, but so full of kindness and love, like Rocco himself, he'd found himself very much enjoying them.

"Things are going to be changing around here," he told Meredith as he got dressed. She meowed back, clearly unamused and unmoved by this proclamation.

"Hey," he told her, "you got used to Rocco. You even like him now. You wouldn't sleep on him if you didn't. I know exactly how that works."

Meow.

"Well, you might want to make yourself scarce later, because we're definitely going to be searing your eyeballs with all this *I love you* sex we're going to be having tonight."

Meoooooow.

"Yeah, you're gonna have to deal with the imposition. Sorry."

Meredith shot him a look from her blue eyes that spoke volumes. *You're not very sorry, at all.*

And he wasn't.

At all.

After scooping out Meredith some kibble as an apology, he put on his coat and scarf and took off towards Jolly Java.

On Sundays, Rocco usually closed about two or two-thirty, depending on how busy they were, and it was maybe a little bit selfish, but Taylor was happy when he pulled the door open to find that the coffee shop was quiet. Rocco was leaning against the counter, next to the register, typing on his laptop.

He looked up and Taylor was struck again by the way Rocco looked at him.

The way he'd been looking at him for awhile now.

Now he knew that look was love.

His heart clenched.

And the words, which had felt so trapped before, wanted to burst right out of him.

"Hey," Rocco said. "I was just getting ready to—"

"I love you, too." Taylor hadn't been able to keep it in a minute longer. He'd had some pipe dream about waiting until they were alone, until he could try his best to make it as romantic a declaration as possible.

But maybe that didn't matter at all, because Rocco practically ran around the edge of the counter and just *jumped* into Taylor's arms. "I love you, so much," he murmured into Taylor's ear, and nothing had ever felt so right.

Then Rocco bit gently on his earlobe and murmured, "Rebecca offered to clean up and close today, because my family's in town. So we can go upstairs right now, if you want. I have to take a shower, but—"

"I'm happy to get you as dirty as possible before getting you clean again," Taylor finished.

Rocco beamed at him.

"I thought," he confessed as they walked up to Rocco's apartment, "that maybe they all might have scared you away. You know, with their Moretti-ness."

"Hardly," Taylor scoffed. "They're a bit noisy, yes, and excitable, but they all mean well. They're good people, your family. Not that I ever thought they could be otherwise."

"I can't believe they all just showed up, for Christmas," Rocco said, unlocking the door. "I knew I missed them, but I didn't even realize how much until they were all in my coffee shop."

"Of course you did," Taylor said.

Rocco shot him a look as they headed towards the bathroom. "Is that how you and your dad are?" he asked.

Taylor supposed he should have expected the question, especially with how close Rocco was with his own family.

"Sort of, I guess. I do see him. But he's always so busy during the holidays, on all these committees, that I don't want to push him to come out. I've got a family here, too. Trust me, I'm never alone on Christmas."

"No, you won't be," Rocco agreed. "Come on, let's get me all clean."

"Dirty first," Taylor insisted and lifted Rocco's T-shirt off, tossing it onto the bathroom floor and then tugging his jeans down next.

It felt so right to follow them down to the floor, pressing a palm against Rocco's bare chest, feeling his heart begin to beat faster, his cock hardening as Taylor leaned in and gave it an experimental lick.

Rocco's hands buried in his hair, and the look of pure bliss on his face as Taylor let his dick slide between his lips was all Taylor ever wanted to see.

"God, you're so good at that," Rocco groaned as he took him deeper, sucking him hard.

Taylor's own cock was a hard, pulsing line in his jeans and it was usually easy to push his own desire aside so he could make Rocco feel good, but he wanted him too badly, wanted to be so close to him he couldn't even remember where he left off and his man began.

He wanted to be buried so deeply inside him, giving them both everything they craved until there was no way they could mess this up.

"I'm good at other things too," Taylor murmured, sliding a spit-slick finger up, circling Rocco's hole. "I was thinking of bending you right over here, making you sob with it, but maybe instead . . .on the edge of the counter so I can see you. When your eyes go blurry with pleasure like that . . ."

"Yes, *God*, that, yes, yes, *yes*," Rocco chanted. Fumbled in a drawer in the vanity and pulled out a bottle of lube. "Come on. Get in me."

Even as desperate as he was, Taylor wasn't ever going to be careless. He took his time, pressing one long finger inside Rocco's heat and then another until Rocco was babbling and swearing, trying to fuck himself on his hand.

"You're gonna make me come," Rocco cried out. Like that was a bad thing. And it wasn't. Not even close. But Rocco couldn't come, not until he was inside him. Buried all the way inside.

"Condom?" Taylor asked, voice rough as he helped Rocco up onto the counter.

"I was tested about six months ago," Rocco said, the corner of his mouth tilting up.

"And you know, it's been forever for me. There . . ." Taylor tipped his forehead against Rocco's as his legs wound around his waist. "There was never anybody I wanted to take that risk for. But you? You're another story."

"A new page?" Rocco teased, his lips nipping at Taylor's mouth.

"A whole new book," Taylor said, exhaling hard as he slicked up his cock and then lined up.

Rocco gasped as he slid inside, and Taylor was pretty sure that very undignified groan echoing in his own head was from him.

"Kiss me," Rocco groaned and Taylor did, locking them together every way he could, tongue delving into his mouth, loving the sugar-spice flavor on his tongue and the way Rocco's body pulled him inside, the hot clench of him, but more than anything loving the *man*.

It was amazing and overwhelming and Taylor knew no matter how much he tried to make it last, he couldn't.

"God, yes, move *please*," Rocco pled, and Taylor did his best, thrusting hard, his knees buckling at the waves of pleasure cresting through him.

Reaching between them, he wrapped his fingers around Rocco's cock and tried to jerk him with the same rhythm, even though his own was highly compromised.

But that didn't seem to matter, because a minute later, Rocco was crying out, clenching around him, and he was following him right over the edge.

Taylor had never had a *lot* of sex, but the sex he *had* had, had never felt like this before.

Like he was being emptied out and filled up, all at the same time.

But he wasn't alone. Because Rocco's head slumped onto his shoulder and he murmured into his skin, "We need to do that a hundred more times. A thousand. It's never . . .*never* . . ."

"I know," Taylor agreed.

"A whole new book," Rocco mused. "That seems about right."

And even though he was on new footing, it felt fine—better than fine, it felt fucking incredible, in fact—because they were both there together.

CHAPTER 14

"I can't believe all these people came," Rocco said incredulously.

Maybe a little too incredulous, but Taylor loved him for it anyway.

After all, he knew well enough how free food and drink could get people in the door, even when they were set against something. Even in Christmas Falls.

Bright balloons in purples and pinks and greens were gathered in bunches in the corners of Jolly Java, and Rebecca had hung a hand-lettered sign in the same colors that read "Happy Birthday, Marjorie" over the main counter.

The birthday girl herself would be here any minute. She'd been thrilled when Taylor had stopped by her place and invited her for coffee. He hadn't let on that he knew it was her birthday, hoping to preserve the surprise.

"Well, at least a quarter of these people are your family," Taylor teased.

Rocco laughed. "True. But I had a number of people tell me they weren't invited by me or you or even *them*, but the Secret Santa? He sent invitations out."

"Do we even know if it's a *he*?" Taylor wondered.

"I don't think we know *anything*," Rocco said. "And you'd be in more of a position to know than me."

"If I know something, *you* know something," he said, nudging him.

Rocco had piled plates of cookies and scones on either side of the birthday cake he'd asked Joel McArthur to bake. Rebecca was manning the espresso machine, and they had a big bowl of punch, Nicoletta Moretti manning the drinks table, as well as two dispensers of hot chocolate and hot cider.

"She's coming!" someone hissed. It might have been Enzo, or maybe Joel.

The crowd switched their expectant gaze to the door.

A minute later, it opened, framing Marjorie, her hair in riotous gray curls in a halo around her head and a bright red scarf wrapped around her neck.

"Surprise!" the crowd exclaimed.

She looked floored and thrilled and a little overwhelmed.

"What is this?" she said, exhaling sharply.

Taylor and Rocco walked over to her, gently guiding her to the table of honor where Rebecca had decorated one of the chairs with brightly colored streamers. "We heard it was your birthday," Rocco said. "And we thought you might want to celebrate it properly."

"I . . .*yes*," she said, her eyes glimmering with tears. "How did you know?"

"A little bird told us. But you can thank the Secret Santa for making sure your party was so well-attended," Rocco said. "He sent out a bunch of invites, and everyone came."

"Probably wondering if *you're* the Secret Santa," Taylor said with a knowing grin.

Marjorie's smile was wide, even as a tear wound down her cheek. "Goodness, I wouldn't even know where to begin. But this is . . .this is special. Thank you two. I'm all atwitter."

"How about I get you some punch?" Rocco said. "And a piece of cake?"

"I made your favorite. Pumpkin spice with cream cheese frosting," Joel said. "But before I cut it, we'll have to sing. It's tradition."

Marjorie glowed. "I don't know," she demurred. "Aren't I a little old for a birthday song?"

"Never," Taylor said, reaching out and taking her hand, squeezing it.

It felt like the rafters of Jolly Java shook a little with the sound of the crowd singing Marjorie happy birthday, and if Rocco was being honest, his heart trembled, too.

Joel cut the cake, and after Rocco helped distribute it, Luca cornered him.

"This was a special thing to do," he observed quietly. "And a pretty special community to come together to do it with."

"You'd know, you're part of a pretty special community yourself," Rocco said as he picked up empty coffee cups and piled them in a bin.

Marjorie was holding court at her table, surrounded by Marlene, Mrs. Lil, and not surprisingly, Murphy Clark.

He'd brought her a present of her very own wooden gnome. And since Murphy's waiting list for his custom carved gnomes was about three years at this point, it was even more special.

"Indigo Bay *is* special," Luca agreed, referring to the small coastal Carolina town he and Oliver had settled in. "And your parents' restaurant in San Francisco is special. Nonna's, in Napa, is special. The food truck fleet Gabe and Ren have in LA is special. There's so many special places you could have found a place in, and for awhile, I thought you'd made a mistake, not picking one of those and carving out your own place in one of them."

Rocco knew his cousin had felt that way. Just as he'd known he'd *had* to make his own.

"I couldn't," Rocco said simply.

"I can see that now," Luca said approvingly, patting him on the shoulder. "This is the right place for you to be. Just know, we'll miss you terribly. We *do* miss you terribly."

"Which is why you all ended up here for nearly two weeks at Christmas," Rocco retorted lightly. "But I know, I miss you too. And still, I know with a family this size, I'll never be lonely."

"Never," Luca said, his smile knowing.

"Plus there's that guy over there," Rocco said, glancing over at where Taylor was talking to Joel. "He doesn't have the kind of family we do."

"He does now," Luca said firmly.

"He sure does," Rocco agreed.

Rocco had a feeling that just him would have been enough for Taylor, but then the Morettis were an extra bonus, too.

Along with one other surprise Rocco had up his sleeve, for Christmas Eve.

Christmas Eve

"It's called the Feast of the Seven Fishes," Rocco explained to Taylor as Rocco's aunts set the two long tables they'd created in Jolly Java with mismatched dishes and silverware. "Fish because traditionally Catholics were discouraged or even forbidden from eating meat on the eve of a feast day, like Christmas."

"You Morettis don't do things small, do you?" Taylor knew that was true. But it was another to see it in action. The many dishes that would be set out, full of delicious food, and the sheer number of seats at the table.

All the Morettis would be here, of course, but not surprisingly they had invited a few other members of the community to celebrate with them.

Rocco laughed and shook his head.

"No, we don't," he agreed. "Hey, I'd better go help Luca and the rest with getting dinner on. Are you okay out here?"

"I'll just help the aunties and your mom," Taylor said, gesturing to where Nicoletta Moretti, Luca and Gabe's mom, and Giana, Enzo's mom, and Rocco's mom, Bea, were setting the tables. "I'm sure they can find something for me to do."

"Just don't let them kidnap you forever. They might. They love you," Rocco said. Leaned in, brushed a kiss across Taylor's mouth. "And I love you, too."

Taylor took one last kiss, making it a good one, before he finally let Rocco go and reported for duty.

Nicoletta asked him to grab the wine from the walk-in, and he was on his way in when the Jolly Java door opened.

He nearly called out that they were currently closed, so sorry, when his words died in his throat.

Because they weren't some random Christmas Falls resident or even a tourist, unaware of what the coffee shop hours were.

It was a very familiar face, wearing an uncertain expression. Like he wasn't sure he'd be welcomed.

Taylor was lucky he didn't drop the wine.

Instead, he set it on the counter and rushed over to where his dad was hovering in the doorway.

"Dad!" he exclaimed. "You're here!"

Taylor didn't hesitate, just threw his arms around him. Not realizing, just like Rocco had said, only a week before, how much he hadn't realized he'd missed his family until they were right here in front of him.

"Taylor." His dad smelled the same as he always did, of peppermint and books. He'd been an adjunct professor of literature at the University of Chicago before retiring two years ago.

"I'm so glad you're here." Taylor realized, to his surprise, that his throat was actually tight with emotion.

"Really?" Walter looked surprised and that hit him harder than Taylor had imagined it would. "I wasn't sure . . .but your new guy sent me an email and said, maybe I'd want to join in with the family celebration. I guess he's from a big family?"

"A huge family," Taylor agreed. "And of course I'm thrilled you're here. I just thought . . .I thought you were busy. I didn't invite you, even when I wanted to, because I always thought you'd be too busy—"

"Too busy for you?" Walter asked the question a little sharply, and Taylor realized how stupid that had been. "Never too busy for you."

Taylor swallowed hard. "I think that was kind of dumb of me," he admitted. "I was . . ." He wasn't sure he could explain it.

Like he'd been encased in a thin coating of ice, since Teresa Hall had died. Like he'd been too afraid to put himself out there, too afraid to take chances, too afraid to even embrace the family he had left. He'd tried, once, with Michael, and that had only reinforced the bad assumptions he'd carried with him.

But Michael wasn't everyone, and he'd never been right for him. Taylor could see that now—but only because Rocco with his heat and his passion and his humor had melted all that ice right off him, when Taylor wasn't even paying attention.

"It's alright, son, we all deal with grief in different ways. I shut down too, after your mother died." Walter Hall's back straightened. "But that's done with now. I won't do it any longer."

"I won't, either," Taylor promised, and he was suddenly dragged into another big hug.

"Now," Walter said, when he finally let him go. "I want to meet this new man of yours. He seems pretty great, when I talked to him."

"He is." Taylor swallowed hard. "He's incredible. I love him. And I think you'll love him too."

"Best Christmas present I could have asked for, for you," Walter said with an approving nod. "You've been alone too long."

"Not anymore. Neither of us is alone anymore," Taylor said, reaching for his hand and squeezing it. "Come on, come meet my boyfriend and your *many* new relatives."

"Lead the way," his dad said, squeezing back.

The table was strewn with the remnants of the many, many dishes the combined culinary talents of the Moretti clan had produced.

"I'm so full I think I'm going to burst," Enzo said, leaning back in his chair. "Those mussels?" He kissed his fingers. "*Bellissimo.*"

"If you'd believe it," Luca teased from the other side of the table, "that recipe wasn't even from us. Will made those."

Enzo looked over at his boyfriend, who just flushed pink. Or maybe that was from all the wine they'd drunk with dinner.

It had been an incredible meal. Rocco wasn't sure in all his years of Christmas Eves there'd ever been a Feast of the Seven Fishes quite like this one.

It wasn't just the family and friends lining each side of the big long table, or the incredible variety and quality of the dishes they'd scattered up and down them—the mussels, of course; two huge branzinos that his dad had had flown in and Luca had stuffed with lemon and thyme and garlic; a delicate lobster and shrimp bisque that Joy and Giana had made, or even the enormous dish of stuffed calamari in tomato sauce that Gabe and Ren had made together, pureeing fresh tomatoes down and then simmering the sauce all day—it was the way they'd all come together to do it.

And, of course, it was the love in Taylor's eyes as Rocco looked over at him.

He'd been a little bit worried that his big Christmas surprise might not be well-received, but when Taylor had come up to him in the kitchen, tears and joy in his eyes and had introduced him to his father, it was clear that not only was he forgiven for interfering, Taylor was actually grateful that he had.

"Best meal I've had in as long as I can remember," Walter Hall said. "Son, you hooked up with the right family."

Taylor laughed. "I think so," he agreed.

"I think," Luca said loyally, "the bread was amazing."

Everyone laughed, because of course he did. Because Oliver had baked it.

Oliver elbowed him hard. "You're ridiculous."

Luca's smile was soft, affectionate. "You love it."

"I love *you*," Oliver retorted.

"You two are almost as sappy as the two brand-new love-birds," Enzo exclaimed.

"Oh, you no longer get that title, then?" Luca challenged.

Enzo spluttered. "Oh, we never gave it up," he said.

"Speaking of that," Taylor piped up, "did I ever tell you that Rocco suggested we fake date first, using you two as an example?"

Will laughed out loud. "No, he didn't! Oh my God, you *didn't*, Rocco!"

Rocco shrugged. "It was a good example. And okay, your whole fake relationship was never very effective."

"Or fake at all," Luca inserted.

"But it worked out," Rocco claimed. "Why shouldn't I want a little piece of that success for myself?"

"Oh, I think you got it," Enzo said.

Rocco met Taylor's gaze. "I think I did." He leaned in to kiss him and Taylor just grinned.

"Goat cheese," he murmured under his breath.

And nobody at the table knew why on earth Rocco laughed so hard he couldn't stay upright—or why Taylor joined him—but really, all that mattered was that *they* knew and they were happy and life was actually, surprisingly, very, very good.

EPILOGUE

It was another surprise party.

These were becoming kind of a Jolly Java trademark. Rocco had thrown five of them in the last four months, and during that time period he'd been gone for three weeks, in Indigo Bay, to help Luca and Oliver with their Sweethearts Festival. He and Joel were even discussing putting together a special menu and price list just for these parties.

But this surprise party wasn't for a birthday or an engagement or an anniversary.

It was something a lot more special. And a lot more intimate.

Rocco checked the candles he'd scattered across the empty room, in nooks and on tables, making sure they were all still lit. Walked over to the panel that controlled the lights and sound, turned the overheads down to only a faint glow, letting the candlelight flicker across the walls.

He'd picked out a slow, soft romantic playlist and it echoed through the room, making it even cozier.

Ten minutes ago, Joel had dropped off a little six-inch cake, with *Congrats, Taylor,* written across the top. Chocolate with chocolate ganache, his favorite.

Rocco had baked a batch of Taylor's mom's almond cookies, and there was also a plate of ham and cheese pastry swirls, just in case they went into sugar overload. Next to the pastries, he'd tucked a bottle of Taylor's favorite prosecco, a perfect reminder of their first date, into a makeshift ice bucket.

He checked his watch and everything was ready, with at least five minutes to spare.

His phone dinged and it was Mona, letting him know that the council meeting had just broken up and Taylor was heading in Rocco's direction.

That meant Rocco had ten minutes to obsess about whether this was the right move.

Of course it is.

Even if this meeting had been merely a formality, it was still a very big deal.

His phone dinged again. It was the mayor again.

And don't worry about Walter. I'm taking him to an early dinner at Rudolph's :)

Walter moving to Christmas Falls had been so good for Taylor. At first Walter stayed with Taylor, but the first time he'd walked out of his bedroom in the morning to find the mayor there, hair mussed and a bright smile on her face, with his dad, he'd suggested that maybe until Walter found a place of his own, he could stay in Rocco's apartment over the coffee shop.

Since Rocco was barely there anymore, it had been easy enough to move the rest of his belongings to Taylor's house and let Walter stay here.

There'd been a lot of changes in the last four months, but this might have been one of the biggest.

Still, Rocco found himself excited for the future and all the new challenges it would bring.

He texted Mona back. **We still don't want to know what you're doing after.** She sent a laughing emoji, and he'd just slipped his phone back into his pocket when the front door opened and Taylor strode in, the biggest grin on his face.

He practically ran over to Rocco and hugged him so tight.

"I got it! I can't believe I got it."

Rocco couldn't help *his* smile. "Of course you got it. You were the only qualified applicant. This meeting was barely a formality."

"I know, but I was still nervous. And they did grill me a bit, about some of my older projects and being new to the town—"

"You've lived here over four years," Rocco interrupted, frowning. How could anyone not see how much Taylor loved Christmas Falls? How much he *belonged* here?

"I know, I know, but they see that as a blip of time. But one of the council members—that old grumpy guy, you know the one, he actually spoke up and said that I'd been doing more forward-facing outreach lately, and he was glad to see it. That it had swayed him and I'd gotten his vote because of it."

"Mr. Richardson, who looks like he yells *get off my lawn* at every kid who walks by?"

Taylor laughed again. "Yeah," he said with a nod. "That's the guy. Of course he said something disparaging about my youth, but then Mona reminded them that young blood who care about this town is what'll keep it going, and they all seemed to agree with that."

Taylor let out a breath. Like he was diffusing all the pressure that had built inside him. And Rocco had felt it, these last two months. Even though they'd been admittedly incredibly happy, he knew Taylor had worried about this meeting. Had worried that somehow the worst might come to pass and they wouldn't vote to give him the city manager job.

But they had.

It was over.

And it was just beginning, too.

"Come on, let's celebrate." Rocco pulled him over to the table.

It was only then that Taylor seemed to look around and take in all the decorations and the cake and the pastries and the bottle of sparkling wine, chilling in its bucket of ice.

"You did all this . . .for *me*?" Taylor gazed at him with awe and love.

Rocco didn't think Taylor looking at him like that would ever get old. Like he was a magical miracle that he couldn't quite believe really existed. He'd worried that eventually that look would fade from Taylor's face. That they'd get used to each other, that the honeymoon period would end, but the truth was, Taylor gave him that look more now than he had when they'd first met.

"Of course I did. It's not every day my man gets a seriously awesome new promotion," Rocco said, lifting the prosecco from its bucket, wrapping a towel around the neck and ripping the foil off. Popping the cork, he asked, "Now, what should we toast to?"

Taylor helped him by picking up the two champagne flutes, holding them out for him to fill. "Oh, that's easy enough." He paused. Lifted the glass to his nose, enjoying the smell of the wine as Rocco set the bottle back into the ice. "Goat cheese."

Rocco nearly choked on his own saliva.

"*What*," he said, laughing. "I meant a *serious* toast, Taylor."

But Taylor's gaze *was* serious, his blue eyes intent on Rocco's face. "If you hadn't had the intrepid idea to make goat cheese and turmeric scones and remove pumpkin spice lattes from the menu here, you never would've gotten worried about your business and never would have suggested to me that we fake date to fix it." He paused, his smile turning intimate, his eyes full of adoration. "And we never would've ended up here. Me with my dream job and you with your dream business. And us, together, madly, completely, totally in love."

"You think goat cheese was responsible for all that?"

The corner of Taylor's mouth tilted up as he lifted his glass. "It's a lot to put on a dairy product, but I think it can handle it. What do you think?"

It was easy to answer. Rocco lifted his glass and tipped it against Taylor's. "I think I love you. To goat cheese!"

-

To read a sexy short about Taylor and Rocco flipping the script, click here.

-

To grab a copy of Teresa Hall's Almond Cookie recipe, click here.

-

Interested in the Morettis? These are all standalones, but don't miss a single entry about this entertaining, interfering, and much-beloved Italian family:

On a Roll, Gabe & Sean's book

Ride or Die, Ren & Seth's book

Sweet as Pie, Luca & Oliver's book

Cherry on Top, Enzo & Will's book

INTERESTED IN READING MORE OF
BETH'S BOOKS?

CHECK OUT A FULL LIST OF TILES
BY SCANNING THE QR CODE
OR VISITING HER WEBSITE

WWW.BETHBOLDEN.COM/BOOKLIST

WANT TO FOLLOW BETH?

MAKE SURE YOU NEVER
MISS A RELEASE?

SCAN THE QR CODE BELOW
OR VISIT HER WEBSITE
FOR A SOCIAL MEDIA LIST,
NEWSLETTER SIGNUP,
AND SO MUCH MORE!

WWW.BETHBOLDEN.COM/ABOUT